AMERICA IS A ZOO

ANDRE SOARES

Elijah, Isaiah, I love you dearly. This is our shared legacy. The blueprint to a bluer sky and a greener earth. Forget the dark clouds that once cluttered the sky vault. The depressions have passed.

CONTENTS

1. LOOPHOLE

WASHINGTON, D.C. - THE CAPITOL

There are very few creatures on this earth matching the shameless character of politicians.

They scarf down rich courses and sweet delicacies, building unhealthy fat as the pressure applied by their ever-increasing weight is felt under the opulent flooring patterns of their offices.

Down below, the frail frames of the working class keep pushing upward to prevent the Calacatta Carrara marble from sinking in, as its beauty and rarity requires preservation, above. The working poor are told it matters; naturally, their conditioned selves keep the hamster wheel spinning.

As the fat builds up and the oppression persists, the blinded, misguided, and putrescent souls walking the Capitol see only one viable solution.

"Bring more of the regular people. More bodies to support the structure."

"MORE."

T he top two State Department officials set foot inside the Capitol's coveted spot, an urban footpath to the throne; they came to rectify an injustice, to release a war-torn country from the U.S.' increasingly repressive chokehold.

To them, this place held no other value, no significance. The polished floors across the National Statuary Hall projected a wavy reflection of the two men's silhouettes, unable to provide clarity in details. One of the two was short and heavy set, the other tall and elegantly athletic. The superior and his subordinate, their feet planted on the floor and heads swaying to the flow of synthetic smiles and rubbery eyes, stood out from the remainder of the crowd. They were visiting a deceitfully sophisticated farm whose sheep were shepherded inside the House of Representatives chamber by a seductive prospect: power beyond limits and the shade obstructive of accountability.

A charming evil inhabited this place, running on timed laughs and strategic touches.

The two outsiders looked up above the brainwashed masses and noticed patterns on the high ceiling: circles woven into a patchwork of loops; an observation that triggered complex thoughts in the tall one, a young, chiseled face of a tan complexion with wavy lose curls arranged in a sophisticated cut.

What is the definition of insanity?

His tapered fade complimented a subtle five o' clock shadow.

Dismissive of the quiet reflection, a distant voice produced a rapid-fired question. The tone was worshipping, the sound unpleasant in its squeak.

Cafe Milano, 7 PM? I have a proposition.

The State Department's subordinate did not belong to this place, a den of long in the tooth, double-chinned white men who built and acquired assets through negative leverage and corruption.

Oh, and their chained-up minority tokens used to distract the public opinion from the lack of access to wealth building for those very same minorities.

The touches intensified, shoulder taps and arm squeezes depicting a decidedly sexual ritual. A lust for political capital transpired through the forward-leaning stances, the bobbing heads, the creepy smiles. It was a spectacle of unchained genies granting each other wishes.

The athletic figure, one of understated elegance, found the wary gaze of his superior, stubby and plump. The latter seemed to fit the congressmen and congresswomen's profile yet displayed a grounded behavior the others lacked. They both kept looking up, finding the sight of well-dressed flesh-eaters nauseating.

The ceiling definitively offered a vision of dreamish gold patterns running its surface to then return to their starting points. The two men's eyes eventually met, and they agreed, in a conspiracy of silence: *This will never end.*

Click... click. Beneath them, the rare and expensive marble saw crooked figures walk its surface. They were bent, challenged by an incurable disease: the loss of their humanity.

A conversation sparked a few feet away from the two State Department outsiders. Secrecy was optional in this space; the system now openly supported debauchery and deviant practices, restricting access to those willing to break the rules or at minimum tolerate the crooks who did. There was no countermeasure in the general population, a feeble force the politicians fed off of.

An old white man whose melted porcelain skin begged to be let loose said, "They offered me thirty years. I beat it on a loophole. The rape kit was compromised."

The two parties involved in the conversation erupted in crass laughter. Their shadows were all that remained of their organic print, out here in this palatial hallway. Their diseased black eyes blocked the path to finding anything potentially human. Gesturing was theatrical in its wide movements. The pigs did not experience stage fright, instead confident in their delivery. Some eyes turned but morals and integrity were chased out of this cursed place like invasive rodents. No one dared intervening nor recording.

"How old was she, anyway? Fifteen? She craved a more experienced hand. I know she enjoyed it," the other added.

Click ... click.

"She did. Her legs were shaking when I dug in. Her first time. I wanted more. But she lacked stamina."

The inflated belly of the perpetrator threatened to burst in his expensive navy suit and striped shirt. His red tie bounced to the beat of a sinister laugh as both decaying monsters were engulfed in the chamber.

In the hallway, a woman passed by the two astonished State Department officials and nodded. Her skin was of an umber tone, a rich dark yellow brown that struck the face of a refined beauty.

Her smile was unsettling, however, more... artificial. Oversized veneers created a *Joker-ish* grin running from ear to ear; one frozen in time, engineered for the same purpose with each and every encounter.

She stopped before the gargantuan mouth of the chamber's main access further down, to address an older white woman in a black pencil skirt and blazer. Her bob cut and its razor-sharp trims accentuated her narrow, penetrating stare.

A humming sound blended inaudible whispers and side conversations. The unsettling noise distracted the two standouts from a lingering fragrance opening with a note of citrus. Their sense of smell finally took notice of the heavy amber floral scent, and their eyes followed its trail to the same black woman who had just casually nodded at their disbelief.

"Should I move forward with diverting the capital?" she asked.

Malicious eyes sparkled as her Caucasian counterpart, the *bob cut*, answered, "Yes. Report most of the revenue through the for-profit. Private companies aren't legally obligated to disclose their financial statements. Which also means you can easily work the numbers ... to your favor."

"And I will shout *Black Lives Matter* at these fools and use the non-profit for PR?"

The white lady let out a silent laughter and replied, "Indeed, Patrisse. Make your urban features appeal to them. A lot of these people are diehard consumers and will give to one of their own, no questions asked. They crave for representation, whether it's purely performative or genuine allyship. Race hustling 101. I do the same with my people. Throw them a couple of bones, some community programs, maybe. Or merchandising. And watch the profits skyrocket."

The ladies shook hands and parted ways when entering the chamber.

The two individuals from the State Department, or "Foggy Bottom", were adjusting to the booming sounds of absurd statements, outrageous propositions, and the darkness of a place where the burning flames of justice and decency were swiftly extinguished by the whiskers running a demonic rat race. Both were familiar with the culture in Washington, D.C. but always felt foreign to it. Like a few isolated cases, they were a beacon of integrity fighting to sustain its light amidst the chaos of a cataclysmic storm.

Capitol Hill was a refuge to the scum and villainy, the men in power; those who bent the law for their own personal gains, shaped new legislation to attain more political capital and quiet the hunger of the lobbyists whose sharp teeth craved a piece of the pie. Those who feared no retribution. Those whose moral compass never accounted for the shattering of innocent souls.

There was no end to the madness, no boundaries for the parasites who leeched off of a broken system that only benefited the monsters peering from above.

Tap... tap... tap.

The two public servants walked in.

The House of Representatives chamber screamed *old money*. Its blue carpet, golden seals, and dark brown leather seats, a byproduct of French influence, as well as the intricate wooden pillars fixed on its walls gave it an austere look prone to conservatism.

The room had heightened perspectives. However, the high ceilings and the half-circle seating layout appeared smaller now that it was occupied by some of the biggest decisionmakers in this country. Somehow, however, the space still carried historical significance for the two outsiders and proved almost... intimidating.

The State Department officials continued walking straight down the middle aisle and turned left to a set of tables equipped with wireless conference microphones. They dropped two black binders right next to the devices; the Saffiano leather coatings starkly contrasted with the surroundings. It was elegant, unique, and modern.

The *Foggy Bottom* superior scanned the room, his eyes dancing on the fifty-three souls attending the oversight hearing. Many of the crooks here were gauging one another, looking for something to exploit in the others' behaviors.

The tall, handsome one looked forward, seeking his audience. His fingers drummed on the edge of the brown table and finally rested on the solid wood structure, helping the man find balance in this swaying chaos.

He found *your* gaze, as you also found yourself *pulled* into the belly of this underworld, through the lens of his unique perspective. Around, time and space stilled. Quietness settled.

"This is the U.S. Capitol. The seat of *Power*, the theater for some of the most impactful decisions this country has ever made and will ever support. Inside these walls, men and women gamble with your life savings, with your taxes, with your labor. And although today's session is an oversight hearing, it will still impact your lives for generations to come, in the upmost secrecy. Indeed, you have no idea of what is at stake, that the rumble of war already pulses through the flesh and veins of this city. You crave escapism, blinded by the lights of consumption, gluttony, lust, an unregulated capitalism and the newest form of an untreatable cancer, social networks. What have you done to educate yourselves on politics, to understand the process in which your lives are molded, shaped, transformed, bruised, cut, beaten, and violated? The pigs whose glistening skins stretch tight are crassly laughing as they sit in these chairs finding newer, more creative ways to profit off of your poverty wages and false hopes. There are no greys in this dynamic.

"You are the *Blacks*, and they are the *Whites*. In this regard, History has taught us one thing: They have failed you. Yet you keep yearning for more beatings, moaning as you reach climax in pain. Some of us try to swim against the treacherous currents of politics to warn you, since you're feeding them upstream. But it would require an institutional shakedown and a massive shockwave to shape a new landscape. And most of you, comfortable with the established order of things or unaware of how rotten this government is, are unwilling to push or call for a change. And each year, as a reward for your obedience, you get a temporary fix, a brief release of dopamine as you spend your income tax on designer clothes and flat screen TVs, forgetting—for a flying instant—about your misery and a cost of living you can no longer afford on a single income.

"You could at least renounce to instant gratification and build generational wealth, positioning yourself in a more favorable predicament, where, as a society, you would gather enough influence to make a lasting change. But *that* requires patience and focus, and the short content pushed by algorithms on social media —surprise, a practice supported by big corporations and the government—as well as the get-rich quick schemes advertised by influencers and gurus who are themselves victims of the system made you believe you could attain substantial wealth overnight, making a big break in an elusive viral moment. How do you feel, knowing that the rotten corpses and minds of those surrounding me are byproducts of your vices, the *people*?

"Ladies and gentlemen, welcome to the United States of America. A broad-scale loophole."

2. SAD PAG

WASHINGTON, D.C. - GEORGETOWN

There is nothing more satisfying than operating unseen, unheard,
impervious to any form of legal prosecution. However, the Boogeyman
whose shadow ran the globe began questioning the impunity he
enjoyed.

ichael Hoover entered the steamy kitchen of an exclusive fine dining establishment in Georgetown, a curated experience tailored to French cuisine lovers with deep pockets.

A heat wave had struck the city a week earlier, yet the tall figure walked the deserted place in a turtleneck sweater, slacks, and creeper soles, all black, in a modern spin on the personification of death. His round-shaped reading glasses, emaciated facial structure, and rich dark skin were all contained in the coldness of his demeanor. His eyes were devoid of life, almost synthetic. There was no fog on his lenses, like those of a ghost visiting the world of the living, unaffected.

His sharp senses picked up light accents of bleach and the low buzzing of appliances in sleep mode. He examined the kitchen's double galley layout, carefully reviewing the stainless-steel counters and custom racks running alongside the stone walls.

Voices inside his head whispered, *There are a few discrepancies.* A set of *Wusthof* kitchen knives was placed onto a hanging magnetic strip. Michael recognized the signature craft, the trident on the classic black handle, the hardened steel forming a sharp blade. But whoever had sanitized the place prior to leaving was guilty of a grave violation, a transgression yelled at by the competing voices of Hoover's split personality.

"See, *Ben Ben*. This cutlery is a cultivation of refinement. Its precision, the attention to detail, the standards, the quality control, the *brand*. Everything about this particular line of products is designed to achieve the best results, to perform at the highest levels. Many world-class chefs have adopted them. *Ben Ben*, they deserve recognition, may I say *respect*. The latter is crucial," he said to himself.

Michael Hoover, a specialized skill officer for the CIA's Political Action Group (PAG), felt a tingling in his extremities. His spiderlike fingers felt compelled to approach the blades. He straightened two of them out, adjusting the angles to achieve a precise parallel. The tingling ceased.

The man, almost mechanically, turned left into a wide corridor whose neutral-toned walls housed expensive-looking abstracts in gold frames. At the end, he engaged a small private room whose surrounding glass panes floated above the herringbone-patterned hardwood floor. A single table occupied the space.

Michael retrieved a tiny circular device from underneath it and sat down. The strange object was of a matte black, a six-inch diameter disc housing a round rubber pad in its center.

The slender CIA figure reviewed the equipment, lowering his frames, his eyebrows raised. He set it down on the expensive white tablecloth projecting its damask patterns on the ceiling and readjusted his eyeglasses. Here again, the device was placed parallel to an exquisite set of porcelain tableware with golden floral shapes. The entire setup was curated to Michael's preferences, each piece of silverware, glassware, and plate combinations positioned with a remarkable precision.

It was surgical, uncompromising. *Perfection, Ben Ben.*

A silhouette approached from across the table. Its contours took the shape of a grimy-looking man. His Mediterranean features were rough, his beard chaotic, and beads of sweat escaped through his dilated pores. He reeked of spicy bourbon. The man sat down at the table. Michael felt disgusted as well as bothered; the individual lacked symmetry, refinement, cleanliness.

"M. Charles, got ya file." The dirty face handed the CIA agent an orange folder marked *TOP SECRET//HCS*. Michael opened it, keeping the spine straight, perpendicular to the table.

Inside the madness of his sick mind, the voices quiet down, leaving space for a proper review of the document. Photographs of a young man whose complexion was of a warm almond tone drew his attention. The person of interest was at a café, delicately sipping on a small porcelain cup.

"Libyans?"

The guest cleared his throat and answered, "Yeah, or meddlin' witcha suits."

The folder also contained a written report. A single page.

HUMINT.
KFRA connection.
1st SFOD-D was ODA.
Gypsum trade with lobbyist firm.
Objective not clearly defined.
HUMINT from OP Sand Wave suggests elevated threat level.
HVT is in Washington, D.C.
Location unknown.
HVT bypassed CCTV sweep.

S&D. Title 50.

Michael redirected his attention towards his guest and asked, "Good. Drink?"

The man nodded in approval and licked the sweat flooding his upper moustache. A bottle of *Basil Hayden's* stood in between the two.

The drunk must have exercised a considerable self-control in order not to look at it, Michael thought. He said, "Be my guest. Take a few sniffs of this bourbon before tasting and you'll find aromas of toasted oak, creamy vanilla, and peppery rye. The first sip is filled with buttery caramel, sticky toffee, toasted marshmallows, and cracked black pepper. It all ends in a nice, warming finish with just a hint of smoke and spicy pepper. A complicated profile geared towards connoisseurs like yourself."

The man answered, "Thanks. It's nice o' ya." He poured himself half a crystal glass of the high-rye bourbon and held it in his hand, contemplating the golden treasure. A crooked smile drew wider as his chapped lips touched the liquid. His puffy face opened to the explosive flavors of a ten-year old bourbon. *Magic.* The man continued sipping, his eyes conveying gratitude and excitement.

Soon, the volatile element of questionable hygiene began tensing. He put the glass down as his eyes began rolling left and right. His neck muscles protruded from his fat frame, and his mouth expanded wide. Nevertheless, he maintained silence.

"Tetrodotoxin. A biotoxin. I managed to maintain its colorless crystalline form at a liquid state. It interferes with the transmission of signals from nerves to muscles. This one is particularly potent. Instant paralysis. I appreciate your contribution, but my employer deemed you unstable." He paused. "And ridden with vices," the CIA agent explained.

He left his chair, retrieved the black device he had left at the table, and closed the folder in his left hand. Three individuals erupted from where the victim came from, a backdoor access to a killing trap designed by the most powerful intelligence agency in the world. They wore blue Hazmat suits with integrated ventilation circuits. A hissing beat accompanied their steps. Michael nodded at them and turned around, gracefully walking back to the kitchens.

His steps followed a strange pattern. He was skipping. *Left... right... right... left... left.*

His face remained of clay, cold and smooth, polished and devoid of imperfections. Life seemed to have left his shell, now only driven forward by the momentum of a delirious craze.

Outside, the sun radiated power. It was bright, penetrating, viciously hot. Vehicle traffic was minimal in the mainly residential street, but afar, the city called with muffled honks and comical shouts. The bleach scents and the dry bourbon smells left room for delicate floral fragrances and the distinctive print of freshly cut grass. Brick houses extending to both sides of Hoover's peripheral vision produced a visually stunning patchwork of colors; the personalities caged *within* fought to observe the spectacle, requesting access to his lens.

Michael ignored the mind parasites and crossed the small paved street and its tree lines to reach a three-story row house. The white façade was smooth and elegant, complimenting the massive windowpanes that begged for natural light on its surface, swallowing the sun in their enormous mouths.

To the neighborhood residents, Michael Hoover was an eccentric artist with a signature look à la *Steve Jobs* enhanced by colorful variations. His strangeness offered the best covert identity: Who would suspect a rich bizarro in such a culturally charged area?

The agency had arranged a past, and the specialized skill officer had an acquired taste for art. He was also proficient at painting. His visual treatments and brush strokes suggested those of *Lubaina Himid*, the British prodigy whose work took the world by storm in the 1980s.

Michael unlocked the entrance door of his residence with the slight pressing of his thumb and traversed a large vestibule whose white walls amplified the sun rays shining on the structure. The interior design was artsy, minimalist, and purposeful; it was a blend of traditional, mid-century, and contemporary influences.

Tap. Tap. Tap.

His carefully manufactured stride led to a greenhouse in the back of the property. He slid the access open. The glass roof towering over the plush jungle that occupied the space remained surprisingly cold in its conveyance as the sweet scents of the passionfruit trees and the banana shrubs poured indoors.

At the center of this wild development, the CIA agent stopped and allowed his creeper soles to sink in the soft evergreen grass. His round-shaped frames and glacial eyes found *you*. There was a strange beauty to his perspective: He saw the world through a mosaic of squared frames.

Some panned out, others zoomed in.

"Most of the general population, *you*, tends to believe that the intelligence community and law enforcement agencies are benevolent forces driven by public servants of unquestionable ethics and effective checks and balances. Ah. Many of our people, the melanated skins who die by the hands, soles, or knees of police forces and covert groups only trigger short-lived reactionary movements with no sustainable impact. Then, you quickly move on as the next casualty awaits in the streets, or inside their own home, car. This indifference, this 'numbness' to the killings committed by the country's most powerful institutions ... well, it serves me. My agency benefits from the lack of oversight, from the disinterest in our operations and practices. Creative mediums paint us as superspies infiltrating high-rises abroad, equipped with fancy Walther PPQs or HK45s, mounting a suppressor onto a threaded barrel while approaching our target in the concealing shadow of the night. The reality is far more concerning. We operate on U.S. soil and shape the dynamics of *your* world, unseen, unheard.

"Sometimes, I rapidly shift between emotional states, and my distorted self-image begs to join the regular people, the lesser ones, *you*. It suggests I should educate the zombified masses, the corpses who lost faith in life. As I reach the edge of a mind that feels foreign, looking down into a dizzying void, I remember. I have medication engineered for my particular condition. And as the chemicals pour into my system, I find myself again. The Boogeyman in a zoo."

3. THE GERMAN

Himmel und Hölle in Bewegung setzen. The three-headed wolf casts a snow-white fur on the forest greens of the woods. His muscles are tensed, and his pounce leaves the soil weathered. The magical creature knows no counterpart in the animal kingdom; his relentless advance and diabolic efficiency meet no match.

A middle-aged Caucasian male walked alongside the cascading fountain of the Meridian Hill Park. On the surface, the muddy waters were covered in green residues beaten by small ripples. Mark Wagner, a German national, advanced up the stony stairs flanking one of D.C.'s wonders. He was tall, fit, and clean-shaven with a wavy blow dry whose volume and proportions made an optimal use of his salt and pepper hair. His nose bridge was straight and sharp, his jaw line suspiciously flawless as it blended a masculine squared shape with a slight angle. His blue eyes were swept by a red fire.

He exuded composure and a result-driven culture. The muggy sixty percent humidity and the triple-digit temperatures would not penetrate M. Wagner's linen suit. The fixer, a feared force in the highest political echelons of the U.S. machine, was in total control of his environment, cool, dry, and purposeful in his motion.

He stopped by a set of brown pillars, looking down through the formidable perspective of an upstream being. The man reached for his jacket's inside pocket and grabbed a burner phone. A *clap* followed, and the antiquated model revealed its small keyboard and pixelated screen.

The German pressed and held the call key. A pre-recorded message blasted from the old cell to his ear. He quickly released the button and gave the automated prompt his undivided attention.

"Thank you for contacting Alawi Holdings, a subsidiary of Kent Braggart Enterprises. Building the present of your future."

An on-hold music struck a delicate sound.

A few seconds passed. The blooming shades of the summer gave Wagner a pleasant distraction. The sugar-rich golden nectar of soon-to-be pollinated flowers produced a sweet scent battling the pungent filth of a nearby homeless gathering. The automated message resumed.

"We have identified your account. How can we help? Please press 0 to speak to a customer representative."

The German pressed the 0 key.

"Hi, my name is Brent, ID 38.8899.77.0091. May I have your name please?"

"Der Krake. DOB 09/06/1990."

"Thank you. How may we help you today?"

"I'm looking to confirm the status of a transfer I scheduled three weeks ago."

"One moment."

The conversation left room for rapid keystrokes.

"Confirmed. Would you like a transaction number for your record?"

Mark Wagner lifted and pressed his right shoulder against his ear to hold the flip phone in place. He grabbed a small notepad and a pen from his slacks' left pocket.

"Yes, please."

"ID 38.784976.8721"

Mark's pen danced on the yellow paper. The handwriting was legible, fluent, and efficient.

"Thank you."

"My pleasure. Enjoy the rest of your day M. Krake."

"You as well."

The conversation ended with a *clap* as the flip phone closed. Mark smiled, revealing a set of pearly white teeth engineered to stun. He left the landmark to exit the park and reach Chapin St, a residential area that bore a striking resemblance with Brooklyn's most common layouts.

A row of tree lines escorted the man to another intersection, further east. He turned left and continued until the next carrefour. Another left led him to a quiet street, along with a bench bordering a brown row house.

A sign in the front lawn read *Tapper's ministry*. Mark rang the door's bell twice and left the entryway to sit on the wooden bench; its bamboo structure was still cool on the touch.

The door behind him opened. A black male in his sixties or seventies found his way down the stairs, fighting a limp by stiffening. His features were patriarchal, benevolent. He projected goodwill and a sensibility to others' pains. He sat next to Wagner, the German. They both shook hands and exchanged genuine smiles.

The Black man asked, "It's good to see you, Mark. How are things going on the *Hill*?"

"Great, *alter Freund*. There are adjustments made."

The Black man smiled again and waved at a pedestrian across the street.

He said, "We're ready for George?"

"Indeed. We break the news."

The two remained quiet and contemplated the landscape. Around, the restless people coming to terms with their inner demons and challenges were unaware of the importance of this conversation, but Wagner strongly believed in the cause he was hired to support.

A few minutes prior, in Meridian Hill, he received the green light to launch an offensive that would forever alter the country's trajectory: a nationwide revolution of countless political ramifications.

The German's blue eyes met his partner's warm gaze. They once more shook hands and parted ways.

Tap... tap... tap.

An all-black Suburban with diplomatic plates was on idle a few houses down. Wagner approached the vehicle and opened the back door on the driver's side. Then, he entered and closed it out.

The vehicle quietly took off.

The German fixer sat straight, shoulders relaxed, fingers interlocked. Outside, noon's rush hour fed the scorching streets of D.C. with a massive portion of agitated commuters; the *Hill* and White House rats, the high-end prostitutes on the way to a lunch fix, the suburban working class infatuated with the city's quiet display of wealth. Mark knew the town's main political players would not leave their office on a weekday. The battle was always raging, and soldiers would never leave their posts unattended, instead more fearful of missing overlooked opportunities.

The Suburban navigated through the traffic with ease, pacing itself to maintain a constant speed. A blue façade appeared to Mark's left. The SUV stopped. The German opened the door and stepped out of the vehicle, his brown loafers tapping on the freshly repaired concrete. He entered the blue building. A basement access to the left led to a fireproof door.

Wagner pressed his right thumb against the glassy surface of a fingerprint scanner installed on the right side of the frame. The door clicked and slid, disappearing in a cavity.

The space ahead was massive: A digital wall of epic proportions covered three of the four partitions, while an off-white couch's edges ran the last, unused surface.

At the center of the room, a minimalist desk with an elegant monitor, a landline, and a legal pad offered the German a chair. He sat down, his blue eyes meticulously combing the walls: the city's CCTV feeds.

Wagner's eyes fixed on a specific footage and looked *beyond* the *fourth wall* to find *you*, the pages' travelers. His stare was a cautionary tale, his vision sharp. It issued warning shots as the icy blue optics refocused on an exterior footage: white stairs that led to a bright dome. The U.S. Capitol.

"Capitalism and patriotism. Two mutually exclusive concepts here in America. I'm a fixer. A strange title considering I usually break bonds to tip the scales in favor of those who pay the right price. This city is mine, and as I walk the grid like a giant leaping forth, *meine macht* grows stronger. America is a zoo, and although I profit from walking contradictions, I could not resist the offer I was presented with. Someone with a vision approached me. They want to cage the beasts. It is time I take a less neutral … stance?"

4. ABEBA

*Among us are those who carry the Torch. They are an eternal beacon of
light in the darkness of our days. Their optimism and willingness to drive
change are perceived as misguided idealism by the cackling birds
flapping their wings; nightmarish creatures trapped in invisible cages
and covered in their own feces.
Abeba looked up and saw the vultures circling around the corpses of
those who possessed the same gift as she.*

"There are clusters all over the continent. Central Africa's is the most enduring. Thousands killed, 620,000 displaced. Charred bodies along the routes. The motives? Complex. Religious, ethnic, economic ... I have ties to the African Union. I plan on reshaping the geopolitical landscape. Today, Africa is the world's second largest and second most populous continent. 1.3 billion souls hindered by instability. Recurring and reemerging conflicts. A lack of global leadership. The ghosts of a colonialism that has conditioned most of the heads of state and left an unaddressed trauma lingering in the shared history of the motherland. 125 billion dollars would reach the locals, who would benefit from a better allocation of resources. Ten-year plan. A workforce of 123,000. Military-grade equipment. Top notch training. Thirty-five UN officials have showed interest in the project. 4500—"

Abeba's boyish beauty and above-average height exacerbated her craze as she delivered the rapid and deconstructed speech. The essential tremor running through her slender fingers begged to speak. The world did not understand the ramifications, the numbers, the correlations between them, the projections her brain produced at a dizzying speed.

Why can't the people see? She felt isolated her whole life, trapped in a giant bubble, pushing down against hot air to reach the masses down below: the ones who lived a simpler life.

She was diagnosed with a rare form of autism at age nine, Kanner's syndrome: a high degree of rote memory and visuospatial skills, an uncontrolled speech and a lack of emotional attachment to others. Her case, however, was unique: She showed no learning disability in other areas and was deemed one of the FBI's brightest minds by her superiors, peers, and subordinates alike.

The panel of judges across the newly renovated stage looked up to her. The five faces, covering most shades in the spectrum of mankind, opened up to the speech in astonishment, overwhelmed by the amount of information and the rough transitions. A young Black male in a linen shirt raised a hand.

"Miss Solomon, let's pause for a second."

Abeba nodded and sought her refuge, her mental construct. She called it *home*.

Less data, more human. More human, better data. Better data, less data.

The man resumed, "I follow your career and accomplishments closely and … I have to say, it is an honor. From what I understand, you have a very particular thought process? One rooted in data correlations?"

"Yes, sir."

Her eyes focused on him. He understood her.

yell. Why is data so important to you? So prevalent?"

...e sipped on a tall glass of water and jolted down a few notes on a legal pad. The others were calm, attentive.

Abeba felt compelled to get closer to him. He spoke her love language. Except it was not a romantic interest she shared for him, but a scientific curiosity.

She refrained herself, however, and answered, "The data always leads to tangible solutions. It is drawn from real-life events. An infinite number of small nervure-like circuits carry universal and undisputable truths no one has altered yet."

The man's benevolent smile conveyed a genuine care for her vision. She felt it. He was respectful, methodic in his reasoning. He said, "How can you be sure that the sources you rely on aren't compromised? And does data truly cover every aspect of our lives?"

"I can *see* which sources are reliable and which ones aren't. I shut out the noise, and I can *visualize* the discrepancies, the red flags, the inconsistencies. And yes, data covers every aspect. Pain, joy, life, death, hot, cold, up, down … both ends of any spectrum and anything in between can be translated into data."

The man wrote down a few more words. "But how does your message *translate* with human beings? With flawed creatures who don't have your abilities, your superpowers?"

Laughs ensued from the other spectators, but they were not the products of bullies moving mockingly. They were reassuring, gentle, and steady, accompanied by genuine smiles and happy faces.

Abeba understood the intent but hit a wall. She felt the flames of mankind's limitations consume her pristine input and statistics. They weren't receptive. She remained quiet.

"You can call me Brayton," the Black man added. "Let's try again. This time, I want you to focus on the *people*. How are you going to make this data, this project, of significance to *them*? How are you going to reach them *emotionally*? We are aware of your gift, but that's also why we're here. To help you adjust."

An older Asian lady to his left interjected, "Absolutely. We are here to help you level the playing field for your targets. We already fully trust your ability to perform and manage. Your formal education, track record, your history, your brightness. You also happen to project a dazzling beauty, which, let's be honest, gives you an edge in public speaking."

Abeba Solomon nodded yet found the last comment irrelevant. Her looks had always been a hot topic, but as she saw the world deconstructed, as she identified each component, as she remembered each step … the timeless character of raw life relegated fading and shifting looks to last place.

The Asian woman interrupted her thoughts. "Like Brayton mentioned, you simply need to streamline your speech. Take away the complicated data, the calculations, correlations, and narrow specifics. How will your project make this world a better place? How will it save lives? How will it uplift the bright minds of this continent? Why is it important to you?"

Abeba was familiar with streamlining, but her convictions and excitement trumped the need to vulgarize the message. As the FBI's Counterterrorism Division's assistant director, she had to exercise a simplified communication on a daily basis. The hundreds of men and women under her guidance and leadership needed to clearly understand their objectives in order to perform at the expected standard. Abeba also sought to prove *her* leadership that her diagnosed and well-documented condition did not affect her own performance. She had succeeded thus far.

She tilted her head in agreement to let the panel know she was processing the feedback.

Her thoughts reorganized, shuffled as she compartmentalized the facts by order of complexity. She needed to appeal to a broader audience to get funding and gain traction. Within the past couple of years, she had developed a business plan and a press kit for a non-profit organization. It was time for her to move on from the intelligence community and federal law enforcement; there were too many layers of bureaucratic slow bumps, too many conflicting interests, and... politics. She *despised* politics.

"My name is Abeba Solomon, assistant director at the FBI's Counterterrorism Division. For years, I have strived to keep this country safe from both foreign and domestic threats. But for the past two, I have been doing a lot of soul searching on my own. I traveled to Africa to meet family members and reconnect with my roots, seeking an ancient knowledge. One main thing transpired from that journey. Africa, the motherland, was violated, beaten, bruised. By colonialism of course, but also by human nature, corporate greed, and religious, ethnic conflicts. This is nothing new. We have known this for decades. However, no one ever devised a comprehensive and sustainable plan to address years of neglect.

"This is where I come into play. My political connections in the U.S. and documented ties with the African Union in *Addis Ababa* serve as a blueprint to what I set to accomplish. My non-profit organization and paramilitary force, *Zoya*, will work closely with major African players, free from the shackles of corporate interests and lobbyism, to reshape the geopolitical landscape in Africa and offer future generations an opportunity to grow and sustain that growth in a safer environment."

Brayton took advantage of a short pause and asked, "How do you remain impartial while deploying a force on foreign lands? What is your actual solution? And why should we care as U.S. nationals?"

Abeba forced a smile and answered, "Those are great questions." *Not.* "The paramilitary force I intend to deploy will be composed of skilled contractors who will undergo an extensive training and background checks, as well as weekly reviews. I designed a system to provide checks and balances. Each task force will be operating in a country they have no ties to or no leverage on. It involves complex data, but I will be happy to discuss it at a later time.

"Second, *Zoya*'s overall workforce will be compensated ten to twelve percent above market average, and a comprehensive benefits package will be offered to all, regardless of the nature of their role. Historical studies have shown that compensation and job significance are two major variables in most successful, corruption-free enterprises.

"Third, organizational culture. Studies have been conducted on the subject and demonstrated that a well-communicated vision statement and actions that align with it can have dramatic repercussions on the methods and associated outcomes in an organization. Culture is often overlooked or overshadowed by broken promises and valueless PR statements. I intend to set tangible procedures in motion to ensure our workforce remains faithful to our missions. Those procedures include but are not limited to weekly meetings, training programs, psychological evaluations, personnel investigation and an internal affairs department whose operational specifics will remain secret. One that will be ran by a third party with no affiliation to me or my operations."

Abeba refrained herself from continuing. The panel was absorbed, but they needed time to process. Her rich dark skin shone as her round cheekbones rose. She produced a juvenile smile full of radiance. Her beauty was unique, peculiar.

Soon, she resumed, "The solution we offer is a comprehensive suite of resources and a uniformed vision both developed to attain one goal: economic independence and political stability in Africa. This would unfold in three ways: peacekeeping, civil affairs, and a data-driven diplomacy effort. The human component remains important to us, however. Each member of *Zoya* will receive an intense sensitivity training geared towards preserving the cultural integrity of local populations and governments.

"The mission is also beneficial to all foreign nations, including ours. Although my objective is to assist Africa in gaining more independence and achieving a more sustainable growth, it will have a positive impact on U.S. affairs, as well. Under our guidance and the local leadership's direction, Africa will become the largest and best-coordinated economic block in the world. By seeking neutrality and autonomy, the motherland will break free from conflicting influences, such as massive Chinese investments, our military presence, and the remnants of European colonialism.

"There will be no policymaking in our favor, however. I want to make that clear. But healthy relationships do not exist, nor subsist, on the basis of one of the parties being in a position of power. The same should apply to geopolitics. Also, there's potential for a positive environmental impact worldwide, the preservation of an eco-diverse habitat, access to natural resources war conceals from us, the neutralization of public health threats, improved diplomatic ties ... the ramifications are countless. Some we can't even foresee. This is the opportunity of a lifetime. A real, meaningful change."

Abeba squeezed her hands in a ball. The auditorium was massive, the three balcony levels undulating in the shapes of wooden waves. The lighting was dimmed, embedded in the ceiling in a representation of the city's *Federal Triangle*. Her world was full of hues and grains, pulled apart in a grandiose 3D schematic. She could tell how each element connected to the other: how it was built, engineered.

Brayton smiled at her contemplation and cleared his throat. Her gaze turned to him as he spoke, "There you are. The psychological connection, the relatability. We've studied your business plan, your projections, your reports ... they are flawless. But you need to sell your future financiers on the idea as well. Features and benefits, your ability to rally an entire continent to your cause, the halo of a transformational leadership. You need to differentiate execution and representation. How do you feel?"

The rest of the panel members were taking notes, their pens silently gliding on their papers.

"Better, Brayton. I understand the needs and the expectations."

"Fantastic. I will follow your project with great interest, Miss Solomon. It was an honor having you in the program. Remember, data must also convey your sentiments."

Abeba thought, *Some relevant points but a bit idealistic. Execution remains crucial, and credibility is a priceless asset. Four billion in initial investments. Fifty-four sovereign countries. 123,000 employees. A silent battle against corruption and appropriation. 11,730,000 sq mi. Five main ecosystems. Over 3,000 tribes.*

The thoughts kept pouring in as she was dismissed. A narrow hallway led to the entrance of the Cathay Williams Hall. The walls were covered with wooden panels transformed by intricate carvings: mazes and crooked bodies overlapping one another.

One-inch protrusion. The grain ... growth rings, no repetition in patterns. Dark red tones, high density. Pink Ivory.

Abeba located the artist's pseudonym in a flash and searched him on her phone. She found his work and portfolio. The art that surrounded her was now also on her screen. A brief description served as a caption underneath the digital slideshow.

Varume. Men seek purpose and truth. How do they fit in the grand scheme of things?

———

Commissioned by the George Washington University (Washington, D.C.) with the financial support of Nigerian curator Ode Adewebe. Made from repurposed Pink Ivory wood panels.

Repurposed Pink Ivory. Abeba felt relieved. She squeezed her right hand into a ball and counted backwards from ten. She was ready to face the world once more.

Tap, tap... tap... tap.

Outside, the courtyard was hot and muggy. Cherry trees were of lighter shades, a washed-up pink whose petals turned slightly maroon at the extremities. Heat waves led to an adjacent street. A pretzel stand doubling as an ice-cream parlor drove its owner to court the passing pedestrians. Abeba ignored the man's call and turned left to an expensive-looking vehicle parked under a plush tree line, its glossy black strangely refreshing in the feverish early afternoon. A butterfly door opened to its owner, and the car powered on without a sound.

Miss Solomon entered, her evergreen pantsuit elevating the off-white interior and Italian stitching. The door closed back up as she manipulated a wheel on the middle console.

She was whole, anew, as all things fell in place.

Around, the jam-packed street displayed the oblivious smiles of downtown visitors. There was this facet of Washington, D.C.: the uninterested, the outsiders, or the ones who never craved power but instead cultural enrichment. Brayton was one of them. She could not feel love or attraction, but she felt oddly close to him.

As she engaged in traffic, she found the road's patterns were erratic.

23rd St's ongoing flow of commuters, towards the Lincoln Memorial, was experiencing a peak, she thought. *773 vehicles per hour per lane.*

She glanced at a slick display above the center console. "Zoya."

"Administrator," a British-based voice answered.

"Barometric pressure within 2.8 miles, please."

"17.65768 psi."

She looked forward: Dupont circle's canopy drew afar. The famous roundabout had undergone a massive makeover. Its tall banana shrubs dominated the forest floor, and Kapoc trees cast their shadow over proximity traffic. She saw the landmark in a unique light, torn apart by meticulous hands, each variety and floral arrangement isolated. *Heat wave, increasing atmospheric pressure. Irrelevant.*

She said once more, "Zoya."

"Administrator."

"Distance by car from Dupont Circle to the National Mall."

"Nineteen minutes. Heavy traffic. No accident reported. No blockade reported."

Unusually slow, she thought.

"Zoya, please call NTAS."

The line rang. In the vehicle, the ATMOS system relayed high-fidelity sounds.

"NTAS, the natio—"

Abeba interrupted the automated message, "Extension 1990."

The call was transferred to a woman whose platonic tone starkly contrasted with the nature of her position as a high-paid alert system. "Operator. ID?"

"Charlie Tango Delta Alpha Delta. Tango Sierra Hotel Uniform Mike India November Tango Tree Tree."

A brief silence followed. Abeba began circling around Dupont, towards R St. The pavements were smoking yet a steady flow of pedestrians walked the city. College students, artists, wealthy corporate wigs, high-ranking politicians, and workers in the trades blended in an eclectic mass. The energies collided and the people dispersed, swallowed by the smaller arteries of one of the most expensive and exclusive neighborhoods in the country.

"ID confirmed. There is no current announcement. Threat level brown."

"Thank you." Abeba hung up.

Bodies were moved to the city, she was certain of. *What did they want?*

She turned right to a smaller street with a cozier vibe. A contemporary, single-block house radiated in colors in the historically and architecturally conservative neighborhood. Abeba parked out front, under the shade of a massive tree that expanded over to the street. Her property featured two stories whose front façade consisted of a giant glass pane. The front lawn was manicured to perfection. A soft and lush grass covered most of the space, with the exception of a small pathway leading to the entrance: a creative exercise made of hexagon tiles, ranging from white to a light pink.

Abeba stepped out of the car and disappeared in the shaded concentration. A hot stab poked her skin as she looked left and right before heading to her residence. The transition from a cool, quiet cabin to a hellish, loud jungle felt heavy and pressing.

Yet she continued. Abeba opened a stainless-steel gate with an electronic key and set foot on the colorfully tiled pathway.

Inside, she found a ceramic bowl on a small accent table to her right. She dropped her keys and wallet into the bowl as a massive blast-proof door locked itself up behind her in a formidable display of domotics. And there, a new quietness settled, leaving the strange noises and shifting shapes of the city behind, sucked into the void of an outer space, shut out by the concrete and the steel.

The temperatures dropped, and Abeba found her feet planted in a safe environment built to accommodate her hypersensitivity.

She looked around and let out another juvenile smile. *Home.* "Zoya."

"Administrator."

"SEC report, please."

"No movement recorded. Sensors did not report any fluctuation beyond 1A model."

"Thank you. Play C Span through ATMOS."

A news anchor blasted through the house's state-of-the-art sound system. The crystal-clear voice was that of a middle-aged woman, judging by the inflexions, Abeba thought. She reached the upstairs through a floating stairwell made of a light-shade wood. The floor plan mirrored the lower level: It was open, modular through the implementation of sliding panels and uncompromisingly symmetrical. The entire house, a squared layout, reflected Abeba's dynamics: She was precise, orderly, and efficient.

Today, September 6, 2023.

An oversight hearing has been scheduled at the House of Representatives. Fifty-four members of Congress are reported to attend. The program is confidential, but sources claim the matter is of national security. We cannot confirm nor deny the veracity of the statements made earlier on social networks.

Abeba entered a massive walk-in closet in her master bedroom and undressed, carefully hanging her business attire. She was alone yet shied away from an invisible presence, covering her chest as she found her workout gear. She quickly slipped in, anxious to leave her naked state.

Across her bedroom was a small gym space, beyond a mezzanine platform with a built-in library and a lounge chair. Abeba slid a massive wooden panel to the right and entered in.

The room looked like a strategic command center, the face of an aggressive campaign for the digital age. A sophisticated-looking breathing apparatus hung above a sleek treadmill at the center of the layout. In front of it, an electronic wall broadcasted C-Span and displayed textual content at the bottom: vitals levels and health indicators, all reset to zero. A crunch machine, a pull-up bar, and a yoga mat completed the setting.

The President and Vice President, who will be attending as well, promised the session will be fruitful and bear long-term benefits for generations to come, according to the White House press secretary in an earlier statement this morning.

She stepped on the treadmill, stretched her legs, wrist joints, and rotated her neck a few times. She took a sip of the water that was left in a cup holder to her right and reached for the breathing mask overhead.

This was her ritual: the climbing of mount Everest, the crossing of the Mojave Desert. A painful chapter as she fought the icy winds and heated storms, emerging stronger every time. She donned the device, her fragile eyes gaining in intensity and resolve as the straps tightened up, slightly pressing on her skin. A chime indicated the breather was now active. She pressed *Mountain* on the treadwheel and began walking.

Is partisanship dead? A recent survey from Nielsen shared its results on their official portal this morning at 9 AM eastern time. The initial query was, "Do you believe in political parties?"

The unequivocal prompt indicated a downward trend in the public's trust in our system. Among 254,000 subjects from various demographics, 52% answered "Yes", 37% "No", and 11% "I don't know". The poll emerges in a complicated climate where the White House is facing a few scandals, including one that directly involves the highest echelon of the Executive branch.

Abeba began running. The treadmill gained in incline and speed, reaching ten mph. She was racing against her own thoughts. Her mind had recorded the last twenty-four hours: the interactions, the information acquired throughout, the environmental specifics, the feelings; it was all *within*, stored in a memory that never ceased to expand, one limitless in growth.

Her posture was straight, her thoracic cage open, and her mid-foot strike light.

At this very moment, Abeba had landed on Earth, temporarily freed from the curse of the gifted. She was exploring a simpler construct, among men.

5. THE ROTTEN CORE

WASHINGTON, D.C. - HOUSE OF REPRESENTATIVES

Black mold runs through these walls. Its spores threaten the nation's young children. Where did it come from? How does it propagate? The answers lie within the men and women in charge, the outlined profiles, the politicians disfigured by the Disease. Down a sinkhole of lamenting cries, short-lived victories and broken dreams, you found a voice.

And it tells you, WASH THEM AWAY. RID THE NATION OF THE FLOODED BASEMENTS AND THE FUNGUS-INFECTED FOUNDATIONS. It is overdue.

The heads and trunks leaned back on the leather chairs, an assembly of wary wooden figures. The seats were treated and serviced on a weekly basis to avert a potentially game-breaking squeaking. The chamber was like a pit of horrors, full of snakes gravitating around a bigger snake who served even bigger snakes. The Chairman presided the oversight hearing, demanding silence in the room.

The crowd quieted, and the eyes sharpened.

"Welcome, everyone. This is the first hearing of the Kufrans Committee. The chair will recognize himself and then the ranking member for purposes of making an opening statement. The Committee on the Kufrans exists because the House of Representatives voted for it to exist and, in the process, made it very clear what is expected. If you have not read the House resolution authorizing this committee, I would encourage you to do so. The resolution asked this committee to investigate all policies, decisions, and activities related to the attacks on Al Jawf Kufra, Libya circa 2010, the preparation before the attacks, the response during the attacks, efforts to repel the attacks, the administration's response after the attacks, and executive-branch efforts to comply with congressional inquiries. The operative word in the resolution is the word 'all'."

The Chairman, a fast talker in a jittery state, met a few pressing stares before he resumed. His slender silhouette arched over his microphone, à la *Tim Burton*.

"I would like to address specific points today. The chair must note that the President and Vice President are attending this committee. This exceptional measure is due to the highly sensitive nature of the associated operations conducted in Libya and the extent to which national security is concerned."

The President and his VP, two short figures on the opposite ends of mankind's emotional range, sat in the front row. The other attendees, fixed on the Chairman, refused to acknowledge their presence; for those sitting directly behind, they were faded traces of very little significance, minor props to a grand production design.

"The events we will discuss began on June 11, 2010, in southeastern Libya. Presidential findings recorded on May 12, 2010, sanctioned a covert operation led by the Combat Applications Group (CAG), referred to variously as 1st SFOD-D, Delta Force, The Unit or Task Force Green. The mission was the capture or killing of a high value target, Bin Allah, also known as 'The King of Kufra'. Intelligence provided by the CIA at the time of the operation and attached to this hearing's resolution confirmed that Bin Allah posed a significant threat to national security. The CIA uncovered evidence that a massive, coordinated attack on seven urban concentrations in the U.S. was set in motion by Bin Allah's organization, a tribe known as The Kufrans."

The jittery bug laid his globular eyes on the State Department officials. The two were stoic and composed. Heat rose in the room.

"Today, we have a primary and expert witness who will, in accordance with the House rules, provide a testimony on the motives, methods, and outcomes of the attacks conducted on Libyan soil and targeting Bin Allah in the remote location of Al Jawf Kufra. Witness one, please stand and state your name, current occupation, and relation to the events."

Andre Seraos, the tall and handsome-looking official from the State Department stood, borrowing a posture he acquired during his service in the armed forces. The looks were deceiving, however; Seraos' pedigree inspired respect and admiration at *Foggy Bottom* and beyond.

A military hero of quiet demeanor, he showed both intellectual substance, physical prowess, and acquired a massive amount of knowledge during his special forces rotations.

Today, one of the deadliest assets ever birthed by the U.S. military had become a masters graduate fluently speaking five languages and offering a pertinent and sharp insight on foreign policies and international relations. The corpses in the House of Representatives shifted to lay eyes on him; they were concerned and fearful, their flesh melting on their pale skin or stretching their dark undertones. Some were looking sideways.

"Chairman, my name is Andre Seraos, born September 6, 1982. I am the deputy secretary of state for the State Department. I was a CAG weapons sergeant at the time of the events, and I led the direct action, capture or kill, on Bin Allah, beginning June 11, 2010."

The Chairman's right eye betrayed a slight twitch as his shoulders shrugged.

"M. Seraos, under whose authority?"

"Title 50. Ground operations were supervised by JSOC, and intel was provided by the CIA Special Activities Division."

The bodies tensed. The rats smelled the cheese. The Chairman's oily optics combed the room. He resumed, "M. Seraos, this extraordinary committee was assembled upon the State Department's request. Can you state the reason behind this request?"

Seraos looked to his left, stealing a glance at his superior, a man whose short stature was offset by an undeniable yet intangible authority.

He said, "The State Department has credible evidence that the CIA used Bin Allah or his affiliates to train and finance an indigenous force. This highly skilled group of local combatants ran amok and crossed frontiers to settle in Syria. They are known as the Caliphate, or IS."

An uproar conquered the space. Papers flew, showering the attendees in a white thunderstorm. Men and women yelled unintelligibly. The voices overlapped and mixed in a deranged cacophony.

The suits creased, the mouths spat, the eyes darkened to reveal the monsters within.

The Chairman blinked, renewing the glossy texture of his large eyes.

He called, "Order in the room!"

"Order in the room!"

The monsters had surrendered to a dormant bloodlust. They were caught in a momentum, unable to don the pretty white façades they usually displayed, out there in the world.

"I repeat, order in the *room*!"

The Chairman's voice rocked the space. The human creatures stopped. Andre Seraos, who remained still, raised a hand. The Chairman motioned for him to talk.

"Chairman, the evidence was provided in the discoveries annex of the resolution."

The bodies and suits were readjusting, the teeth licked. He turned towards the mass to his right. To him, they were parasites of this host country, the relics of an ancient time when the wealthy would use the lower classes as a shield from deadly diseases and war. He felt no concerns for his own safety, his political advancement, or the demise of those who shamelessly fed off of the dying poor, *his people*.

He looked at the bloated faces, the decomposing structures, and said, "It seems this hearing borrows a similar model than the one you all share on your day-to-day operations. Childish behaviors and counterproductive internal disputes to conceal your lack of integrity and spineless frames."

Another uproar ensued. Seraos' superior locked him in his peripheral vision; the silent authority looked forward towards the dumbfounded Chairman and failed to repress a smug look.

Proud of you, son.

6. THE BEASTS WITHIN

WASHINGTON, D.C. - BARTHOLDI PARK

Many argue that mankind is above all. Human beings are capable of self-analysis, mental time travel, imagination, abstract reasoning, cultural establishment, and morality. These higher-level skills separate us from beasts and form the basis of our global culture as a species.

In politics, rape, sex trafficking, embezzlement, corruption, war, murder, defamation, blackmail, and other destructive behaviors add to the aforementioned differentiation factors.

Be aware, however: Yes, often, the suits in this city cross the threshold to bestiality. And some never come back.

The afternoon sun breached the blockade imposed by the emergent layers of the eye-catching botanical garden; its rays, emissaries of its all-powerfulness, crashed onto a collection of thick and radiant foliage. Vibrant pinks, reds, greens, whites, yellows, and blues covered various shapes of many sizes. Petals swung about their legs, moved by the gardeners' gentle interventions and the light, rising winds.

Bartholdi Park was a safe haven, a place of introspection, a wrinkle in time whose neighboring crazies fast-forwarded through life. The sweet scents that characterized the shrubs, bushes, and lush grass matched most of the visitors' inclinations: D.C.'s suits were the *sugar* of this world.

Indeed, their primary mission was to *please*; it was for others to develop a dependency to their *sweetness* through false promises, bribes, and lies. But often, in gardening, sugar proved to compromise the soils' balance and integrity. It also brought about a steady flow of pests. Salt, on the other hand, tasted bitter yet made for an effective nutrient. Here, in this mad city, no one wished to take that route.

Tap, tap, tap, tap tap, tap.

Underneath the explosion of colors, scents, and textures, frames took shape in the darkness of the underground.

The black tactical vests, combat shirts, and assault rifles concealed the bodies; the unconventional gas masks, sleek and ceramic-coated, hid the faces of a ten-man team whose swift yet precise cadence warned of death.

The unit's men and women advanced towards the Capitol under the radar, virtually shielded from any potential repercussion. Should war break out on grounds once owned by the slave runners who founded this country, they were ready to die in the escalation and take with them as many adversaries as possible, in the embrace of a friendly death. The tunnels they ran were cartel-like, as if carved by millions of spoons. It was the work of a clandestine force with a worldwide reach. Years of small brush strokes and pathfinding defined this very moment.

The combatants lowered their profile, splashing the muddy browns of the water that infiltrated the rocky layers above head. The mysterious foes were foreign, born in circumstances that the locals could not fathom. Their concealed eyes met a more sophisticated man-made tunnel that offered an exit shooting upward. The leading element raised a fist as he stopped at the bottom. The unit halted its course.

————

One mile east, a local pharmacy painted a more idyllic picture.

A small shaded front housed petunias and roses arranged in rows, running along a white picket fence. The drugstore's wooden structure was an anachronism; it belonged to the underdeveloped towns of America's infancy.

A motherly figure ran the business. She was a local staple and a warm soul who had conquered the hearts of even the most troubled people. Her pale, rosy skin, curly gray blow-dry, and inviting smile reminisced of a feel-good movie on a Sunday afternoon. Her operation ran smoothly, as her likable and relatable persona attracted new clients and accumulated an impressive list of regulars.

Mama Joy, as nicknamed by the locals, had been serving Washington, D.C. for over sixty years, perpetuating the legacy of a century-old institution.

She was fronting and facing her shelves, reorganizing and consolidating after a hectic noon rush. Her contagious benevolence met the smiles of her clients. Her wrinkles conveyed affection, like the effects of time could never supersede the baking of a warm apple pie.

The clock above the entryway of her store read *1:45*. *Mama Joy* walked to the registers and disappeared in the back room.

Beyond the pristine storage space ahead, a narrow corridor led to multiple doors. She stopped at the first one on the left and retrieved a set of keys from her floral-patterned pharmacist coat.

The door opened and revealed a spartan setting. A small table was erected in the middle of the floor; ten burner phones were lined up with care, forming satisfying parallels. She picked an older model, one whose size betrayed the remnants of an ancient technology, and pressed the call button.

"It's a bit early for dinner."

Mama Joy answered the soft-spoken man, "Sweet tooth."

"The package has been dropped. Make the call and keep this device on you."

"Understood." Her loving persona and joyful demeanor still radiated in this exercise of spycraft. There was no mask. Something *else* drove her. A single, unswerving ideology, maybe?

The truth was, *Mama Joy*'d had enough. The country she so often celebrated had washed off its heavy makeup and revealed an ugly truth: the corruption, poverty, the crumbling infrastructures, the darkness in people's souls. Her moral compass was a line in a chart; the transgressions of those who ran the U.S. formed a second line on the same axes. And it no longer followed hers but instead trended upward.

She keyed *911* using the massive plastic buttons on the phone.

"911, what's your emergency?"

"A bomb was planted at the intersection of Third and A Street Northeast. Another one at the intersection of First Street and Independence Avenue Southeast. They have a cumulated killing radius of two miles. Two brown backpacks."

"When are the bombs going to explode?"

Mama Joy hung up and returned to the front, showcasing the clientele a genuine and good-natured smile.

———

A series of silent measures hit a bustling D.C.

The United States Capitol Police, who had concurrent jurisdiction with other law enforcement agencies over a 200-block area that included the Capitol grounds, was on the move. Its "Executive Team" began assessing a threat received by the D.C.

Police. The FBI's Counterterrorism Division also offered assistance, closely monitoring the situation.

First reports on the ground revealed a credible threat in at least one of the two locations provided by an unidentified individual thirty minutes earlier. Law enforcement agencies were unable to trace the call; the cell phone utilized was, inexplicably, using a foreign network. Domestic operators did not have any record on their calls and access logs. The voice of the caller was also altered through an analog system directly at the source.

The methods and meticulousness indicated it was the work of a well-organized individual or group, a thought that drove fearful prospects.

The Capitol Police, plump birds whose wide span wings failed to support flight, proved unusually efficient and coordinated, however.

Ground teams had cordoned the Capitol, sweeping the lawns in an inverted V-shaped pattern, looking for additional explosive ordnances. They quickly reached Independence and Constitution Avenues, as well as First St, moving with purpose and precision. Other teams conducted sweeps around major federal buildings east, closer to the presumed bomb sites. Clusters of cops, quiet professionals, expanded, laying the groundwork for a future evacuation.

The American public, a walking contradiction numb to violence yet damaged by the compounded trauma of mass shootings and bombings, had fled the sectors; the stern faces, dancing eyes, invisible tears, and drumming fingers painted a broad spectrum of emotions.

But there was one common variable: The panic was internalized rather than shown. The masses moved quietly and in an orderly fashion, distrustful of one another.

From the sky, a migratory movement drew a darker concentration.

There was a strange character to the police officers who

repeatedly failed to contain and neutralize various attacks from uneducated hillbillies; the ones who had mistaken domestic terrorism for patriotism last year, the QAnon cultists producing wild theories of a secret world order hunting *their* president. They had rushed the Capitol to further damage the democracy their *Orange Man* had already compromised through existing as a gross, incompetent, impulsive, and sexist figure of leadership.

Security failed to contain the mainly white crowd, a mushy blend of various supremacist groups. Or maybe refused to: conflicting accounts painted the *January 6* officers as undertrained, understaffed, complacent, or complicit.

But this time around, the Capitol Police exuded authority, leading the charge on the ground and at strategic command level. The entire force projected strengths, both in communication and tactical execution, reducing the radio chatter to executive orders and pertinent information related to the incident. They were decisive, composed.

Other agencies witnessed the blooming of seeds emerging from crisp ashes.

———

Beneath the marble surfaces and bright white stones of the U.S. Capitol, artificial lights shone on a procession of confused visitors. The underground access they were led to was unfinished, cold in its concrete coating. But there was light at the end of the tunnel, and the tensed facial expressions found relief in the flourishing brightness.

Above, in the House of Representatives, a structured sound, a coordinated set of steps interrupted Seraos' valiant crusade. The Chairman's froggy gaze now followed the Secret Service agents who surrounded the President and his VP. A second group of special agents ran alongside the chamber's curved wall to lock every access.

There was no movement among the men and women who proved to be as resilient as cockroaches, as resourceful as the most hardened pest, the politicians and advisors; the most dominant sound was the strange tapping of the walls by the presidential protection detail's floaters.

Tap. Tap. Tap tap tap tap.

The sounds resonated beyond the separation, leading to the hallways and spaces that housed non-essential personnel. The latter barely noticed the chamber's lockdown as they were grappling with an evacuation and pushed out through a maze of stones and woods. In the crowds, a young woman stopped and looked back at the chamber's dignified access. A nametag on her concierge uniform read *Yared*. A set of hands gently guided her back to the exit points, as she laid concerned eyes on the flock of *Hill* rats.

Out in the world, giants sat in thrones the heights of skyscrapers, pulling strings connecting to the wooden puppets at their feet.

———

The black ops team was patiently waiting, stacked in a file formation, underneath the Capitol's National Statuary Hall. The leading man had his rifle directed at a vent grill, up above. Light struggled to breach through the small apertures of its metallic structure. After growing distant a few minutes earlier, the rumble of fleeing preys above head had ceased.

A soft-spoken man echoed through their radio: "Green to green. The chamber is sealed. Proceed forward with the Kufrans."

"Strausberg moving."

The lead climbed a set of cold, stainless-steel bars and opened the vent, trailed by the wolves of his pack. The unit infiltrated the hall like a silent flood, bubbling from behind Mary Jane McLeod Bethune's fine marble.

They formed a herringbone and rushed to a hallway across the room. A couple of Secret Service agents spotted them around the corner and raised their gun; one of the two struck his forehead with his right fist. The group advanced towards him and identified a two-pane door further down: the House of Representatives chamber.

The covert detachment approached the access, their shadows gliding on the walls like menacing visions. They split in two files, left and right of the massive entrance door; its wood carvings and smoked glass had trapped elongated shadows that swung left and right, like the coordinated frenzy of a cult.

The point man raised two fingers in the air and waited a few seconds. He received a light tap on the shoulder. The female soldier across the frame, one whose revealed left eye marked the beginning of a deep tissue scar, nodded a *yes* to him as they both began to mount canisters onto their rifles' threaded barrels. Two clicks ensued. They proceeded to open the door and aimed up at a forty-five and sixty-degree angle.

The steady fingers found the triggers' walls and squeezed. A *swoosh* erupted as the gas canisters flew into the chamber, drawing a curved trail of smoke in the air.

The death squad closed the door back up, stealing a brief glance at the rotten politicians sitting in their leather chairs. Their perched necks were turned; they betrayed widening faces and frozen stares.

Inside, Secret Service enjoyed the monopoly of safety. They had donned gas masks seconds before the attack and let the attendees fend for themselves. There were no oxygen devices underneath their chairs; what constituted a known measure against bioweapons in the Capitol was missing.

The metallic gas canisters hit the crowd, landing on the carpet in muffled thumps.

A green smog filled the chamber; the committee and its attendees began rushing towards the exits in a chaotic craze where natural selection operated undisputed. The Secret Service agents in charge of the President and Vice President's protection details motioned all to stop, at gunpoint.

The politicians and officials complied, in a confusing turn of events. Their usually eerie smiles turned into half-shut mouths and widened eyes; the hunters were hunted.

The poisonous toxicant breached the targets' airways through respiratory droplets-like particles. They froze, inhabited by an intense tremor, their eyes blackened by monstrous vessels that progressed inward. The Secret Service accomplices left through a side door while the others suffered the toxin's unique properties. One last tall shadow escaped, and the secondary access shut close.

A strange metamorphosis became the greatest showman on Earth. Cracking bones shifted under the thin membranes, moving in an oscillating motion. Hairs grew, becoming coarse and furry. Extremities extended and retracted, driven by claws and paws. The eyes of the then-powerful changed, acquiring new details in the pupils, irises, and sclera. Facial features became inhuman, giving their inner demons a material form for the world to see.

Pores dilated. Screams and shrieks were lost in an animalistic cacophony. Heavy masses rocked the grounds, crashing the nearby walls and woods. The politicians regressed toward more primitive states, being carved and cut into more primitive forms. Creatures of darkness established a stronghold within their hosts; they found an angle to breach, one hidden within the triggers of a mysterious neurotoxin.

Outside the chamber, the black ops unit signaled the two Secret Service agents to continue pushing towards the lawn. The masked soldiers remained attentive to the developments inside. The House of Representatives was now sealed and had long been reinforced to withstand the destructive impulses of *literal* animals. The plan was in motion.

Without any warning, the last element of the operational detachment returned to the National Statuary Hall and turned right to find a small room the size of a janitor's closet. Inside, an individual was patiently waiting, fingers interlocked, straight and inflexible. He wore a tan vest disfigured by embedded blocks of explosives. A timer was sewn onto the fabric. It read *00:00*.

The plump man was sweating, his fat burning under the heat generated by the suicide device. He was composed, however. The black ops soldier met his moon-eyed gaze and raised her fists at eye level. The man nodded and left the room, trailing behind his escort. The latter reunited with her unit, bringing the kamikaze to the House of Representatives access.

Behind the massive door, a new biosystem produced strange, alien sounds.

————

The attack on the House of Representatives went unnoticed, camouflaged in the outside noises of a bustling city challenged by a terror cell and the repeated attacks of a nightmare. No one questioned the timing nor looked elsewhere, instead obsessed with and blinded by self-preservation.

News outlets covered the events; networks theorized about the reemergence of foreign terrorism, the shaping of new domestic hazards or even a government-led hoax. Sensationalism was the order of the day, prioritized over a deep, insightful, and accurate journalistic approach whose focal point would revolve around a yearning for and seeking of a universal truth.

The airwaves were cluttered with an incomprehensible chatter, conflicting retellings driven by the news outlets' shifty political affiliations. Until an unforeseen external force took over, shutting the noise out.

An unidentified frame sat behind a layer of smokey plexiglass. It appeared to the general population as being elusive yet inevitable. It had no distinctive features. Its blurry edges belonged to various body types, a multitude of potential profiles. A synthetic voice of a low pitch broke the silence left behind by the hijacking of cable networks, social media platforms, and online video sharing hubs.

"This is the *Watchmaker*. Today, at 01:45 PM Eastern, D.C. Police Department received an anonymous call reporting that two bombs were planted east and southeast of *Capitol Hill*. The Capitol Police, which has jurisdiction over a 200-block area expanding outward from the pits of snakes that are the House of Representatives and the Senate, has proved surprisingly effective in cordoning the sector and taking appropriate measures towards a potential evacuation. It's almost like ... January 6 was never a thing.

"But like everything in this city, the truth is always concealed, or at best, underlying. The suits and decisionmakers shaping your lives exercise a narrow vision, preoccupied by the preservation of their benefits and a position of power that allows them to build generational wealth through questionable practices. Politicians lost their humanity a while ago, when the system became a rat race where the fat worms now justify status quo under the pretense of a new form of 'body positivity'. I'm aware this message outlasted your average seven-second attention span, but it is necessary. You have been fed content from ill-advised medias controlled by a handful of wealthy partisans who fight one another to drive favorable optics for reelection.

"When's the last time you questioned the system? The last time you took action, tangibly and purposefully? This country is broken, shattered by a tale of two worlds on the opposite extremes of capitalism's spectrum. The men and women ruling this nation feast over your decaying flesh. You are served at their table, medium-rare, by systemic design. Drink those words, reread my transcripts if necessary; we will make them available online at *americaisazoo.com*."

A pause provided a dramatic effect.

"A prime example of this State being a house of lies: The

incidents reported earlier this afternoon are nothing but smoke screens. The real fight broke out inside the walls of your Capitol, once more. This time, however, it was executed with consideration and professionalism, with pure motives lightyears away from the nonsensical actions of uneducated demographics born into generational racism. Further details are coming. Note to law enforcement agencies: Do not breach the U.S. Capitol or interfere with our process. M. President and his VP, trapped inside, would face grave consequences."

7. STATE OF EMERGENCY

WASHINGTON, D.C

Collective tragedy is one of the strongest bonding agents. To a mass of brain-dead followers, it is the antidote to a poisonous neurodegenerative disease.

Hundreds of thousands of Twitter fingers searched for answers on the Internet of Things.

The brains were driven by impulses, by new basic instincts molded by social media platforms and interconnectivity. All over the city, *Pinocchios* danced to the rhythm of pulled strings, frantically typing in bubbles. But the founding fathers, the *Zuckerbergs*, the *Systroms*, *Kriegers,* and *Dorseys* lost control of their people. Their servers and data centers were all compromised, hit by a formidable hacking force, one from a network whose reach was global and ideology impervious to capitalistic temptations, to corruption.

Google.com was attacked as well: The homepage displayed a shiny piglet with an equally polished kitchen knife cutting another pig in pieces, the scene immortalized in a vector art. The imagery lacked subtlety, but the smartest minds understood why.

A website withstood the storm: *americaisazoo.com*. The landing page featured text on the left side. Random words made for chaotic thoughts.

Rebuild.
Reform.
Question.
Systemic by design.
Oppression is a monster of a thousand processes.
A platform elevates, so they lied.

A video feed was embedded into the website, as well. A message displayed four words in a loop.

Hey, you, wake up.

People feared the disruption, blinded by narrow-minded beliefs, reactionary jerking, and emotional responses, unable to see life through the countless shades of greys introduced by the *Watchmaker* and his enterprise.

There was a beauty to the global panic: From the unseen, a mysterious anthropologist, or a few of them, began examining the humans through a magnifying glass, over a fishbowl.

Abeba Solomon was one of the few exceptions, a rogue ant who ventured outside the colony's boundaries. Her post-workout beauty care routine was interrupted by a call from her office; the Capitol Police contacted her FBI division through a secured pipeline, reporting multiple incidents of significance. Two of them were already relayed by the media.

The other was initially missed. Until the *Watchmaker* made himself known, as the spokesperson for a potentially dangerous revolutionary movement.

But what had happened inside the Capitol?

Abeba's thoughts ran amok as she grabbed her service weapon and cell phone. She needed to connect the dots, to fight her way up the stream and locate the source. *The video feed is still inactive. No claims. No known casualties. The focal point seems to be politics and policymaking. No criminal property damage.*

Inconsistencies made for a strange pattern; there was more to discover. Abeba zoomed full-speed to Independence Avenue, southwest of the *Hill.* There, FBI vans and police officers in wasteful muscle trucks took over the area, set up in the shape of a massive sunflower. The Joint Terrorism Task Force was waiting for its last missing piece: Abeba Solomon, the Queen.

She arrived a few minutes later, after breaching through a paralyzed traffic. *Twenty-six vehicles. Thirty-two human assets. One command center. One armory. Four RQ-11.*

Logistics was already a finalized strategy. Abeba's brain yearned to cruise faster, beyond the technicalities. *I need to understand.*

The personnel under her command were hiding in their vehicles, running from the scorching heat of the sun's hostile takeover. Abeba could regulate her temperature, compartmentalizing portions of her brain concerned with heat factors: another benefit of a cursed gift few could comprehend.

She stepped out of her vehicle and walked through the stressed engines of cars, vans, and tactical wheels; the noise was like the fluctuations of a displaced beehive.

The personnel identified their leader and followed her to the lawn, effectively shutting the hubbub.

They continued two hundred feet west. Abeba stopped in front of a large patch of grass flanking the right wing of the Capitol, grandiose in its bright whites and bronze.

The entire area had been evacuated, leaving silence exposed to the ghosts of the slave builders who still haunted the collective memory. The grounds were drenched in black blood and liquefied body parts, yet the grass was lush, neatly trimmed, and soft underfoot. Vectors and numbers flooded the woman god's sensory input as she came to a halt.

Abeba faced her assets. Her baby eyes were offset by a quick, chopped speech that conveyed knowledge and decisiveness.

"As you know, a credible bomb threat was communicated to D.C. police at 01:45 PM eastern. One explosive device was found at 02:12 PM eastern by the USCP. Highly sophisticated. DCPD's bomb squad is still working on it a few blocks east. We allocated people to assist with the task, and the area has been evacuated. The mayor received a formal State of Emergency request. We're shutting the city down."

Concerned eyes failed to understand the correlation between an isolated incident and a city lockdown.

Abeba raised her right hand, palm outward, and said, "I know. I know. There's more. You reviewed a video feed from an individual self-identified as the *Watchmaker*. He or she, or it, is your priority. Public enemy number one on the board, *PO1*. And this is where the SOE request comes from. Twenty minutes and seventeen seconds ago, the CTD received HUMINT that the attack referred to in the footage could be of biological nature. We are unable to trace the source of the feed, but details on operational procedures inside the Capitol make it a viable threat."

A young woman holding a tablet-like device asked, "Is it a national security threat?"

Abeba answered, "From the data we've collected so far, no. It's local. But ramifications on a systemic level could be national, maybe even global. We've seen regimes fall and take others in their collapse. Think *Arab Spring*. The general population has a right to access information. The things they will see or hear could lead to long-term shifts. But our sole purpose here is to restore order and address the threat. How? Transparency, constant communication with the general public, and a channel with whoever's inside that building."

She pointed at the Capitol behind her. Its massive dome shot upward in the clear skies. Its aura radiated; it was the wellspring of magic waters, the guardian of terrible secrets, the provider of many answers.

A tall, white male inquired, "Any update from the SAD?"

Abeba joined both hands together and replied, "Classified as of now. But I will let you know if I get anything of relevance from the CIA. The SAD usually doesn't disclose their assets coverage or SOPs."

Abeba pointed at her feet. "We're going to start here. I want a 1.32-mile cordon around the lawns with HAZMAT containment. Our strategic command here, 13.53 feet from where I stand. I need drone feeds in the rotation, southeast, northeast, northwest, southwest. Lines with the USCP, DCPD, and our office's liaison. I want a window to the *Watchmaker*'s landing page, and I want to know everything about the IP's specifics.

"Where are the servers hosted? The intention here is not to shut down what constitutes our only communication channel with the perpetrator as of now but to understand the nature and origin of the threat we face. I also want another monitor on PO1's previous message. 173 individuals were evacuated by the USCP. Fifty-four are left inside, including the POTUS and his VP. I want a file on each and every one of them. Travel logs for the past month and travel patterns to and from the city. Boat, plane, train, car, bike, flight balloon ... whatever it takes to identify suspicious movements. Any questions?"

Pens scraped on papers in a muffled frenzy. Abeba felt the need to absorb more data, to pull her men out of the water and sail to deep sea. But she had to wait, to work within their scope and processing capabilities. No questions were formulated as the Joint

Terrorism Task Force, or *JTTF*, began working the logistical details together.

Abeba took over, curling her hands into fists alongside her toned frame. "Good. SITREP meeting with all internal leads in two hours and twenty-two seconds. Go."

8. THE ZOO GALLERY

WASHINGTON, D.C. - UNDISCLOSED LOCATION

It's eclectic art, from a broad range of sources. It's horns, it's claws, it's scales. It's a slithering motion, it's a paddling, it's flight.

"Welcome to Hell, where you are welcome to sell," Wagner muttered to himself.

His glacial eyes swept his digital wall's feeds and stopped at the sight of Abeba's FBI's demonstration of force. An improvised crisis coordination center took shape on the screen.

Production design on a set. There was an attempt at masking the operational details with hardwood panels, but lone wolves from blogging outlets provided various angles of the scene, livestreaming from online platforms that survived the *blackout*. The concealment measures were outmatched by rogue drones and well-connected freelancers. Wagner had various footages of the scene displayed on nearby screens.

How can you deliver on the promise of national security when the nation itself lacks discipline, instead participating in the obstruction of the due administration of justice?

Mark Wagner rubbed his brows, expelling the thought. The network he employed knew better, he was sure of.

The Alpha in the pack shared no emotional connections with this country. *Amerika* was a business partner, a provider, a clueless client willing to pay full price out of sheer laziness. But the U.S. nationals who contacted him were different, enlightened, hard-working, decisive. And their plan was sound.

Mark found himself wandering in his memories, picturing his beloved Germany positively impacted by the public lynching of corrupted politicians. He longed for his return to a culturally rich nation whose ingenuity outmatched a troubled past. *Mutter Deutschland.*

A call came through the landline on his minimalist Swedish desk. He pressed the speaker's key.

"Glossy black?" the synthetic voice asked.

Wagner answered, "No, evergreen."

"What did you think?"

The German let out a half-suppressed laugh and gave his opinion. "A bit theatrical, very American. But the content and its shock value fit the targets. For an introduction, at least."

The mysterious caller inquired, "How should I proceed next?"

"Shift tone. Less antics, more operational details. It's a quick process on a tight window. You can still remain provocative at key points to keep the thread tension high."

"Fine. Will beam you a draft in thirty-five."

The call disconnected and Mark Wagner returned to Abeba; her file detailed a condition that could prove a formidable enemy. She shared the perspective of a thousand gods.

At this very moment, in the eye of the storm, the German fixer was developing countermeasures.

Washington, D.C. - The House of Representatives Chamber

Feathers stuck to the wet coat of a massive bear who chased an adult-size panda to the nearby wall. The Bear's footsteps marked giant leaps as it inched closer to its prey, ripping the blue carpet off in the pursuit. The Panda was brave, facing its potential murderer, pinned against a hard surface.

In their peripheral vision, heavy feet with opposable big toes approached and rocked feces-covered leather chairs in the chase; a full-grown silverback gorilla rushed and intercepted the Bear, dealing powerful blows that sent both flying across the space. On the opposite side, by the Chairman's stand, a raging bull stood his ground, bellowing to the wilderness, to the center of U.S. politics.

His thick bone structure and large, muscular frame concealed a majestic lion of gold undertones whose darker mane was royal in appearance. A grasshopper was perched on the stand, much smaller in stature yet defiant, ready to be catapulted by its big, back legs.

A flock of migratory songbirds flapped short wings above, feeding the ongoing destructive rampage with a thunderous cackling foreign to their species, almost *human*. A peregrine falcon circled over the murmuration, recording the entire scene with sharp, dark eyes.

A foul scent of urine, fecal matters, and bodily fluids gave the chamber a more suitable fragrance. A unicorn, its shiny white coat still sparkling under the dimmed lights, was contemplating the supernatural chaos from the balconies overlooking the Bull and his clique.

There were apparent bonds; a dynamic of clans that shaped the strange battlefield. The walls eroded under the impact of poundings the strength of ten humans. Beneath the stone, a steel frame prevented the creatures from escaping. The doors were also reinforced following the same method, quickly modified by the black ops unit standing outside the chamber, one unmoved by the eruption of a new animal kingdom.

A wolf blended with the darker furniture of the balconies. It roamed the upper floor, searching for a non-existent pack. Below, cheetahs, dogs, frogs, snakes, insects, and other mammals of various classifications had already succumbed to deadly wounds, bleeding in one last raspy cry.

The smell of iron now blended with the offensive scent of the loose bladders and fast-processing stomachs. The souls and motives of those who had once ruled this country shapeshifted their shells, and Evil left its horrendous print on the seat of power.

Boom. Boom. Boom. Boom. Bang. Boom. Boom.

Inside the organisms of the transformed, hormone levels stabilized. The new brain tissues quickly matured; the optics adjusted. The fight lost its intensity, its vigor.

A frightened pig hid underneath a bench, terrified of the menacing buzzing of a murder hornet. The latter flew away.

With the physiological adjustments came another threat, more insidious: self-realization. Through the lenses of zoo attractions, of the jungle's and desert's inhabitants, the beasts remembered their human forms. The rocking and seismic movements of a wild fight still existed, but something else lurked in the shadows, a fear beyond primal. What was the science, or the magic, behind the revealing metamorphosis?

The new sights, scents, and urges raised another yet interesting question: Why were the politicians and government officials now *more* recognizable?

9. THE HOROLOGIST

WASHINGTON, D.C. - UNDISCLOSED LOCATION

He became the voice of the heroes. The leading charge against the world order. Hidden behind safeguards, fail-safes, covert identities, and a multi-billion-dollar network, he was still braver than the power-hungry monstrosities suited in Argent, Ermenegildo Zegna and Hart Schaffner Marx.

Washington, D.C. was robbed of its oversized veneers. A crooked smile set an awkward PR damage control op in motion. But the world *knew*.

The *Watchmaker*'s first recording and landing page quickly became the most-viewed content and visited platform in the world. Many foreign heads of state questioned the nature and potential impact of the attacks. Will they also need to make adjustments in their repulsive habits, or could they still feast on the general population, the underpaid field operations people?

The *Watchmaker* began providing answers as its blurry edges appeared on *americaisazoo.com*.

"This is the *Watchmaker*. I know some of you perceived my prior message as demeaning, insulting, highly offensive, or even theatrical. But just like this operation, it was necessary. It was the defibrillator's charge to your flatline, the lustrous light to your darkness. I mentioned an interest in the Capitol's lockdown earlier, and now, I am ready to deliver on the promises I implicitly made, on closure and transparency. The message.

"The actions I will soon be taking with the people I partnered with may not appear justifiable to you at first. Your moral guidelines may find the kidnapping and *transformation* of 'law-abiding citizens' outright illegal. But the frame of the law was constructed by the very people on this *Hill*. Embezzlement, drug trades, sex trafficking, statutory rape, bribes, tax fraud, and murder are among the countless crimes they committed, stimulated by an environment that encourages malpractice in the pursuit of power, interests falsely labeled as 'national' and political capital.

"My team's objective is to clear the smoke screens, the PR stunts, the soporific speeches that never clearly deliver. What did we set to accomplish here, you may ask? I will tell you, a complete makeover of the U.S. political and governmental machine. A chance at survival for the working poor and the lower classes who turn to crime to supplement their income and feed enough to keep their body in motion. A better redistribution of wealth, better infrastructures, a more advanced education, better zoning and environmental policies. I am working for your future selves, the self-aware and the proud, the critical thinkers who desire a better world.

"We'll have no involvement in politics after this event, leaving you with a blank slate to fill. We have no economic interests in this either, but simply the resources and skillsets to make it happen. And a collective conscience, a flow of a deep evergreen pouring into the pitch-black fabric of your reality. I will livestream a footage of the House of Representatives chamber after this communication. You will see literal animals in a fight or flight mode, driven by impulses that were always present. Those beasts are some of the men and women who rule this country. And yes, the transformation is permanent."

The mysterious messenger vanished to leave room for another feed on the landing page: the vision of a surreal America.

Or maybe the *real* America.

Animals of various sizes and shapes were crashing into each other, fighting for dominance over unmarked territories or evading the cavernous blows of the bigger monsters. Hair, fur, dry scales, feathers, and a lingering mist provided a visual backdrop for the scene.

The chamber was vandalized, covered in layers of light brown and white elements. Some creatures roamed, some hid. Some rushed through attack angles. Dead animal corpses were trampled, rocked, pushed afar. A dark liquid had stained the floor and furniture, offering a stark contrast with the brown and white goo that seemed to have fixed prior. The space had lost its symmetricity, its structural integrity.

All over the world, attentive eyes opened wide to the sight of the first chemical attack of its kind: the shaping of human beings into other species, the manipulation of our very own DNA strands in a unique way, on an accelerated time lapse. Foreign news outlets and online channels ceased the opportunity. Wild theories were formulated, from the viral promotion of a new reality TV show to a takeover by alien lifeforms.

Conspiracies of secret orders and hidden figures returned for another desperate shot at fame. Once more, sensationalism had trumped the need for an unbiased and accurate reporting.

A Swedish network offered the closest to an objective angle.

Is America a zoo? The United States Capitol in Washington, D.C. was attacked once more today, September 6, 2023, with grave consequences. A mysterious figure self-identified as the Watchmaker announced it had a plan for what it deemed was a rotten, corrupted government, a 'rat race' to the preservation of power and related benefits. The face of the attack on the Capitol is now on the FBI and Interpol's most wanted and red notices lists. In a process that still remains shrouded in mystery, it appears that fifty-four attendees of an oversight hearing in the House of Representatives chamber underwent a deep physical and psychological transformation. A livestream of the events is available on americaisazoo.com.

The authenticity of the feed was confirmed by the U.S. State Department, whose top two representatives are listed on an official casualty report. No further comments were made on the nature of the attack and its associated methods. Please stay tuned for further updates. Tack så mycket. Hej då!

———

Gigantic industrial drum fans kept the FBI improvised outpost from overheating, their white noise loud yet pleasant, grounding.

Abeba laid eyes on the Capitol building after the *Watchmaker*'s intervention gave her a clearer picture of its insides. The new development brought more data, numbers, probability factors, vectors.

A hot breeze bent the nearby leaves to its will. The sun was setting, yet the temperatures were still abnormally high. A massive, framed canopy shielded Abeba's rich dark skin from the attacks of the star. The crisis coordination center was buzzing in a blend of pencils gliding, keystrokes, animated exchanges, and radio communications. Abeba employed her workforce to gain a better understanding of the threat. Soon, she would explore emerging leads.

At the left edge of the sunshade, she turned towards her team. They were at war with the hearts and minds of those who shook the country, with the mysterious figure who made America look like a helpless child. Her agency was adequately funded, and she was their biggest asset. It was just a matter of time before she uncovered the truth.

Will they be ready for it? In her vivid imagination, a porcelain hand danced in a chopped motion, swallowed by frosted quicksand. A voice reached out from beneath the surface.

"Please."

But as Abeba swept the barren lands around, she noticed corpses were paving a passage to the quicksand; shards of porcelain had punctured their dead, rigid flesh.

"Please."

Letters were carved into the palm of the spiderlike hand, its outer layer chipped.

Amerikkka.

Abeba connected the dots. Anger was crashing the walls of her deeply logical being, failing to infiltrate her conscience. But she still felt like this country was a flawed project that required revision. Was this attack relevant to the bigger picture? To the greater issues?

She shook the contemplation off and ordered her team, "Alright, listen up! We have a direct feed on the chamber. I need answers. Any visual identifiable for the victims? Any clue on the PO1's identity? Is it female, male? Its psychological profile? Where are the servers located? Find me a negotiation channel with the PO1 or its affiliates inside the Capitol. *It* had to have relied on outsourcing for certain portions of the operation. I want a full background sweep on USCP and DC Police personnel. The New York City bureau agreed to lend us two-hundred agents for clerical tasks. You have four hours."

The special agents returned to their posts, finalizing the setup of the strategic command and executing the new orders. Abeba looked ahead. The white dome darkened.

A young Black woman with short finger waves and a reddish-brown undertone approached Abeba. She said, "Ma'am, I have the flight patterns and visitors' logs for the past month."

Abeba grabbed the two dossiers and laid them on a metallic table to her right. "Good."

She turned the hundreds of pages at the speed of light, recording each number and name in milliseconds, like a god meddling with its creation phase. The data danced on the paper, offering itself to her. She accepted, drinking in the input as her subordinate observed, astonished.

A name came up twice in the flight manifests and once in the Capitol's visitor log.

She asked her agent, "Abdul Baaqi. Is he in the hearing's resolution?"

The young FBI asset raised an index finger and swept the crisis center with her mesmerizing green eyes. They found a red-taped laptop. She rushed to retrieve the device and struck the keys frantically, sweat beads crashing her bulletproof vest, like rain drops on a glass dome.

After a few seconds, she confirmed, "Yes, ma'am."

10. THE PARALLEL STATE

Often, shame is weaponized by questionable characters. It is far from genuine, instead more like the twisted manifestation of their inner fears. The men and women raping the dead corpses of the working class were caught in the act, genitals out, the stage lights shining on their sloppy, sweaty flesh.

Belch vocalizations shot from the Gorilla's wide mouth, sending a vibrating note through the chamber. The beasts were panting, dry heaving, producing ghostly echoes that haunted the casualties of an otherworldly battle.

At this very moment, nothing mattered. The minds and brains found themselves at the junction of humanity and... something else. The Panda began *seeing* its black and white coat, stroking the fur. The fuzzy texture was soft yet thick. The weight of massive organs was felt throughout its big-boned structure. But the muscles buried under the fat seemed to support the heavy machine.

Mankind's cognitive functions were tightly intertwined with animal instincts and features.

The Gorilla laid eyes on the Bear; the latter was licking crimson-red wounds on its side, stealing sporadic glances at its opponent.

They all came to a full stop, drowsy from the chemical imbalances, from the costly metamorphosis. Some were shedding tears, aware they perpetrated unspeakable crimes. The stench of blood flooding their heightened senses operated as a reminder, as a vector to a painful realization: They did the dirty job themselves. It felt appalling, unsettling.

Some mammals whose behavioral design was not geared towards evading predators fell asleep, snoring on the smelly and damaged carpet.

The room was unrecognizable. Splintered woods and ripped leather worked in concert to recreate the aftermath of a category five tornado.

Something terrible happened here, the creatures observed.

For a brief instant, they felt connected to one another, through an unexplainable channel that tapped into a collective conscience.

Roaches were covering a portion of the chamber's right section. They were crushed dead yet disgustingly wet, leaving a trail of small translucid eggs in their wake. The Songbirds had touched down, motionless, hungry. They were staring at the shiny bugs, their widened eyes zoning out to a seductive prospect.

Behind the stand, the Lion and its loyal protector, the Bull, conspired in silence. Their minds were navigating through the situation, exploring their defined muscles, wide jaws, horns, and keratin claws. They felt *split*, torn between two worlds, two perspectives. The synergy charted a course to a million stars, a billion universes.

Finally, the Lion found the strength to talk. Was it motion economy that allowed it to acquire speech? Or the inner workings of its own transformation? Or maybe it was God who made it special, above all?

This must be the latter, it thought. The beast roared. "Who deserves the medal of freedom here? You arrrrreeeeee beneath me." The disillusioned stared at the Lion and drew a blank gaze.

It resumed, "I am the President of the United Fucking States! You arrrrrreeee nothing!"

The voice was altered, deep, cavernous, thunderous.

The Lion lifted a paw and swatted imaginary flies. "Just like everyone else, you serve me! Get me out of here, nowwwwww."

The last words roared in the space, sending a tremor traversing the others.

The Bull tossed his head about forcefully, widened his stance, and pawed the floor. He rushed forward towards the main access, trampling on mutilated cadavers, squishing their soft and warm flesh. His head lowered, and his horns found the wooden panes of the door, which had survived the initial brawl.

The wood shattered into hundreds of splinters. But the Bull saw black specks; he had run into a metallic frame then concealed by the wooden layers. The metal clanged. The others jumped. The Panda sat nearby; it had rolled on its side, pensive.

The President jumped off the Chairman's podium and advanced towards the Bull. A high-pitched squeaking followed his path, trailing behind; a shaky pig stood on its back feet, its belly fat shamelessly bouncing. It caught up with the Lion and stood beside him by the metal frame, and by the mature male bovine, still shaken after the collision. The President showed long, razor-sharp teeth and licked his massive canines. He inspected the layer of metal, sniffing the edges. His snout twitched. His layered eyes sharpened.

"Whooo theee fuuuuckkkkk is behind that?"

On the other side, the black ops team had flanked the access, weapons up, directly aimed at the door. The suicide bomber, facing the den of thieves, looked at the unit's lead standing to his right. The fat, corporate-looking white male drenched in sweat underneath his wearable IED was looking for the mercenary's approval. The latter nodded; his eyes grew dim under the black ski mask.

The once composed kamikaze instantly shifted emotional states, tensing his facial muscles and jumping up and down. He finally retired the motion and advanced closer to the door.

He said, in a shaky voice, "M. President, I-I-I-I woulddddddn't do tttthat. Theyyy made me wear ... this ... this ... th ... this *explosive* vest. They are listening and the metal shell ... it ... it won't budge. They said you need to count your dead and ... identify your ... group *members*."

Inside, the Lion turned towards the Gorilla, still recovering from the prior fight. He shifted back to the door and answered, "Youuuu will pay!"

The Pig timidly asked the suicide bomber, "What is it that you need?" It squealed the last syllables.

"Count your d-d-d-d-dead firsssst," the suicide bomber replied. He added, "Who are you?"

The Pig answered, "U.S. Department of State legal counsel. My name is no longer."

11. THE ANACOSTIA PROJECTS

WASHINGTON, D.C. - ANACOSTIA

A key for 35. Answers for 10. The glasshouse for 25.

Crack, overgrown vegetation and busted windows possessed the trap houses, lined in a row a mile from the historical Douglass' Estate. All-black big body trucks and old Buicks occupied the street. Incoming traffic swerved between massive potholes. Lookouts were posted outside the white brick stashes, sitting in long chairs, Glock 19s tucked in their basketball shorts.

Michael Hoover, dressed in loafers, linen pants, and a black-and-white-striped shirt with rolled-up sleeves walked Anacostia's dilapidated neighborhood. His nonchalance and joie-de-vivre were a tactic he employed in this section of the *script*. He knew the local hustlers and gangsters had a silent agreement with the D.C. police: No hits on outsiders and the officers would look the other way. Here, crime was foreign to the upper middle white class that snatched properties and land at a low cost, to drive a *costly* gentrification. It was foreign to the visitors passing through, to the history buffs and locals' relatives. The flooding drugs killed with a delay, hence the emaciated faces and decaying teeth.

Gunshots only erupted in the dark, like a sweet serenade. Bodies were disposed of in the river before the sun rose.

As with most *ghettos*, the government profited off of the social and economic hardships endured here; the democrats saw those hoods as breeding grounds for new voters and the republicans used them as leverage for budgeting propositions. Stuck in the middle were brilliant minds who would have chosen a better path if legal money was matching the drug trades'; or if they could finance strong business ideas with equally solid cash reserves within the local community.

Once more, the rats up top had snatched all the cheese.

But the Watchmaker set a trap, Michael thought. The sight of America's failures made him nauseous. He felt out of place yet so close to home. *Ben Ben, this is awful. So... asymmetrical.*

A small, fenced lawn housed a couple of lookouts who stood right away upon his arrival. Michael seemed unbothered, casually opening a small metallic gate that creaked at his passage. The lockdown was poorly enforced here, yet the hope dealers were antsy; the suits they supplied out west were caught in a storm.

Michael said, "I need to talk to Moses." He joined his hands behind his back. *Click.*

One of the men tucked a hand in his short and asked, "Who that?"

The CIA agent read a lie behind the stoic face; the frowning gave it up. He also knew there was no CCTV coverage in the area. And the *dawgs* barking on these corners... well, most had never seen combat.

He drew his HK45 and squeezed the trigger twice, the hollow points quietly leaving his silencer to find the skulls of the watchers. They collapsed, bending the long chairs' thin frames. Michael looked around and met the defiant stares of other cliques.

He shouted, "See? That's the issue with you hoodlums. You think you're qualified to kill. It takes skillsets and an unwavering commitment. *I* am fully committed. Are you? Because I'll take each and every one of you with me, to *Allah*."

The dope boys and lookouts were weighing the pros and cons, puffing their chests and mean-mugging the CIA agent, the disruptor. They did not understand who or what he was, how he could be so lethal yet so *gentrified*. To them, he was a Black man speaking and acting *white*. A thought process inherited from being cursed by the slums, from a new form of cultural slavery.

But his demeanor and the professionalization of his killings demanded respect from the small entry-level distributors who dreamed of moving kilos and retiring in the sunny South.

They all backed up and looked around, scanning their corners for police presence or unusual patterns. Michael added, "This is not a sting operation. I came to visit a friend. I will be out of your way shortly."

Tap. Tap.

He entered the brick house and yelled, "Mos—"

The barrel of a Sig Sauer P 226 found Michael Hoover's right temple.

He smirked and spoke. "Good. You have the upper hand, keeping in tradition with the oddly inspiring feminism transforming the landscape of those who sell death."

Moses, an attractive woman of a darker complexion, betrayed no reaction. She was a lioness of deep, layered eyes and sharp features.

"Hoover. You owe me two men. *Allah yil'anek!*"

He still had a grip on his HK45. His wrist was twisted, aiming the handgun at her throat.

"Look down, Moses. Squeeze the trigger and we're both meeting our creator. And why not employ female lookouts? Equality should also apply to exposure, right? We're *all* expendables, after all."

Moses quickly looked down the outer tube of a silencer. She met Michael's manufactured eyes and said, "Nice toy. Another overkill from y'all black ops bitches. Oh, and for years, women been on the frontline catchin' the shots and sucking dicks for a crack rock, a Birkin, or a New York Times bestseller. So, I get to decide now."

"It's a bit more complicated than that, but touché. You look lovely."

She smirked and raised her brows. "What do you need?"

"A conversation. And answers."

"'Bout what?" She was steady and controlled, a product of the concrete, a response to the mounting expectations associated with being a drug lord.

"The attack on the Capitol," Hoover said simply.

She shrugged. "The feed crazy."

"Yes, indeed. Maddening, isn't it? I need leads, and I know you keep tabs. Behind this hood slang hides a bright young woman. Quite resourceful, from what I recall."

A brief silence accompanied Moses' thoughts. A burn-plastic-and-cleaning-chemical smell lingered in the air, threatening to compromise Michael's expensive fabrics. In his head, witches perched on gallows shouted incomprehensible words. Their mouths foamed in an obscene display. Soon, their speech became more coherent.

Kill her.

Footsteps grew louder, towards the central stairwell. Hoover added, "It is not worth dying for, young lady." Moses' juvenile energy concealed a formidable brainpower. Michael reminisced of her rise in the echelons. He had bet on her early as a ground asset, knowing she would exceed expectations and break boundaries in a male-dominated line of business. While he never developed a paternal love for her, he grew fond of the *Iron Lady*, the young adult who defied all odds.

She looked deep into his soul and found no trace of fear, apprehension, or frustrations. His window gave on an empty, colorless room. She said, "Ight nie. Dre, we straight!"

The footsteps grew feebler this time, widening the gap.

Moses resumed, "The room to ya left."

"Yes, ma'am. Lower your weapon. Please."

She obliged and shoved him forward. He crossed the space, his gun at an unorthodox angle, covering his rear.

The room was a journey into the past. The floral wallpaper projected a pink glow through a vintage lampshade, cream or perhaps off-white. A sofa and loveseat were wrapped in plastic, shining in a light brown. The carpet was of a dark green shade.

Questionable design choices. But the smell is gone.

Moses kept an eye on her guest as she moved the loveseat to face the sofa. On the right, a hole in the dry wall revealed wooden studs. She noticed Michael shamelessly peeking. "Hoover, eyes here."

He was now facing her, sinking in the sofa. He straightened his posture.

Moses deep, supernatural stare penetrated his flesh. She inquired, "So, what makes ya think I got intel?"

Michael was studying the young woman, a hand on his gun. She had grown into a sharper figure, and the frightened eyes that had met his years ago were no longer. There was a determination, a self-confidence in her posture, in the way she pridefully displayed her scars. The kid had gone through hell and back, but she was still breathing.

Her jumbo knotless braids led down to a partially burnt neck adorned with a gold necklace: the Hand of Fatima. Michael wondered if others also relied upon supernatural protections in encounters with her.

He led the conversation. "Biggest supplier east of the river. Resourceful. Attentive. Muslim with strong ties to the community. My superior gets it straight from the source. There's this Libyan national."

"Slow down. What do I get in return?"

"Fish scale, highest purity, no middleman, no dependency. You own the entire production and distribution chain."

"How much?" she asked.

"Ninety-six keys a week."

Her eyes opened wide, stretching her battle scars. She asked, "Ninety-six? How?"

"Irrelevant. But national security is worth the trade."

She laughed. "National security for who, motherfucka? Them suits are a threat to national security themselves."

"There are further ramifications to this attack. Civil war, infiltration by foreign elements, those proud boys visiting your hood…"

She grimaced and observed a brief silence, her eyes evading his probe. "What's his name?"

"Abdul Baaqi. B-A-A-Q-I."

Two knocks were heard through the ceiling. Moses stood, her gun pointed at Hoover's chest, and motioned for him to exit. She said, "I'll look into it. Same burner?"

"Yes, young lady." He passed her and crossed the doorless frame. "And you'll be compensated for those two, maybe three men. Our little secret."

She slammed the door behind him and yelled, "Dre! Get yo a—"

A whizzing sound breached into the house from the upper level. Soon after, a body dropped, in a loud thump. The wood screamed in pain.

Moses rushed upstairs to find her number two on the floor, his white t-shirt stained by spatters of blood. His forehead bore the mark of a long-range caliber. *Fuck.*

Michael left the front yard and crossed the threshold to the street, unbothered and stern. He stopped and looked around; the locals were hiding behind the wooden planks and smoked windows of the *bandos* they claimed to fiercely defend. Kids were tucked in and shielded from the Boogeyman who practiced his preaching. Michael Hoover could see the eyes dancing left and right, the wet grips on the nine millimeters, the chaotic pacing. He tucked his gun in his trousers and retrieved a small in-ear bud from his front chest pocket. The miniature device found his sharp organ of hearing.

He tapped it twice. A channel opened. "Overwatch 1, you're green to green. Proceed."

"Good copy."

Hoover removed the earbud and placed it back in his pocket. He continued walking right to a dead end and disappeared into a narrow trail, swallowed by the neighboring woods.

'But Grandmother! What big teeth you have, said Little Red Riding Hood, her voice quivering slightly.

As Hoover progressed through the forest to his extraction spot, he thought of Abdul Baaqi. He knew about the man's past and background but needed Moses to understand the connections the Libyan national fostered with DC.

Underfoot, the soft, shaded grass bent and morphed into a light herringbone hardwood floor. White walls cracked the grounds and shot upward. The skies lowered above Hoover, shaping the memories of the past. Sophisticated chandeliers lit up a vaulted ceiling. Michael Hoover's black leather loafers clicked on the floor. He was back in Libya.

Libya - Tripoli - Bin Ashur Neighborhood - May 1, 2006

"Can we trust them?"

Hoover answered the Chief of Station, "Yes and no. They're very territorial so this may work for a bit, but we risk exposure once the assets mature."

"What do you suggest?"

"We enter talks. 'Rent' the basin of Kufra from them through local assets and under *their* guidelines. Once we're done with the trainees, we send them to Egypt, where the climate will be more favorable to scaling."

The Chief of Station, of a massive stature, paced back and forth, looking down at the crowded streets of Tripoli from a high-rise embattled in a brutal duel with fast winds. The picture windows showed a shaky reflection of Michael Hoover, discreet, still, like a black bird perched on a branch. Or the very personification of death: inflexible, relentless.

"Okay, Hoover. How do you plan on addressing the potential political fallouts?"

"I'm going to compartmentalize. Our local asset is part of a dissident group that shares common interests with the tribes down south. They're both against the deployment of pipelines in the basin; both Sunnis and some of our allies fought al-Qadhdhāfī before he was terminated. With the promise of a discreet training program, resources we'll wire through … they will agree, and the central government will never know. They don't even have coverage in these areas. Tribal culture is still going strong and is feared by many."

A personal assistant knocked on the massive marble door behind them, a vestige of an unparalleled wealth the scavengers from the West preyed upon.

America had set a firm foot on Libyan soil, its luscious lips ready to suck it dry. The U.S. was horny, ready to indulge in orgasmic, deviant practices.

The Chief of Station called out, "Yes?"

The door opened, and a tiny old Black lady engaged. She was wearing a pantsuit and holding a blue dossier in one, firm grip.

She stopped by Hoover and addressed the Chief of Station, "Your 12:15 meeting is here. Your operational details, sir."

"Thank you." He grabbed the folder and nodded at Hoover. The latter exited with the executive assistant.

12. THE VENTRILOQUISTS

"Mom, why do they look like animals but they talk like humans?"
"Divine justice, Zay Zay."

The night gained ground, broadening its unpredictable impact. Field LED lights snapped in the quiet darkness, beaming the U.S. Capitol in an all-around coverage.

The *Watchmaker*'s live feed was the main source of intelligence for Abeba's FBI, a vector for crucial information controlled by the perpetrators. Her brain underwent overclocking; she saw the world manipulated in an accelerated deconstruction, a countermeasure to her sleep deprivation. Her surroundings were flooding the fabric of her reality, stretching the boundaries of what was real and what was not. Colors were dissected and reshaped into codes.

The Capitol had a light swaying to it. The temperatures were still quite high, but the moonlight gave the grass a luscious evergreen tone it had lost in the burning day. Her team had rotated, offering its initial members a break from an excruciating work of investigation.

The video feed provided by the *Watchmaker* had revealed the identity of a few beasts of prey. Strangely, they were borrowing patterns from mankind: speech, self-awareness, and a shared hierarchy. The Lion was the POTUS, the Grasshopper his VP. The shining Bull a protective and territorial Chief of Staff. The Bear was the CIA Deputy Director; he seemed to be at war with a massive Panda, the Secretary of State.

A frightening silverback gorilla protected the weaker links: he claimed to be the Secretary of Defense. The Pig, whose tight skin twitched from fear, was the State Department senior legal adviser. The Murder Hornet and Falcon buzzing and flying above head were the CIA's Libya Chief of Station and the JSOC Commander. The Wolf roamed the space, sniffing various tracks. He howled his title under the repeated demands of the Lion's clique, "National Security Advisor."

Abeba had created a board to keep track of the Capitol's hostages and their respective identities, motivations, and behavioral tendencies. There was a correlation between their physical forms and inner dispositions.

Narcissistic tendencies.

But the Unicorn was Abeba's main point of interest: it was Abdul Baaqi. The Libyan national was surprisingly passive, observing the other creatures' power struggles from afar, contained and still as the night.

None of the animals recalled their government names. Their past was shattered into millions of strobing visions. Abeba found the metamorphosis almost... *elegant.* The creatures were tied to their roles and functions and only existed to sustain a dynamic of conflicts and allyship.

They revealed themselves to the world, shouting the ugly truths untamed, unfiltered. Their words struck the general population like hot blades in bubbling, open wounds.

I killed Leyla Johnson! I raped Marjani, a teen I was grooming for my partners! I appropriated some of the Baltimore Waterfront Project funds to finance my lifestyle! I ordered the assassination of five Libyan nationals in the U.S.! I had sex with my secretary and diverted congressional funds for a pay raise! I have three offshore accounts in the British Virgin Islands!

The involuntarily impulsive confessions kept pouring throughout the evening, serving the press corps with juicy meats to sink their sharp teeth in. Investigations were already ongoing in various divisions of Abeba's agency.

However, she refused to let her personal beliefs crash the party and cloud her judgement; her primary mission was to ensure the safe recovery of the hostages and the neutralization of the immediate threat. She clapped a few times to get her team's attention. The fresh faces snapped and shifted towards her.

"Okay, listen. I know there's been a lot to process within the past several hours, but I want to remind you that our sole purpose here is to defuse the situation and support a swift recovery. A biochemical weapon of a unique design has been unleashed in the political capital of the world. Let that sink in for a second, let the implications cascade. As far as the information we gather through the PO1's feed, we only use what's relevant to the current situation and objective. To *our* parameters. The rest is dealt with by Violent Crimes units and the White-Collar Division.

"Now, how do we solve this? We look at the patterns and isolate the rogue elements. So far, our hottest lead is Abdul Baaqi. He is a Libyan national with rumored ties to the royal family and members of the Kufran tribes. He was called upon to testify. The rest of the information about his relations is redacted, but some were given to our division. It is VITAL that you maintain OPSEC while discussing the intel. It should be arriving in ten minutes and thirteen seconds. M. Baaqi has been using a Gulfstream G800 with custom specs to fly to D.C. on three separate occasions, and once to New York City in the past month. The PO2 has diplomatic immunity so there are no immigration records, but I believe he is tied to PO1 or other members of his network.

"The Kufrans are known to exercise ownership over massive

AMERICA IS A ZOO   **83**

natural resources and long-standing cash reserves in southeast Libya, but there's no financial trail connecting Baaqi to them or the central Libyan government. In preliminary checks, the CIA found no links either. We are still looking into potential domestic transactions. Given the attack's MO and PO1's speech patterns, we are looking at a group involving both foreign and U.S. nationals."

The team members were recording the information on legal pads, in a race against time.

Abeba added, "It seems the hostages are communicating with someone on the other side of the chamber's main access. Thermal readings were inconclusive. The perpetrators employed some sort of thermoregulating technology, most likely. They are highly trained and highly coordinated. Leave no stone unturned. As of now, we are still working on triangulating PO1's broadcast signal. Questions?"

The team remained calm.

"Dismiss."

They returned to their posts, looking for new intelligence and new angles. Abeba faced an unparalleled threat. The godly visions and the visual connections between organic and synthetic elements gave her an edge; however, she was still in the dark, seeking a better understanding of the aggressor's motives. She looked forward, her eyes plunging into the lawn's greens, and smiled.

Her work phone, a secured line, vibrated in her pocket. She jolted awake from the contemplation and retrieved the device. A text message appeared on the screen.

We have a pipeline with the CIA. They have new information. A PAG awaits @ 700 7th St SW Unit 4B, Washington, DC 20024.

The code is 2024. Usual Protocols.

Abeba struck the keys with supernatural speed.

Good copy. On my way.

It seemed her former employers at the CIA sought to repay a political debt contracted with the FBI, which let the civilian intelligence agency operate on U.S. soil and collect data under the Congress' nose.

Ironically, the men and women in Capitol Hill were also campaigning for a broader surveillance; they just did not want to know who or *what* was operating it.

Abeba said, "I'll be back." The rest of the team acknowledged, silent.

She drove off the site and headed towards the Ford House Office Building to catch 395 South.

As she passed Bartholdi Park, a giant glass dome turned its googly eyes towards her, tracking her progress. Soon, she engaged on the expressway to reach the Waterfront District.

Visual data was still flooding her senses. She did not feel the need to shut the input out, however; the city was a ghost town, purged from the majority, rotten souls whose journey on Earth was only temporary, transitional, inconsequential.

DC was now controlled by the police forces, the federal agencies, EMTs in transit, and diplomats of critical value. Checkpoints were set up on main interstate accesses and around landmarks of strategic significance.

The wealthy from downtown and the west side benefited from a rather quick resolution, Abeba thought. They cooperated with the authorities and lockdown order, feeling and fearing the wrath of this *Watchmaker*.

For some, it was a targeted attack on their way of life, on their ill-gotten gains. Abeba could see the shadows peeking through the windows, seeking a savior who would not require them to repent.

Indeed, how can you expect saving without a deep transformation? she thought.

Inside her genius mind was a clash between titans: her current mission, the validity of the *Watchmaker*'s views, and her own personal dreams. She was certain things would align in the aftermath.

Her marked vehicle with federal plates skimmed through checkpoints, reaching the densely populated Waterfront District. There, families were gathered for dinner, and lone wolves and bachelors scouted the city up in their towers and contemporary row houses.

It was midtown money. It was redevelopments and mixed-use compounds accommodating a standardized gentrification. It was daddy's bank wires funding housing for a young student whose sole responsibility was the acquisition of knowledge.

The neighborhood was the poster child for America's failure to adhere to a more unique, historically sensible approach to urbanization.

Dull, Abeba thought. *A suitable rendezvous point.*

She parked in front of a red brick building adorned with white balconies. In the streets, poorly trained national guards and DCPD patrolled the sector, relying on the collective fantasy of a strong and disciplined armed force to maintain control. Abeba walked to a thick glass door and struck the keys of a digital pad to the right of the frame. *2024*. A buzz sound deactivated the entrance's electronic lock.

She nodded at the front desk manager, who motioned for her to continue left. The lobby was humble, a maroon-themed space with an off-white carpet flooring and art deco carvings on the walls. The brass-coated elevator she faced opened to her.

4.

On the fourth floor, the hallway she stepped in was narrow yet well-lit. The stone building provided great insulation; Abeba's surroundings were quiet, devoid of the typical muffled chatter. She reached door *4B* and knocked.

"Oti yaju fun ounje ale," a voice from across the door said.

Abeba replied, "I wan chop."

The door opened, and a young white woman with massive,

black cat eyeglasses, ripped jeans, and a black sweater offered a quick smile. Inside, Abeba followed her to an adjacent room.

The interior design was very *new age*, with dashes of an organic print.

Bamboos, Bonsai trees, and roses complemented the light interior, neutral shades, and contemporary furniture. The room Abeba found herself in was spartan: a queen size bed with a wooden headboard, a safe box laid open on the white sheets, and a cylindric nightstand.

The young lady struck a few keys on her cell and addressed Abeba, "It's an honor to meet you. I'm sure you're aware of protocols, but I'm contractually obligated to run the sequence. You will leave your belongings in this safe box. Your service weapon and any other weapon you may carry must be unloaded and cleared. The safe's biometric lock is tied to your fingerprints, more specifically your right thumb. No one will see the content of this box besides you and me. Your ride will arrive in exactly two minutes and thirteen seconds. After your briefing, you will return here. Should any issue arise, there is a pay phone at this address." The young CIA liaison handed Abeba a business card. "It has been prepaid, and you also have my number on there. You can call me Issey."

The FBI's assistant director slid the card into her pocket and drew her Glock 19M. She pressed the magazine release and caught the mag to drop it into the safe box. Her delicate fingers racked the slide back. A black-tipped bullet popped out and landed on the sheet. Abeba held the slide back and showed Issey the empty ejection port. She placed the gun, the rogue bullet, and her personal belongings into the box and closed it.

Issey added, "Please attempt to open it once."

Abeba pressed her thumb against the biometric scanner on top of the box. *Click.* She opened it and closed it back up.

Issey said, "Thank you. You are good to go. B SUV with Diplo."

Abeba smiled at her and turned around. She headed for the door and disappeared in the hallway.

Tap... tap... tap.

Outside, a black SUV with diplomatic plates was idle in front of the lobby. The windows were blacked out. She entered the vehicle and sat next to an individual whose identity was concealed by a ski mask and black clothing. The driver was hidden behind a dividing partition tinted in a dark shade.

A male voice erupted to her left. "Good evening, Miss Solomon. Usual OPSEC. You will find your hood and noise-cancelling device in the center compartment."

She answered, "Good evening." She retrieved a thick, coarse black hood and black earmuffs from the console to her left.

As she put the hood on and adjusted her earmuffs, the world around stilled: there was no data flood, no disturbances, no seismic shifts.

She felt relieved, unburdened, walking on soft clouds, floating in the quietness of a lazy river. She lifted a thumb up. Hands in the dark checked her head covering and ear protection.

A few seconds passed. The SUV drove off into the night.

**

The ride was pleasant. The chauffeur was remarkably considerate in his stops and turns. After what to Abeba felt like ten minutes, the vehicle finally came to a halt. The other passenger stepped out of the car, betrayed by a light bounce on his leather seat.

Her door opened. A wide hand gently tapped her right shoulder. She extended her own hand and was guided out of the vehicle. After a few steps, she felt the dry coldness of a powerful climate control system.

The moisture-free hand released its grip on hers, and she stopped. Her earmuffs and hood were removed, and the world welcomed her back with sounds, visuals, and layered textures. *It* spoke fast, released from its shackles. Abeba's eyes and ears adjusted to the transition. The CIA's protocols were a bit theatrical, but she understood confidentiality was their most powerful weapon.

She was standing in a giant warehouse, or maybe a test site. The clean concrete flooring displayed black-taped Xs arranged in columns, and a table with four chairs was set up in the middle of the space. The walls were rudimental metallic panes. Three ski-masked individuals stood by the table a few feet ahead. They advanced towards her and waved. One of the CIA's officers offered a handshake. She accepted. A male voice greeted her; his eyes were glacial, fear-inducing in their stillness. He moved with agility and purpose. There was a certain sophistication, a swagger to his walk.

"Thank you for your time, Miss Solomon. I am quite impressed with your knowledge of our protocols. But you're navigating in familiar waters, I suppose. Please sit."

They all sat at the table. A few folders were laid out.

The man continued, "We came across some information that could help you in your investigation. I figured we would share it with you and your agency. Any questions before we start?"

Abeba shook her head. "No questions. Your help is greatly appreciated."

Beyond the ski mask, the man's cheek bones raised higher. "Don't mention it. We are big fans of your work and track record. I believe you have an interest in a certain Libyan national. Abdul Baaqi?"

"Yes, indeed, the *Unicorn*. We are currently looking into his financial records. I suspect he has a domestic contact and is in fact involved in the attack. Even considering he was also targeted by the chemical agent."

"Shared belief. I was investigating him before the attack. That is classified information, but it supports the theory of his involvement. What did you find out so far?"

"Flight plans. Three to D.C., one to New York City. All within a month. No immigration records. Diplomatic immunity. His political affiliations and behavioral profile, following the ... *transformation* match. He has the motive, the intent, and the resources."

The CIA officer agreed, "Precisely. I understand you are still reviewing recent transactions. There will most likely be no paper or digital trail. He is far too smart to get involved directly. But we found something this evening."

Another CIA officer took over. The voice was soft and feminine, with a strong London accent. "Abdul Baaqi fosters strong ties with our Muslim friends, here in D.C. Particularly on the eastern bank of the Potomac River. He has been quite generous to an Imam running a mosque close to Anacostia Park. Among charitable contributions that were cleared, we found a couple of transactions that raised red flags, ones initiated by the mosque. They were finalized right after two of Baaqi's contributions and sent to the same individual for an amount under the specified thresholds for the Bank Secrecy Act. 4,500 each."

Abeba ran probabilities in her head. *There are more transactions coming.* "To whom?"

The male officer spoke again. The third silent member of the CIA unit seemed to have been tasked with recording the interaction. "That's where it gets interesting. The wires were sent to an account that belongs to an EMT. A resident of DC with no criminal record and no known affiliations."

Abeba clicked. "A proxy. And he's essential personnel who can still move through the city freely."

The male CIA officer tapped the bridge of his nose, like he was readjusting invisible glasses. He answered, "Good point. I think he could be of interest to you."

She agreed. "Absolutely! Do you have a file on the individual? It would save me time."

The female officer met her lead's calculated stare. "Yes. I've prepared a dossier," she answered. "Last known address, travel patterns, contact information, financial specifics." She handed Abeba a blue manila folder. The latter thanked her.

The male officer asked, "Any other questions, Miss Solomon?"

"No, thank you." She stood as they shook hands. Abeba knew not to ask about the Political Action Group elements. They were individuals who operated under a very strict confidentiality policy. She turned around and walked towards the exit. Her feet stopped over a X mark, closer to the egress. Behind, steps grew louder and louder.

A purposeful walk, an elegant stride.

The coarse hood and earmuffs found her again.

Then, the world turned pitch black once more.

13. BIN ALLAH

LIBYA - HARAT ZUWAYYAH - JUNE 11, 2010

*"Americans and our own Muslim fundamentalists misunderstood or …
instrumentalized the term 'Jihad'. It is an exerted effort, the striving for a
better self. And even in the most violent contexts, it remains only a
defensive stance. Islam is a religion of peace and brotherhood. It has
even been influenced by early Judaic law and Christian models.
America's wild capitalism fed off of the religious conflicts it helped
sustain. It is time we fight back and let love and a mutual understanding
heal our wounds."*

- Bin Allah

A red glow poured into the airframe of a modified M-28 Skytruck. The Libyan airspace was moonless, pitch-black and vacant. Five soldiers, black figures of death whose oxygen masks quietly hummed, stood in a file formation, facing an open cargo bay drinking in the surrounding skies.

Andre Seraos stared at the edge of where chaos began. He was leading his men in one of the most ambitious covert operations ever executed.

Seraos asked through his in-ear transmitter, "Roger, this is Evergreen. Are we still above SAM engagement levels?"

The pilot answered, "Evergreen, this is Roger. Correct. You are green to green."

The soldiers' oxygen tanks hissed. Seraos continued, "Pre-breathing is over. Prepare to jump. ALT 37,000 feet. Initial interval five seconds. Canopy fifteen seconds at 27,000. Recorded?"

"Mark 1, recorded."

"Mark 2, recorded."

"Mark 3, recorded."

"Mark 4, recorded."

Seraos raised both arms and struck the top of his helmet with his right fist. He waited a few seconds and received a light tap on the right shoulder.

The weapons sergeant, the jumpmaster, ran along the ramp and took a dive into the mouth of a quiet monster.

Ten. Nine. Eight. Seven.

He straightened his arms back to gain speed.

Six. Five. Four. Three.

His gloved right hand found the parachute's ripcord at waist level.

Two. One.

The black Kevlar chute flaunted its majestic curves as Seraos' body tensed then stabilized, gliding over the graceful Sahara Desert. Below, endless dunes formed a sea of shifting waves punctuated by herbal notes and earthy scents. Shadows danced on the hills' steep sides. The occasional creature journeyed alone in the search of foods and water. The expanded viewpoint complemented a turbulence-free ride in the cloudless night. A series of *pops* indicated his men had followed his route.

Al Jawf Kufra was still a blurry mark, its lights a distant tale of seduction. It was Seraos' objective, thirty-three miles east of their position.

The Delta Force detachment leader pressed a small rubber pad attached to his left shoulder strap. "This is Evergreen. SITREP?"

"Mark 1. On course."

"Mark 2. On course."

"Mark 3. Deviation .5. Readjusting."

"Mark 4. On course."

Seraos contemplated the celestial vault where billions of stars began revealing themselves. The view was pure magic. He waited sixty seconds and asked, "Mark 3. SITREP?"

"Mark 3. On course."

"This is Evergreen. Good copy, Mark 3. Initiating descent at 8,000. Remember to redistribute your operational load once on the ground. You will stack on me, how copy?"

"Mark 1, good copy."

"Mark 2, good copy."

"Mark 3, good copy."

"Mark 4, good copy."

The remainder of the glide was silent. The instruments of death approached an isolated compound on the outskirts of *Al Jawf Kufra*, one of the most beautiful and vibrant centers of culture in the Maghreb. The structure itself was partially concealed behind high walls and a dense vegetation that flourished all around. A dome still exercised its symbolic authority over the thick greens running alongside its walls. The soldiers found the scenery extraordinary.

Seraos resumed his descent. One hundred feet above ground level, he pressed his feet and knees tightly together, bent his knees slightly, and pointed the balls of his feet downward.

The sand absorbed most of the impact. Seraos seemed to be walking on water as he let his momentum fade. He then kneeled on the frosted sands and detached his parachute. The special forces sergeant proceeded to fold it, keeping an eye on the compound four hundred feet out. There was no apparent movement.

Seraos stuffed his chute in a pouch attached to his tactical backpack. There was no flag on his black thermal suit, no identifiable. He was willing to die here alone, unheard and unseen, in what the average American would define as patriotism. To him, his commitment was a reflection of his core values and a mindset whose focal points were dependability, performance, and completion. It was rather grounded in logic than nationalism or pride, but he often refrained from correcting the people, unwilling to spark a conversation they were not equipped to sustain.

The Delta Force leader turned around and scoped out his men. They were quietly exchanging gear, redistributing it evenly among soldiers. Seraos stood and detached his HK416 rifle from a carabiner clip fixed on his upper chest. He began circling around his men, reviewing the loadouts and checking their surroundings.

The compound ahead was almost entirely devoid of light. The U.S. military chose to strike in the middle of the night, exploiting sleep patterns. Seraos was expected to exfiltrate the high-value target before dawn.

His men stood, blending with the sand waves. Seraos had stopped his rounds and found a focal point in the objective ahead. One of the soldiers, one of a shorter frame, squeezed his lead's right shoulder. They were ready to sanction the evil beasts of a corrupted Islam, or so they were told via a politically charged message from the higher-ups. The men expressed their disagreement with the gross generalization and rather inquired about the operational details.

Andre Seraos reminisced the commander briefing's speech; it was culturally inaccurate, unsurprisingly unilateral, and unwarranted.

But Bin Allah, the *King of Kufra*, was guilty.

The intel linked his tribe to twenty-three incidents worldwide. Four thousand casualties. Entire ethnic groups displaced in eastern and northern Libya.

Bin Allah was the *Big Bad Wolf*, a contemporary of Bin Laden, an eloquent speaker and highly regarded scholar who hid behind deceiving messages of love and unity. Seraos found his persona fascinating. Unlike Bin Laden and other terror cell leaders, Bin Allah sought to educate outsiders on the pure motives of Islam, on its true purpose: to provide guidance to the Muslim communities, to enforce boundaries and rules the descendants of Muhammad ibn Abdullah, the *prophet*, deemed necessary to develop a just and spiritually rewarding society.

The *King of Kufra* never claimed responsibility for the attacks U.S. intelligence associated him with. He never called for the killings of the "infidels" or the annihilation of a *corrupted* West. His followers delivered his message all across the globe, as he fostered amicable relationships with various religious leaders.

Sometimes, Bin Allah would trade his soft demeanor for an iron grip, proving critical of the United States, a nation whose leaders he accused of being expansionist and byproducts of an unregulated ultra-capitalism. The high-value target had hundreds of supporters in the U.S. alone yet never campaigned for an armed conflict.

Strangely enough, he admired the American working class; strong bodies and minds whose sense of innovation and creative outputs offset an unforgiving State.

Seraos, a foreign-born, would often dispute certain political decisions made at his level. But the intel was solid, cross-referenced, and the patterns he studied were sound.

So, why this major discrepancy? he thought.

He snapped back to reality as the men behind waited, quietly. The special forces leader raised his left hand and pointed at the compound. The death squad began their advance. Footprints in the sand foreshadowed the arrival of a merciless menace shielded from the biting cold behind thermal layers; Libya was witnessing the deployment of deadly ghosts, the *tools* of the powerful, meaty fingers pressing on the country's throat.

Their pace was measured; the men needed to ensure they were not entering a death funnel set up by Bin Allah's forces. Ahead, the tall, compressed earth wall they spotted from the skies surrounded the massive courtyard inside its boundaries.

From ground level, palm trees protruded from the emergent layer of the rampart. A forged gate was flanked by two blurry shadows; Seraos veered left and stopped. He kneeled. The men followed suit. The tight file line formation was almost invisible, hiding between the earth and the sky vault.

The leader used his scope to assess the threat. *Two guards. A motor vehicle. Another roaming guard going counterclockwise.*

A voice whispered through his in-ear receiver, "Evergreen, this is Control. Three tangos running the outer perimeter. No other movement inside the courtyard."

Seraos answered, "This is Evergreen. Good copy."

The environment provided the perfect conditions for the unit's ground panoramic night vision goggles. They could see the movements and equipment clearer and clearer as they approached the targets from the southwest. Seraos' men sharpened, their footprints turning darker and darker as they sunk in, looking to gain a foothold in the Kufran market.

The roaming guard met the beast of many heads. *"Aldukhala!"* he yelled.

The Delta Force leader continued straight alongside the western wall while the others shifted right towards the forged gate. Two shots rang, their noise and visual signatures concealed by a titanium suppressor mounted onto the rifle's threaded barrel. The isolated watch collapsed backwards and laid on his right side, motionless.

Seraos scanned his front. There were no other shadows dancing on the neutral tones of the fortification.

Four more shots rang nearby.

The quiet sounds and muffled thumps were unequivocal; they were his men's. He grabbed the dead body and turned around, his rifle up.

Seraos moved forward and pivoted left. He found his men,

flanking the entry point like praying mantises on the prowl; two bodies were already lined up by the wall. They were juvenile forms of larvae picked up by winged beasts of prey.

A third corpse joined them as the unit's leader regained proximity with his team.

Lacking protective measures. Primitive. Seraos approached the access and pushed on the metal gate. The entrance opened a few inches inward. There was still no movement inside the courtyard.

He engaged, his soldiers trailing noiselessly behind him.

A world of a magical beauty revealed its secrets. Date palms provided shading for lower crops. The tall trees also doubled as anchor points for unused string lights, organized in a mesmerizing web of clear glass bulbs. Peach trees shaped a thick middle layer that concealed elaborate balconies whose intricate, see-through balustrades conveyed the tales of the proud Bedouin tribes.

The lingering scent was a poetic narrative; accents of citrus and peach were diffused throughout a narrow cobblestone pathway. The special forces elements shut out the sensory input and focused on the main access to the high-value target, a massive wooden door with traditional Islamic ornaments.

A framework of repeated circular and squared shapes gave it a psychedelic look and feel.

As the operational detachment kneeled in front of the door, Seraos' thoughts began racing, faster and faster. *The RRC guys claimed there was heavy resistance. The DO identified at least ten tangos. Here, we met three untrained elements, no ground measures, and no activity.*

The men he led, however, were reliable factors. They did not have his insight or critical thinking skills, and nor were they raised in a cultural melting-pot of a broad spectrum like he was. They had different... *sensibilities.* Nonetheless, these professionals were still his responsibility, he thought.

After testing the door and confirming it was locked, he turned his head to the left and struck his helmet with his left fist. The number three man broke formation and approached the entry point. He retrieved a standard golden key from his chest pouch and inserted it into the central lock mechanism. *Click.*

The man raised a thumb up, placed the key back in his pouch, and reintegrated the formation. Seraos pushed the left wooden pane and flooded another courtyard.

The architectural print and interior design were a powerful ode to the early Islamic eras.

At the center stood a water fountain that provided a soothing backdrop, in a stark contrast with the unit's intentions.

To the right, a wall featured a mural recounting the journey of a horseman galloping over layered sand waves. There was a plethora of details in the representation of a sky vault, but Seraos shifted his attention towards a couple of doors on the left. He raised an index finger in the air and pushed the first door inward. His barrel met the eyes of a middle-aged woman who seemed to have anticipated the intrusion. Seraos held a finger in front of his mouth. The woman nodded and raised her hands. She was composed, cooperative.

Her *niqāb* left her eyes uncovered; there was no fear, no hatred, no apprehension, no defiance in her stare. The team lead inched closer and searched her. He only found layers of clothing. She was quietly moved around, her hands placed on the wall. The small room was bare-bones; a floor seating sofa and a table constituted most of the layout.

Seraos guided and cuffed her to a nearby radiator. He looked at his number two man and produced another shushing motion. His subordinate gave him a soft, clean cloth he used to muffle her. The detainee sat against the cold ceramic of the unused heatsink, compliant.

The OPLAN mentioned armor-piercing rounds. Heavy resistance. This is not a den of wolves. Seraos cracked a green chemical light and dropped it on the floor. Him and his men left the room and began clearing at a faster pace. A primarily empty ground level floor was under their control when they engaged a nearby stairwell two minutes later.

Upstairs, a hallway overlooking the courtyard featured four rooms. The first three were empty and rapidly cleared. As Seraos' heightened senses sought a deadly mechanism, rushing footsteps or the cocking of a charging handle, perhaps, the quietness of the space foreshadowed a greater danger.

A voice broke the silence across from a door, at the end of the hallway.

"Americans, we are unarmed. There are no traps here." The tone was measured and soothing. *Bin Allah*. The name caused a tremor Seraos contained within tensed skin and a rehearsed breathing pattern.

Inhale. Pause. Exhale.

He and his team almost instantly shifted to the right, hugging the wall. The lead's rifle was pointed at the door at a forty-five-degree angle.

He shouted, "Back against the wall opposite the door, now! How many people?"

The man answered, "Five. We have no intentions of hurting you. We are moving to the back now." The words hit the special ops detachment with the blunt force of a deadly trauma. There was a breaking in patterns, a transparent interaction. No malice.

Seraos tapped on his shoulder strap's rubber pad. He said, "Control, this is Evergreen. Engaging HVT, how copy?"

No response. The man behind the door added, his voice further distant, "Communications have been jammed. There is no ill intention, but I need to talk to you!"

Seraos hid his confusion behind the mask of an ancient wolf god, or a roaring lion asserting his authority over the jungle's inhabitants. He walked closer to the door and checked for heat points.

None. He raised his left hand high. A light squeeze on his shoulder was felt a few seconds later. Seraos stormed through the unlocked door.

He continued straight to the opposite side while his men combed the remainder of the space. Five people, two older men, two children, and a woman rested against the stone, hands up high.

"Clear!" Seraos cracked another green chemical light and dropped it on a small coffee table at the center of the large space. Multiple floor seating sofas were lined up against the walls. A floor sink flanked an aperture giving to an open bathroom.

"Bin Allah?!" Seraos asked.

The first man on the left answered simply, "Yes."

"Turn your jammers off."

"I'm afraid I can't. I need to speak to you first."

Seraos grabbed the man and shoved him against the wall. His body was tall yet light.

The team lead said, "And I'm afraid I can't help you navigate the muddy waters of enhanced interrogation techniques. Very painful. Beyond physical."

Bin Allah smiled. His eyes were probing behind his crooked frames.

"I carry no fear nor hatred towards men. It's against my convictions. I simply want to talk to you and wish you no harm. The dresser there,"—he pointed at a reddish-brown dresser with a glossy finish—"It contains sensitive information that will help you determine the true nature of this operation. And its actual scope. Kill me if you wish. Throw me as a fat bone to your dogs, or destroy the information like it never happened. But I read your file and your psychological evaluations. Foreign-born. High IQ. Still obedient but critical of certain practices. I trust you'll make the right decision. *Allah* be upon you."

14. CONCAVE

*To those who feel no moral culpability and are driven by a bottomless
hunger for power, life is seen through concave lenses. Things appear
smaller and closer. I know you understand what's implied.*

Twenty-four hours had passed since the *Attack*. The general
population uncovered a new link on *americaisazoo.com*.

Sensitive documents were leaked on a secured cloud. The
effort was similar to that of other contemporary
whistleblowers; the *Assanges*, the *Snowdens*, the *Webers*
and *Benmohameds*.

This time, however, a full-blown attack on the *Institution*
supplemented the transcripts and reports. Conversations between
high-ranking officials, foreign contractors, and CIA field officers
were uploaded online for the world to see. The information was new
blood coursing through the veins of the dead; new skin cells grafted
onto the charred bodies of a defaced society.

The people woke up from their vegetative state. The shock value
of this new chain reaction jumpstarted their feeble hearts; a

network of highly skilled and resourceful individuals had dealt a huge blow to the pigs feasting on the *Hill*.

But there was so much more to accomplish, the *Watchmaker* thought. The braindead still needed life support. Until they found the courage to set their bony frames in motion.

Abeba was still up, assembling the last pieces of the puzzle. She had set up a surveillance team on Rashid Saeati, an EMT working for American Medical Response, Inc, a national leader in emergency medical services capitalizing on the privatization of healthcare.

Rashid Saeati. Twenty-seven. No Children. No known relatives in the country. No criminal record. Performing above expectations. No political statements made online or in person. At least none known... a passive proxy. This is about money. He has no ideological drivers.

She drew a few final lines linking his known address to daily schedule and events reported by the surveillance team. Rashid had not broken away from his established patterns, it seemed. There was a prospective flight risk considering the nature and gravity of the potential charges he could face, but he presented no direct threat at this very moment. Saeati had not received military, paramilitary, or law enforcement training. He did not possess any weapons.

Not legally. Abeba's eyes danced on the white board. The pendulum waves of her optics snatched the data to shape it anew. It was time to strike.

She left the markings and turned around. Her right hand raised high; the team members left their computers and think boards to gather around their superior.

"Rashid Saeati. A U.S. national of Syrian origin. No ideological markers. He received two payments of USD 4,500 within a two-week period. I believe it is part of an ongoing structured compensation designed to outsmart anti money-laundering protocols. The source of the wires shares a connection with our Libyan national, Abdul Baaqi."

A young white male with a scruff look raised a hand. "Yes, Jones?"

"What is the source of the intel? Does it fit within our legal framework?"

"It was vetted by the director. It's classified, however."

The man nodded in approval.

"We are going to intercept the target tomorrow at 0500. It is our top priority. I want operational spec—"

In Abeba's peripheral vision, numbers fluctuated. *The Capitol's lawn. Ground waves.*

A vacuum! she thought.

She shouted, "Run!" She pointed at the Rayburn House Office Building, a neoclassical structure erected across the street. The men and women under her direction complied, rushing to the concrete road two hundred feet out. The framed canopy above head adopted a seismic motion. The ground produced a rumble that was felt underfoot.

Abeba waited until the last agent was cleared and began running towards the rally point. Behind her, the soil collapsed, swallowing the state-of-the-art crisis coordination center and the manicured grass. The vacuum spread around in a circular pattern, like a diabolically precise demolition exercise, or a carefully curated experience. *The hand of God.*

The Capitol was untouched, but the surrounding grounds were changed, carved into a more primitive form, into an exposed nexus of tunnels and pipes. Warp-like sounds preceded the explosions. The air was robbed of its oxygen, creating a dead zone all around the animals' golden cage.

There was no smoke, no debris, no projectiles.

Fortunately, the area was already evacuated, and the Rayburn House Office Building offered the FBI agents a refuge. They galloped like gazelles fleeing a storm, grouped in a tight herd of fast runners in dress shirts and bulletproof vests.

Abeba scanned the streets as she crossed the threshold. There was no other disruption, no secondary explosions, no foreign ground force.

A demonstration. Her trainers quietly bounced on the marble floor as she approached her team inside the building. "Jones! Find us three computers and a connection. It doesn't have to be secured. We need general information."

She waved the young male away. "McGuirt, Adebo, Silva, Smith, Diallo, Dos Santos, Myers! Cover the west, north, and east sides. I need a visual report every three minutes."

A group of FBI agents drew their guns out and positioned themselves facing the side windows and the ground level courtyard. Abeba looked around and drank in the input. The building was structurally sound, moderately exposed to natural light, and featured level eight bullet-resistant glasses. *Favorable circumstances against a siege.*

She approached the main entrance and looked outside. The streets were quiet and the damage minimal. Sirens rang afar. DCPD was combing the sector for ground threats, as instructed by the FBI in the event of an attack.

Jones came back with three bulky laptops, treasures of a forgotten era.

Abeba grabbed one and pointed at another agent. She was given a computer.

Jones added, "I have a portable hotspot, ma'am." He retrieved a small black box from his pocket. She tilted her head in agreement.

Thirty seconds later, she had access. The other two waited for further instructions, looking at their colleagues, maintaining situational awareness. They were trained for these situations, but the nature of the technology employed had terrifying implications: They were outgunned.

Abeba Solomon texted her director through her secured cell.

CTD safe. R H O B. Awaiting further instructions. Access to non-secured IPv6 network.

She turned her attention back to the computer she was firmly holding in one hand. Her agile fingers struck the keys with grace.

americaisazoo.com. Her cell vibrated in her pocket. She pulled it out, looked around, then replied.

The House of Representatives chamber's livestream transported the viewers to a wild, televised menagerie. It was now a complex society of half-men, half-others patrolling the space, sniffing the walls and stomping the grounds. Abeba saw a structure, an organizational dynamic.

The Lion and the Pig seemed to act as liaisons to whomever or *whatever* was outside the chamber. The Bull was *roaring POTUS'* protection detail. Others roamed the space and set boundaries between competing instincts and hungers. Some watched over as neutral observers.

The footage disappeared to a fade in on blurry edges and the rhythmic drumming of... fingers?

The *Watchmaker* was back.

"This is the *Watchmaker.* Today, at 6:45 PM eastern time, a new kind of explosive ordnance was employed in a precise demolition sequence. The grounds of the Capitol lawns were swallowed whole, disintegrated at a molecular level to leave a network of tunnels and panic rooms exposed, bare to your sight. This is the next step, fellow citizens. The FBI Counterterrorism Division, although under competent management, has been poking around, chasing leads, and repeatedly attempting to establish contact with me. A negotiation channel of some sort. But the politicians who pull the strings and weaponized your law enforcement and intelligence agencies share a common agenda, under the guise of justice and national security."

Abeba's phone vibrated again. The director.

Standby. CRM and optics in progress.

The *Watchmaker*'s voice reemerged from the muffled limbo of her adaptive hearing.

"They only care about *optics*. Governmental agencies are no longer committed servants to your well-being. They are now the tips of spears whose sharp bone ends contain the dormant disease of status quo, of policies only beneficial to the powerful. As you observed the animals in cage, as you consulted the documents we made available to you, you realized how far the cancer had spread. How shameless your rulers are. It is also why we transformed them. They needed humbling.

"But I digress. The next step, people. YOU are the cornerstone of this phase. YOU now have our support, the backing of an organization that employs weapons unknown to men. A group of selfless servants who have no interest in capitalizing on the situation. It is time you rise against the oppressor. It is time you regain control of your narrative. How? We're going to relinquish access to the TV broadcasts and radio stations. Demand answers for the crimes committed by your officials. Demand a true reform of society. Abolish partisanship and place the well-being of this country and its inhabitants above profit, above a warped version of the *American Dream*. It is time for us to prioritize education, healthcare, infrastructures, and environmental policies over tax bailouts and an inflated defense budget.

"There's a cultural shift that needs to happen. It is beyond socialism or collectivism. It is common sense and human decency. Generations of institutional racism and learned behaviors had some of you programmed to claim those who promote unity and a better allocation of our resources are 'commies' or a 'threat' to your way of life. Unlearn this. It is time to come out new, changed for the better. Demand gun control. The NRA and its puppets on the *Hill* never addressed the root causes of gun violence because they profit off of your fears. A forty-three-billion-dollar industry to be exact. What is their stance on the mental health and opioid crises? On wages outran by a rising inflation. On the lack of basic human rights in the biggest corporations' workforces? What about barriers to higher education for minorities?

"Those are the factors contributing to your brothers and sisters getting gunned down at the grocery store on a weekly basis. Or your kids laying in a pool of blood in the schools' hallways. You lost sight of the real issues in which those events are deeply rooted in. Open your eyes. There is so much more we could accomplish with our resources, with our expertise, our work ethic. You are safe to walk the streets, to defy the lockdown order that has been set in motion to keep you contained. Find the love you are lacking, find new connections with your neighbors and unite. Forget about the crushing weight of assuming the role of company men. Those billion-dollar enterprises find you highly expendable anyway. Why do you think most of their workforce lives under the poverty's threshold? On welfare? Rethink your process. And as far as the caged beasts in the Capitol go, be patient. They'll face judgment in due time."

15. THE JUNGLE

WASHINGTON, D.C. - U.S. CAPITOL

Twenty minutes earlier.

The bird goes, "Tweet, tweet!"

The pig says, "Oink, oink!"

The crooked politician shouts, "Optics. Capital."

T he snouts, nose leathers, and tongues drank from blue plastic barrels found in the House of Representatives chamber. The water was murky, soiled by the competing creatures of various textures and fluids. However, to the transformed politicians, it tasted pure and balanced.

The Lion was spellbound by the ripples on the surface. He thought, *How are we going to recover from that?*

Crack!

One of his paws sunk in a hole on the floor. Soon, he felt the cold embrace of metal. He quickly recovered and moved further right.

The Pig reeked of sweat, urine, and feces, shivering behind the

Lion's fiery tail. The porky legal adviser was sniffing the main entrance edges. The humans' pheromones from behind the door stimulated his thought process. They offered a bridge to a less vulgar state of being.

Negotiations had stalled, however.

The Wolf had begun interacting with the others at ground level. He wanted to offer his expertise and find a substitute to the *pack*, a satisfactory answer to this longing for a collective body.

He was stretching his legs out and wagging his tail by the Gorilla, a few feet from the Lion and his loyal Bull. The Wolf fought an urge to lick the President's muzzle, his eyes fixed on his silky mane.

Inside of this furry body, submissive to exacerbated senses, the Wolf, or National Security Advisor, felt shame.

It cannot be stopped, this compulsive urge to display wants and needs.

He addressed the Lion, aroused by the latter's straight, tall posture. "M. President, what is next? I haven't found any ... structural weakness yet."

The President roared, thunderous and strong-armed. The Wolf and the others crouched. There was a common understanding that trumped the murderous impulses most surrendered to the day prior. The beasts remained still, eyes on the *King of the Jungle*. The Bull and The Grasshopper did not budge as they scanned the small crowd for security threats.

The green bug took over, perched on an improvised stand made of wooden cubes.

"Metal frames everywhere. Legal adviser looking to reopen negotiations. No demands formulated. No claim. Transformation? Permanent or reversible?"

The Lion placed a paw on the stand, sending a vibrating echo to the Grasshopper's back legs. The latter's voice pitch reached new heights as he resumed. "Wait. Wait. Wait. More. No. Just wait.

There. Here. Now. Before. Strange feelings. Something inside, something else outside."

The Grasshopper, the VP, triggered a set of body language specifics among the wildlife, in this jungle of stone. Some were hissing, some beating their chests to the drums of non-communicable pain. Some were standing on two paws, feet, reaching for imaginary things in the foul-smelling air.

The insect continued, his all-black eyes reflecting the chaotic movements of his audience. He knew he was wiser than most. Even wiser than his superior.

"Patience now. Who are the dead? Cannot name names but name titles. Brains are clouded by ... an urge. What are we? I want to jump and hop on tall grass."

The crowd burst in a guffaw. The deep sounds, roars, cackles, and howling provided a relief to the half-human creatures who felt an orgasmic release as they surrendered to a lustful bestiality, to their new reality.

The floors began shaking, unnoticed during the sensory orgy; this was not a result of the pouncing and the sexually charged head-on collisions. The shockwaves were consistent, the tremors gaining in intensity as a distant rumble grew louder and louder. The paintings on the walls flew from their anchors. The Unicorn, posted on the upper ledge, silent, rushed downstairs as the balconies collapsed. The creatures aborted the gestation of wild fantasies and began seeking refuge, guided by supernatural senses that differentiated the big and small vibrations, the least from the most damaged areas.

Luckily, the main entrance was spared. The space continued shaking furiously as the soft furs, smooth coats, wet noses, and coarse feathers met in a joint effort to survive. The Grasshopper leaped all over, inhabited by a commanding instinct.

The shaking ceased.

The Lion's ego drove him to conduct a head count; he was not concerned with *their* safety but the preservation of their functions and strengths. *IIIIIIIIIII need to escaAAAAApe.*

The Pig fought the panic and naked emotions that flooded his round flesh. He gathered enough strength to trot to the door, in a mechanical stride fueled by short legs. He asked, "What is going on?"

Outside the chamber, the human masters refused to make their presence known. The Pig's flappy ears hugged the metal. Tears welled up from his tired eyes. Other caged beasts inched closer to the entryway. Their hearing also probed beyond the veil.

The others had left. There was only one human there.

The realization hit the politicians with the sledgehammer of a cosmic giant. They began rolling, jumping, rushing to crash the door's uncovered metal layer; it was crowned with giant thorn-like pieces of wood, crumbling under the impacts.

The metal remained impenetrable, however.

Bomb. Bang. Thump. Tap. Boom. Bang. Thump.

Some of the smaller creatures zigzagged and leaped to avoid being trampled by the mass of raw-scented shapes. Wings flapped above, flooding ground level with a biting rotor wash.

A shaky voice erupted behind the chamber's main entrance.

"ENOUGH." The animals froze. "I'm here. I-I-I-I'm here! There was an explosion outside."

The fantastic beasts sought comfort in others' non-verbal cues. The man with the suicide vest resumed, "What do ... do ... what you need? I haven't heard anything new. I'm fucking trapped here!" He wept aloud with convulsive gasping. And pitches, highs and lows.

The Pig rested on the now warm metal and said, "We need you to reach out to whoever is ... *oinkkkkk*. Responsible."

A honeyed voice interrupted the exchange. The Unicorn's white glow beamed with magic. The Libyan national was towering over the dead corpses that were lined up alongside the northern wall.

He sang, "One is different. Yet so similar." The prose was poetic, suave, executed in short beats. The Lion, the Bull, the Panda, the Gorilla, and the Bear felt compelled to examine the body in question.

As they bridged the gap with the mythical creature who was left untouched, the man with a suicide vest inquired, "What?!"

The voice was lost in an otherworldly translation. Nothing mattered but the white aura that cast mesmerizing waves crashing the shores of others' sight. Soon, they reached heaven and looked down.

Among the patchwork of dead animals, the collage of flesh, blood, fluids, feathers, hair patches, and bones laid the body of a human. A male. The wavy lose curls, chiseled facial structure, and green almond eyes fought to survive his dead skin. His frame was rigid and crooked.

There was a *moment* shared between Abdul Baaqi's mythical alter ego and the remainder of the transformed; their gazes met as they began a silent conversation. The eyes shifted and the dead body became the focal point. The Unicorn began chanting, "Seraos. Seraos. Seraos. Seraos."

The followers started grooving to the beats of the transfixing chorus and joined, unaware of what the words meant or implied.

Seraos. Seraos. Seraos. Seraos.

16. THE MONSTERS IN MEN
WASHINGTON, D.C.

In this city, all eyes were glued to the men turned animals, the shattered relics held in a captive state for display, broadcast to the world. But among the general population, otherworldly entities still roamed free. They could prove equally dangerous.

0610

The digital alarm clock pulled Rashid Saeati out of a rejuvenating dream rooted in colorful visions of planet-sized canvases and joy-inducing creatures. For a fleeting instant, Rashid stared at the white ceiling and the blades of a sleek metal fan. Thoughts cycled in his head, birthing new possibilities and ramifications for the day. He stretched and sat down on the edge of his platform bed.

A soft shag rug welcomed the young professional, providing a comforting blueprint underfoot. His apartment's interior was modern, sleek, sterile, and minimalist; it was the world of a man pursuing an arduous quest. There was no family picture, no positive reinforcement symbolic nor message, few colors.

Rashid had always felt like the life he was given was meant to be experienced in a utilitarian way; it was designed to be practical and productive, not pleasurable. The mindset he subsequently developed severed forming bonds with others and effectively undermined the growth of potential social skills but brought a new realm of hopes and aspirations for the strange creature within, the pious crusader who sustained on financial advancement and intellectual enrichment.

Tap, tap, tap. Tap...

A few steps led him to the kitchen, a small space with a counter extension that operated as a breakfast and dining table. Rashid smiled and grabbed a nearby water pitcher. He poured the contents into a small pot and placed the latter on an old gas stove. His hands found the burner controls and set it on high.

Rashid enjoyed the process of making French press coffee. It required precision, but the taste was richer and fuller than a conventionally filtered roast. The reward was a parallel to his vision: Quality work and time management produced more desirable outputs.

As the day sprung up, he enjoyed his Syrian/Levantine Arabic coffee and a small plate of dates. Fueling up for a long journey, he began reciting his affirmations in his head, drawn into the oily blacks of his cup's contents.

Life is fruitful. Change must be positive. Actions drive results. Mankind needs to remember its second syllable. Love can be communicated if not felt.

He knew the last statement was contradictory, but it fit within the parameters of his conscience.

Twenty minutes past, Rashid left his unit clean and groomed, dressed in a short-sleeve black polo, black cargo pants, and black tactical side-zip boots. He traveled light, only carrying the essentials of a single working man: keys, wallet, cell phone, and his EMT badge.

In the hallway, a young Black girl peeked beyond her door and stepped out. Rashid, on his way to an old, creaking stairwell ready to devour his tall frame, turned around.

The girl wore a silky evergreen dress, exquisitely tailored and beautifully complementing her rich complexion. Her black Bantu knots shone on her healthy scalp. She held a small package wrapped in aluminum foil, topped by a couple of towelettes in sealed packets. Rashid offered an emotional smirk. The girl reciprocated. Her pearly-white smile radiated joy.

She said, "Good morning, Mr. Rashid! My mom made some beef patties and plantains."

He walked to her and answered, "Good morning, Femi. That's very nice of her. Thank you." He grabbed the food and kissed her forehead. "Beautiful dress, young lady! Evergreen is a great addition."

The girl smiled again, showing a missing baby tooth. She said, "Mom said lockdown doesn't change things. 'A fi mi dawta. A mi no chaka-chaka'." She stood there with a stiffened posture, waving a finger in the air, reprimanding. They both burst into laughter.

For a second, Rashid wondered if he could develop into a great father figure. Femi's mother, a Jamaican transplant, took notice of the Muslim with a golden heart more than seven years ago. She was bold and expressive yet always accounted for Rashid's particular sensibilities, his highly structured lifestyle and religious beliefs. Throughout the years, the neighbors had maintained a fragile balance between friendship and ambiguous displays of affection that never quite scored. There was no other female presence around Saeati, and Femi's single mother fell in love with their dynamic and his commitment, sharing her time between a popular catering business, a daughter blossoming out into a bright future, and him, or more specifically the potential prospect of a *them*.

Despite Rashid's unwillingness to fulfill his neighbor's dreams and set priorities shaping an unconventional hierarchy of needs, they remained the closest to a nuclear family. But his objectives took precedence, overshadowing the dreams of parenthood and sacred unions.

Rashid repressed tears. His lips briefly twitched. He said, "Femi. You and mom are God-given gifts."

Their eyes met, and they smiled again. He looked at his watch.

"But today, I may not come back. You may hear about me on the news. But mi deh yah, yuh know." She frowned. He anticipated her questions and resumed, "I must go now. You are loved, Femi."

He hugged her tightly and offered a reassuring smile. Rashid inspired trust and benevolence with his refined facial traits and clean, tight curls. His beard was thick yet trimmed and moisturized. Amidst the invisible chaos pre-lockdown and through a citywide closure, him and his goddaughter had maintained the standards of a healthy living. She waved at him as he engaged the stairs.

Tap... tap... tap.

Outside, the streets were quiet, save for the occasional patrol or essential personnel. The heat waves had survived the sunless night and reemerged stronger. The façade's red bricks ignited the gray sidewalks. Rashid's steps followed unmarked parking spots and shaded alleys full of homeless outcasts, to whom lockdown was irrelevant.

A few blocks down from his multi-family row house, escalators sloped downward to the underground. Above a glass frame covering the mechanical ramp, a massive sign read *Congress Heights Station*. Rashid entered and subjected to the moving staircase.

Below, the train station adopted a strange dynamic. The single platform was full of essential workers; professionals from the medical field, various public servants, and others waited for the next westbound ride. A group of DCPD officers was checking IDs and badges at the bottom of the escalator.

The place was unspeaking, however, muted by the uncommunicated fears, by the internalized trauma of enduring a potentially major societal change. Rashid showed his badge, apprehensive, and approached the platform.

No response yet. They kept their promise.

A rumbling sound announced a new train. The brakes hissed and screeched as it slowed down to a stop. The commuters entered with Rashid. He found a seat and began unfolding his aluminum wrap, grabbing the juicy plantains and warm beef patty. *May Allah bless your family, Femi.*

His phone vibrated. He retrieved it with his dry hand and checked his notification.

A text. The contact displayed as *No ID.*

They are coming from central. Logistical issues.

Rashid's spiderlike fingers typed a reply.

Understood. Air tag is activated.

The paramedic, falsely labeled as an EMT by his friends at the Counterterrorism Division, enjoyed his Jamaican delicacy, energized by the prospect of a new America.

The train entered a dark tunnel. The ceiling lights offset the shift.

———

Abeba Solomon had reached a tipping point, a breakthrough.

She traveled on the surface in an armored truck. A sticker with yellow letters read *FBI* on the matte black paint. Given the citywide lockdown, there was no need for concealment.

The suspect's cell phone indicated no break from his established routine; a third-party application offered the FBI techies an opportunity to track Rashid's device. He was headed towards the Southwest Waterfront District, his most recent known place of work. Earlier surveillance did not reveal any behaviors pointing to Rashid being a flight risk, debunking prior theories on his upcoming moves. The money trail was still the strongest proof points.

The fleeing pigeons leading the agency are scared, Abeba thought.

She had to fabricate a national security threat and invoke the Patriot Act to receive warrants for arrest, search, and seizure. Her superiors inquired about the suspect and debated for what seemed like ages; they were far more concerned with the optics of detaining a Muslim amid a nationwide crisis than the pursuit of an investigative lead.

The people of this nation had begun questioning the status quo; groups were suspected to have gathered in secret to devise protests. Her bosses feared a new uprising, the emergence of a new revolutionary force. This time around, their vantage point was exposed by the *Watchmaker*, however; they could not commission the assassination of loved figures who simply demanded accountability, like they did with the late Dr. King and Malcolm X.

They told Abeba, "Tread carefully."

But she was more concerned with progress, with a resolution to this conflict. Political considerations did not factor in the exercise of her duty.

Her practical mind also pondered the vital questions of what the general population felt at this very moment, as the strange, emotional creatures she did not relate to. *Some of the ramifications could be the bearing of strange fruits. Some tasty and nutritious.*

Abeba's eyes reviewed the tactical vehicle's cargo. FBI agents from the Hostage Rescue Team rode with her, attentive and restrained. She needed their tactical capabilities; Rashid's apprehension demanded swiftness and a firm grip.

A female voice came through her in-ear receiver, "Suspect is headed north westbound towards Navy Yard. The train is currently UW. Ground surveillance reported no delay."

"This is Solomon. Good copy."

The armored truck was racing through the streets of D.C. Its big body drifted away from the Anacostia River's bank and the Yards, finding more and more concrete, stone, and narrower routes in the inner city.

Another communication came through, "Solomon, this is Control. Ground surveillance reported a stop. The WMATA confirmed it was a standard dispatch procedure. Adjustments to signaling."

"Good copy. Thank you for the update."

Abeba addressed the driver through an intercom nearby, "Stokes, turn around. The Yards."

"Yes, ma'am."

————

Rashid Saeati finished his second breakfast meal. He was inhabited by a feeling of warm contentment. He wiped his hands with a towelette and folded the trash in a ball; it found one of his cargo pockets.

In the wagon, the commuters were quiet. The stops were common occurrences. However, what thundered on the surface was not.

The train's motorist came through the speakers, jovial.

"Ladies and gentlemen, you will soon experience the effects of a sleeping gas. The substance itself is harmless, and most related injuries are usually sustained by environmental hazards and falls. I suggest you sit down to avert head traumas and microfractures. Thank you." The polite and joyful tone did not match the content of the message. The passengers laughed.

Rashid did not. He straightened his posture.

A chime rang in the wagon. He closed his eyes and counted in his head.

Three. Two. One.

A white smoke flooded the compartment coach at a furious

pace. The commuters rose and collapsed, hitting the hard floor in full force. A body leaned on Rashid as he held his breath, his lungs tightening, and covered his nostrils. He remained still. *Motion economy. Twenty seconds.*

Ten seconds later, the paramedic heard the doors open. A mysterious individual in a HAZMAT suit gently squeezed his right shoulder. Rashid extended a hand and grabbed a gas mask he was offered.

He donned the protective equipment and exhaled. His lungs relaxed under the new oxygen intake while the mask's sophisticated filters cleared the gas-related contaminants deposited on his tan skin.

A voice echoed through the breathing device's comms bracket. "Give me a thumbs up if you are ready."

Rashid pushed the old white man leaning on his left side. The inert body tipped the other way and froze. He looked up and gave the mysterious individual standing in front of him a thumbs up. The stranger waved the smoke away and motioned *ten* with his fingers. Rashid gave another approval.

The enigmatic ally turned right and disappeared through the sliding plug doors.

The paramedic and number one suspect in the Capitol's attack investigation initiated a game of cat and mouse with the FBI and its local partners.

May Allah give my partners the strength to complete their mission while I divert their attention. May I survive to reminisce al-Mahdi being brought out from concealment to spread on this earth justice and equity and eradicate tyranny and oppression.

He waited ten seconds and left the train. Outside, a pathway of light bulbs led to a service door. Rashid began his new journey, bound to a call beyond his flesh.

———

The Giant's footprints had sunk in the underwater tunnel. A war broke out, down below.

Abeba and her tactical unit stood by the *Yards'* edge, on the west bank: to the goddess of a thousand eyes, the Anacostia River was generating exploitable data in real-time.

Three inches per second. North eastbound.

She held a blueprint in her hands. Her eyes met the paper. The document began *speaking* to her. Exit routes from the subway line bled on the document, highlighted by divine colors only she could see. She circled them and laid the map on the hot concrete. Her hand found her cargo pocket, and a small device shaped like a standard lab culture tube. Abeba pressed a button on the bottom.

A *click* ensued. She swept the blueprint with the device, from left to right.

Beep. "Transferred," a synthetic voice booming from the portable scanner announced.

Abeba tapped her in-ear receiver twice and ordered, "Control, you received potential exit routes for the person of interest. I want them sealed. And I want the Anacostia River shut and combed within a ten-mile radius. From the subway car. You have ten minutes. Suspect is most likely on foot but healthy and receiving assistance. I'm going in with the HRT."

"This is Control. Good copy."

Abeba folded the blueprint and placed it back in the armored truck. She motioned for her team to leave their vehicle.

"Initially, there were at least fifty-four scenarios in which the suspect could have escaped. After triaging the data in this specific set, it is closer to five. We are going to drive Rashid Saeati to a dead end while the ground teams further restrict his space. Rules of engagement are clear. There is no shoot-to-kill order. Despite the most recent developments, I do not believe Rashid presents an immediate threat. And he may be our best lead in the ongoing investigations. We need a link to the *Watchmaker* and the shadow network that orchestrated the attack on the Capitol. It's vital. In other terms, this *package* is fragile. Tread carefully. Questions?"

The tactical team remained silent, knowing each second bridged a wider gap between them and their prey.

Abeba nodded in approval. A point man led the unit to a metal door nearby. He entered a code on the electronic lock and swung the gateway open.

Inside, the tactical unit, covered by Abeba in the rear, discovered a massive tunnel whose spherical curves suggested the existence of an underground ecosystem, one running parallel to theirs.

No one ever fully understood how Abeba's mind separated the infinite layers of this world. But a proven track record averted further questioning. She verbally led the point man to a series of doors and intersections, like she was *connected* to Rashid, tracking his every step, his every turn.

The suspect's cell phone was turned off or destroyed; the FBI had lost his electronic trail prior to the underground incursion. But Abeba, relentless, perceptive, and uniquely gifted, continued her implacable advance.

Steps resonated ahead. A shadow danced on the weak light bulbs. The point man sped up and shouted, "FBI, freeze!".

The silhouette ahead projected blurry edges. It began running faster, its crooked arms moving like the twisted parts of a mechanical beast.

Abeba broke formation and rushed towards the unidentified individual. Her training and lighter gear allowed for a faster stride and unrestricted movements. She needed to take that chance, to shorten the interval.

As the shadow turned human, she saw him.

Rashid. She gained ground, stomping on the cold concrete with a furious determination. Rashid was only a few feet away when he suddenly veered left to an opened steel door.

The access locked behind him.

AMERICA IS A ZOO   123

Abeba pressed her fingers against the steel; it read *Water Junction ne3423. Safety Chamber.*

A loud thump rocked the metal. She stepped back. Her tactical unit caught up and laid inquiring eyes on their commander.

Panting, she managed to articulate, "Pressurized ... chamber ... suspect ... pushed out into the river."

In the dimmed lighting, the eyes widened. The point man asked, "Isn't that lethal?"

Abeba took a deep breath. She answered, "Yes. Unless you're trained. At full speed, it takes a minute and thirty seconds to reach the river. Another twenty-five seconds to reach the surface. The chances are slim, but he might make it."

The FBI special agent found no alternative to this observation. She needed to confirm Rashid's death or apprehend him. Every other development would prove inconclusive.

She said, "It will take two hours for the chamber to depressurize and give me access. Even if we had diving gear, he would be long gone. Let's head back and dispatch a diving team in the river."

They retraced their steps under Abeba's lead and quickly reached the exit. Suddenly, their pupils retracted, adjusting to the blinding lights of the beaming star above.

Abeba tapped her in-ear receiver, black specks flooding her sight. "This is Solomon. He's in the river. I want him found! Send divers to sweep within a two-mile radius from *Water Junction ne3423*. Keep me updated every five minutes."

"This is Control. Good copy. Also, aerial support is inbound."

The sound of rotor blades churning the air grew louder and louder. Two black helicopters sent ripples to the surface of the Anacostia River. *It's only a matter of minutes*, Abeba thought.

———

Rashid was fighting the seductive embrace of the darkness as he launched into the river.

His gas mask also operated as a breather with a limited oxygen supply, but his body almost failed when he sustained the blunt force of raging waters in a high-pressure pipe, deviating from the given script.

He shook his head and peered through the mask's polycarbonate lenses. The murky waters of the river were traversed by faded beams of light.

Rashid Saeati had trained for this very instant, in the upmost secrecy. The money was secondary. Being part of a major systemic overhaul was the *true* calling. As he swam to the bank, his hands repeatedly reached for the intangible reward. He was close to completion, to evading his pursuers, whose resources and energy were diverted from the *actual* leads.

A concrete slab drew its outline in the blurs of evergreens. Rashid shot up to the surface and emerged, hopeful.

I have to try.

A flock of metal birds ruled the skies. Divers were sweeping the sector, and ground teams were most likely combing the streets nearby. The city was on lockdown. There were fewer concealment options.

But he had an unwavering resolve, an ideological justification that could not be argued or compromised by the promises of material riches.

Rashid ditched his mask on the pier he climbed on and began running, fighting bruised sides, a burning chest, and the weight of soaked clothing. He saw the row houses and subway stations ahead. He needed to entertain this game of cops and robbers until he could find safe refuge.

A thunder of footsteps smashed his hopes to smithereens. FBI teams appeared from behind the surrounding vegetation, converging on his position from multiple angles like a black smoke infiltrating through cracks. There was no way out, but death was not in the plans for Rashid. He froze and tensed, internally praying for survival, for another sunrise, for the comforting presence of his godchild after beating the judicial system.

I am not another martyr.

As the feds circled around, a young Black woman stepped closer and held him at gunpoint. Their eyes met, and they reached a mutual understanding: *The violence must not escalate further.*

She said, "Down on your stomach. Fingers interlocked behind your head. Legs crossed back. Do you carry any weapons, controlled substances, or explosives?"

Rashid complied and turned his head sideways, his golden skin scraped by the hot concrete. "No … weapons, no … dr … ugs, no … bombs."

Her voice reached his ear, "Are you in need of medical attention?"

"No … yes."

Her steps grew closer. Soon, he felt the sharp plastic of disposable restraints cut through his wrists. It was foreshadowing of a painful treatment. Fear flooded his heart.

Rashid added, "I have information that could lead to the *Watchmaker.* I want immunity."

17. U.S. PROXY

"Avoid the company of liars, but if you can't, don't believe them."

- Bin Allah

Seraos took off his tactical gloves to cycle through the documents. The grain was coarse, the paper stiff, the corner and edges darkened by droughts, seasons, and travels.

Bin Allah and his close entourage were blinded by the tactical flashlights of the special forces detachment. They were handcuffed, back against the wall, fingers interlocked at crotch level.

Bin Allah chose to shut his eyes; his beard's shine produced glitters of white gold under the LED beams.

He projected a mystical beauty akin to Medusa's mesmerizing, lively hair patterns. His skin was the color of a gold-hued oil, one binding the ingredients of a sophisticated recipe. His long eyelashes and thick eyebrows drew black eye lines; his hooked nose accentuated a jaw line chiseled in gold. Bin Allah's ears were of a medium size, oval and sharp, engineered to withstand the friction of an adversarial resistance.

After a brief contemplation, Seraos returned to the documents he was given by the *King of Kufra*. One of his soldiers indicated, "Extraction in seven mikes. I'll need at least three for SSE and one for transport."

"Understood. Give me forty-five seconds."

The reports and transcripts were using official identifiers and classification models.

Operation "Sand Wave". Unconventional warfare. Training of a counter-insurgency force well-positioned in the local communities. Political action. Economic benefits found in a direct access to natural resources and political capital. Plausible deniability. Focus is the Republic of Iraq. Model could be replicated through other proxies.

Seraos flipped the pages with purpose.

"ID Bin Allah greenlit the deal, sir. Ten square miles two klicks east of Al Jawf Kufra. The logistical details are being worked on as we speak."

"Legal specifics?"

"A contract has been drafted. Our local shell front fabricated an environmental study."

Seraos continued turning the pages. More recent time stamps came to life in an animated sequence.

"Sir, we've lost the assets. They used a reflective material in the break. No satellite feeds. No vehicle signatures. Our proxy is MIA."

"Activate the pathfinding protocols. Get me the DO on the line."

The last sheet featured a list of names.

Salim Ben Ali
Samir Hourdin
Malik Odewolo
Alif Saprim
Michael A. Bailey
Omar Al Fikri
Medhi Boulefi
Zarwat Alifa

Muhammad Gaffar

Zoya J. Jones

Seraos began shuffling the puzzle pieces, under the growing pressure of an operational deadline. Time was evading his grasp as he attempted to understand Bin Allah's vision and message.

The *King of Kufra* broke his brief silence, his eyes still closed. "Last page. Those names can be cross matched with the incidents your government linked me to. I know you. You are a man of integrity and a good leader. We share common values. You and I."

Bin Allah sighed and resumed, "The entire compound is shielded against thermal readings, and the communications are still jammed. I can give you a body, so you can sort this out back home."

Seraos looked at his men. Their eyes danced between the windows and their target. He asked, "A body?"

Bin Allah opened his eyes, looking beyond the beams. "A wise man joined our cause years ago. He agreed to give me his dead son's body, one we transformed to match mine. I felt a sharp pain going against the principles of the great *Allah*, not letting the blessed Muslim decompose into the earth following a last wash and prayer. But I thought, how do we go back to a state of bliss? How do we heal this broken world? Islam's objectives and doctrine have always been about creating staples and anchorable values in the communities, bringing Muslims and non-Muslims together. We are not waging a war here. We are ending it."

Tears fell from his oval eyes the color of evergreen streams. Was it God, questionable intel from his command, or the award-winning performance of another charismatic Middle Eastern? Bin Allah's stance seemed genuine. He expressed no threat and gave Seraos a choice. It was *unusual*.

The jammer.

The special forces leader addressed Bin Allah, "We have operational contingencies. If we don't establish communication with our command within the next two minutes, we'll suffer the wrath of *hellfire* missiles. There will be no conversation then. I need you to prove to me that you're operating in good faith."

The other soldiers opened their eyes wide and shifted towards their leader. Seraos ignored the silent objection and continued, "Begin SSE. You have three mikes. Release the detainee downstairs. Quietly."

The men nodded in agreement and laid the captives down on the ground, leaving Bin Allah untouched. They began packing forensics evidence and sensitive information in clear pouches labeled *Al Jawf Kufra - BA SSE*.

Seraos stared into Bin Allah's soul, commanding. The latter answered, "Deal, good American." He clapped twice. A chime rang from a ceiling corner.

Seraos tapped his shoulder strap's rubber pad. "Control, this is Evergreen, how copy?"

"Evergreen, this is Control. SITREP?"

"This is Evergreen. Comms malfunctioned. We have the HVT, and SSE will be completed in one mike."

"Good copy, Evergreen. What's the package status? Any residuals?"

Seraos took a second to process the implications of his next decision. He looked at Bin Allah. The older man was consistent in his neutrality. He betrayed no reaction, no expectations.

"Package is KIA. Identifiable. No residuals."

"Roger that, Evergreen. Exfil in six mikes. HLZ two."

"Good copy, Control."

Thoughts were racing in the Delta Force leader's brain as he plunged into a strange abyss of limitless depths.

He addressed his unit. "Leave his entourage here and get ready to exfil. This intel is solid. Are we co?"

One of the men raised a left hand. The remainder of the unit followed suit.

In the United States Special Operations Command, Seraos was a giant few could outleap. His track record in tactical operations and beyond the duty of the uniform was that of a man grounded in logical reasoning and championing for consistency. His men trusted his judgment, regardless of the outcomes.

Seraos addressed Bin Allah, "I need you to be quick. I need to know how this body will match your biometrics and how you plan to escape. I need a point of contact to follow up and through. I need to know what you plan on doing if we move forward with this."

The *King of Kufra* tilted his head in agreement and slightly bowed as his restraints snapped free. He said, "Yes. Follow me."

Seraos ordered his soldiers to stand by and trailed behind Bin Allah. They entered the large bathroom whose walls blended hexagonal tiles and clayish textures. A massive mirror provided a reflection of the two men on a mission. The *King of Kufra* pulled a built-in handle on its left edge; the mirror swung outward and revealed a set of stairs. Down below, a well-lit concrete basement called the visitors in, like the passage to an upside-down world where answers laid bare. Andre saw the potential repercussions of his transgression in the cascading steps.

Bin Allah initiated the descent. He asked, "Your name was redacted from the reports I received. You must be from a Tier-1 SMU, or CIA?"

Seraos found the poking irrelevant. "You have basic knowledge of our procedures. But it's not necessarily true. Now, answers."

"Hm."

Bin Allah stole a brief glance at the American over his shoulder.

He resumed, "This region holds many secrets. Our ancestors received many godly gifts from the prophet himself. *Muhammad* blessed those lands in his travels, guided by the words of the *book*. We were chosen. The men before me built a network of tunnels to protect what Allah bestowed upon us. I will escape through here, to *Harat Zuwayyah*. I will provide you with coordinates and a code phrase to a point of contact. The body we have stored here was specifically altered for these ... particular circumstances. I knew you and I would meet. I wasn't sure you'd be receptive, but my trust in *Him* is unfaltering."

The two men reached the bottom of the stairwell. It was a cache, but there were no weapons.

A printing press, tables, computers, and a large cast-iron tub made for the minimalist layout. An aperture on the furthest wall led to a bedrock on a downwards slope. Bin Allah approached the cast-iron tub. Its glossy, white finish underscored the green liquid it contained, one in which a body was fully immersed. The corpse was immaculate, perfectly preserved; it was the carbon copy of the *King of Kufra*.

Bin Allah said, "Dental records, fingerprints, eyes, even new emerging biometrics your government is testing like ... finger vein recognition, brain and heart patterns. Everything will match. Give me thirty seconds. I must pray, and although I cannot satisfy all the demands of a proper *Janazah*, it is necessary."

The *King of Kufra* pulled the body out of the tub and dropped it on the cold floor. The liquid that soaked the corpse's flesh and its white robe almost instantly evaporated, dissolved.

Seraos stepped back, existing in both fear and admiration. *How?*

Bin Allah began praying in his native tongue. Andre's extensive knowledge of Bedouin Arabic, or *Badawi*, helped transform the sacred words into a romanized ode to the dead, and the living they shared a bond with.

"O God, forgive our living and our dead, those who are present among us and those who are absent, our young and our old, our males and our females. O God, whoever You keep alive, keep him alive in Islam, and whoever You cause to die, cause him to die with faith. O God, do not deprive us of the reward and do not cause us to go astray after this. O God, forgive him and have mercy on him, keep him safe and sound and forgive him, honor his rest, and ease his entrance. Wash him with water and snow and hail, and cleanse him of sin as a white garment is cleansed of dirt. O God, give him a home better than his home and a family better than his family. O God, admit him to Paradise and protect him from the torment of the grave and the torment of Hellfire. Make his grave spacious and fill it with light."

Bin Allah quietly recited a few words and said, "*Assalaamu 'Alaykum Warahmatullah*."

He turned around and gauged Seraos, probing on his eyes through the Balaclava.

There was no malice in the Muslim, Seraos thought.

After a few seconds, a call from upstairs interrupted the silent exchange. "Two mikes!"

Bin Allah added, "The coordinates are on this table. I prepared hard drives for your team. Additional resources for your new journey, *akhi*."

He disappeared in the tunnels, his shadow flickering with the dying lights.

Seraos witnessed an act of God. He was certain there was no technology or substance with such unique properties, and very few men willing to defy the established order of things and elevate above War, above dangerously misguided social constructs, above hatred. Bin Allah was *special*.

The team lead shouted, "Test shot!"

Upstairs, a voice repeated, "Test shot!"

Seraos approached the corpse and shot him twice in the head, unwilling. The skull rattled on the concrete and quickly returned to a motionless state. He grabbed the hard drives and note on the tables and picked the body up in a firefighter carry.

Above, his men were ready. They untied the captives. Bin Allah's entourage rushed downstairs, in the pursuit of their leader, their husband, and father.

"Bin Allah". The son of God.

18. STAGE 3
WASHINGTON, D.C.

*Power to the people! They reached terminal velocity in a free-fall,
breaching through what they believed was an immutable state of affairs.*

Andre Seraos' corpse was celebrated by the strange menagerie of talking animals. Was it because he represented the humanity they lost? Or because of the rally cry his uncompromising integrity shouted at their naked souls?

The beasts felt uplifted, inhabited by a feeling they could not quite identify. It was bringing tears of joy. It was swinging the tails. It was flapping the wings.

Brain-altering pheromones shaped ritualistic mating dances. There was a growing sexual tension as the crass politicians felt disgusted by their own urge to stroke, to feel on, to enter. The beasts were losing the humanity they had recently partially recovered. They were willing to risk it all, to expose themselves to the judgment of surprise visitors whose fingers would press against the glass.

The footwork was that of a boxer circling around his opponent, looking for an opportunity to breach and strike. The Gorilla set famished eyes on the Panda, with whom he was moving in unison;

the latter felt compelled to the primate's dark energy, to his longing for dominance. It was inexplicably *appealing.*

The strange scene unfolded all over the chamber, where improvised couples spread and twirled to a silent beat. The place was in ruins. Dead limbs and faces protruded from the rubble of woods and stones, occasionally trampled by careless creatures driven by insatiable impulses. The air was filled with a thin mist of dust and foul-smelling secretions that evaporated with the rising heat.

Most animals had reached a state of trance, dry-heaving, sleepwalking through a feverish dream.

Inside of their ruptured brains, fragments of who they *were* begged to resist the urges, to continue the mating dances until the heat inside dissipated. *An orgy would add to the irreparable damages already caused.*

It was comical to the viewers. They watched the beasts of furs, coats, feathers, and scales give in to their hidden fantasies. The tension was palpable through the screen, even to those who had very basic knowledge of animal behaviors.

At this very instant, the most powerful elements of the U.S. political class had lost all credibility. They were exhibits from a freak show.

There was a duality, within the nucleus of their shattered minds and flesh: Chemicals were shared, *seductive*, and absorbed, *nurturing.* An accelerated cycle of ups and downs, highs and lows made the beasts feel like proper drug addicts seeking the next thrilling fix to find bliss once more.

The Lion roared as he tensed, on the prowl, eyes on a songbird. The latter chirped, and sang, "You want me? We can make it fit."

"That's how I like my interns," the President thundered, his mane swinging.

A few feet away, the growling of the massive Bear preceded a few words as he fixed on the Bull's glossy coat. "Deep in your tissue.

My rules. No oversight. Like the hundreds we killed on U.S. soil, under the pretense of ... national security. The almighty CIA!" An earth-shattering laugh exposed his sharp teeth.

The ground shook at regular intervals, puncturing the overall tremor. The Gorilla was pounding the floor with massive fists. More words with terrible implications flew from the mouths of the transformed, rid of all inhibitions, robbed of their ability to cheat, deceive, and lie.

"THE WORKING CLASS IS A MEANS TO AN END."

"I will never let go of thissssss power."

"Fuck those PEASANTS. They better run me my money!"

The Grasshopper. "By the people. For the people. FOR THE PEOPLE. No correlation found. Public servant? No. Business. Profits. Lesser expenses. More. More. Morrrrreeee. I told you. You told me. I told them. They told them. We told on ourselves. What. Wait. A. Minute."

The animals continued the twirling, spinning, and pouncing as they erupted in booming laughter. They were urinating and defecating to mark their territory, or to release strange sexual impulses. There was no rule. No boundaries. No reserve.

Outside, law enforcement agencies, a scrambling government trapped in a web of state and federal jurisdictions conflicts, and the poorly trained regular armies lost control of the masses.

There was a beat to this quiet, incoming revolution: the deep sounds of the staircase ramps, the sliding of the windows, the conversations that overflowed the streets of D.C.

In Brentwood, a mother of three peeked outside, eyes on the expressway that bordered her complex. Downtown, the wealthy hid from the storm that was brewing, their shadows shielded from the sun by expensive blackout curtains.

In the deserted streets, dope dealers and military personnel shared the same objective: *How do we serve the masses?*

The city's veins were pulsing through its shell made of stones, woods, concrete, and greens. Community leaders had found each other, relying on texts and calls, finding people who knew people who knew people. *New* old social skills resurfaced, and genuine, distraction-free conversations took place.

"Georgetown University. Healy Gates."

"Anacostia Park. Section F. 21st and C St NE."

"Good idea! We both converge towards the Hill. What about security, Charles?"

"I can provide representatives and security officers. Jamal is the head of our detail. I'll shoot you his number to work the specifics."

"Thank you. Is five hours enough? I'd like to hit some numbers and get the press involved before we head out."

"Give yourself eight, Kenya, so I can pick a route and refine the logistics. With those numbers and the coverage, they won't dare make a move."

A conversation between two of the most powerful activists in D.C. acted as a primer to a foreseen implosion. Fuses the size of city blocks sparked a new hope, seeking their blasting caps: the population centers, the neighbors, the friends, the relatives. A storm was coming.

Shouts roared in the buildings, in the homes.

You will pay!

Cage them!

You motherfuckers.

Oh, we're coming.

Sensationalism regained its place in the broadcasting landscape. An interim government struggled, incompetent and spineless. They also knew their own judgment day was near.

On most TV channels, a young Black woman with geometric cat eyeglasses stood in front of a podium. The White House sign in the backdrop was faded, disfavored by an awkward lighting setup whose focal point was a spot left of the new press secretary.

She wore a mocha blazer skirt set and a white silky undershirt.

The fashion was trendy and the body appealing, but the soul was still rotten, the viewers thought.

Fear shrunk her lashless eyes. She was still as stone, her shoulders slightly raised.

She produced a statement.

"Good morning. My name is Leticia Carter, your new White House press secretary. I am here today to assum—"

The working class, drained of its joyful aspirations after years of financial and mental hardship, only saw a cackling bird serving the usual bullshit from the survivors of an outdated political caste. They pictured a feathered avian sporting a long beak and a wild crest. The mocha outfit remained on her slender frame, her bird legs providing an uncomfortable, nightmarish vision.

The people shaped their own perceived version of the statement.

In their revenge-fueled imaginations, the press secretary laid bare her mask.

"So, what I'm saying is ... I'm playing the clock on a comfortable salary. All I care about is optics, preserving the status of my slave masters so I can get paid and afford this high fashion. You know damn well we have no intentions of resolving this situation in a way that's beneficial to you. You can die for all we care. The corporations who bend us over the lavish countertops of their industrial kitchen for a meal will replace your ass with another underpaid worker who accepted the position out of necessity. I can't wait for the muscles to enter the Capitol and end this situation, so we can go back to how it was before.

"Those Black folks outside the *Hill* aren't my tribe. They're lazy and lack obedience. My white masters fetishize and fantasize on me. And you know what? I'm in control, I can leverage this body for more power, for a lush garden in Georgetown, trips in Turks and Caicos, *red bottoms*. Maybe those old white men are right. Maybe we need new slave catchers. Anyway, let me shower you with more empty words. More containers with no food for thought. You'll give up, eventually."

———

Washington, D.C. - FBI Washington Field Office

"Excuse me?"

Abeba Solomon was arguing with a dashing middle-aged man of Mediterranean descent.

His dark, slicked back hair, golden skin, and double-breasted pinstripe suit screamed *power of a conqueror*. They were facing each other in an empty room of neutral tones. A two-way glass offered them its clear side, giving views of an interrogation room. And Rashid Saeati.

"Precisely, Miss Solomon. My client adds value to one of the biggest investigations this agency had ever conducted. A matter of national security with strong political implications. The future of this country shaped by a single decision: to grant my client immunity or delay the resolution of this crisis with a televised trial."

Abeba deconstructed the layers of wool and silk that made his expensive suit, seeking a structural weakness. But his piercing eyes were telling the story of an inevitable outcome.

Abeba asked, "What are the conditions?"

"Transactional immunity. Release within seventy-two hours. The payment of all associated legal fees. My client has agreed not to sue under the legal theory of emotional distress. Provided you meet those conditions."

"How can he afford you?"

The lawyer smirked and answered, "That's irrelevant."

19. THE SANDMAN
WASHINGTON, D.C.

*What part do you play in this? What possessed you to serve the Devil
himself? Or is it God, in the disguise of a necessary affliction?*

The single father who suffered the biased judgment of a
dysfunctional justice system. The hungry kids whose
bones threatened to rip their skin. The Black woman who
fought a thousand battles since her chaotic introduction to this
world. The homeless. The mentally ill. The drug users who, in a
moment of clarity, acquired a political conscience. The working
poor, to whom job significance was a foreign concept. The strong
ones who never complained, carrying the pain and trauma of a
thousand lives, unheard.

They were gathered in Georgetown University and Anacostia
Park, ready to reclaim the right to forge their own narratives.

The people had endured enough. The *Watchmaker* set the
country ablaze, reigniting a dying fire within. The hundreds of
thousands stretched over miles, coming from all backgrounds and
places. They were gauging each other, greeting one another as they
accepted a newfound connection: a common bond rooted in
struggles and inequalities.

The protesters felt empowered, shaping new possibilities as they built strength in numbers.

Why haven't we done this before? a collective inner voice inquired.

In *Georgetown U*, at the *Healy Gates*, a middle-aged Black man stood on the roof of a security shack. In the background, the neo-medieval Healy Hall Building, a flagship D.C. landmark, threatened to swallow his outline.

But the man with a megaphone was elevating above persecution, carried by a sea of a million bodies. His round-rimmed eyeglasses softened his angular features. His striped shirt, black jogger pants, and white sneakers skillfully blended an accessible intellectualism with an operational practicality.

The timing made him a creature of another plane, a war angel sent to enforce God's decision. Millions of mythical beings readied with him. The crowd stretched out far west; law enforcement agencies and FEMA-like organizations were outnumbered, brought down by the resolve of a united front.

The bright sun made the man squint. Still, he could not find the boundaries of this endless wave. However, he knew that his voice, his message, would be relayed.

He shouted in the megaphone, "Thank you. Thank you. Thank you."

The murmurs and side conversations ceased. A droning sound provided the speaker with a dizzying bassline.

He shouted once more, "We are at the junction of a broken past, a dysfunctional present, and a better future. Although I do not condone the actions of the *Watchmaker*, we knew the people in charge of this country were bound to pay a price for their unforgivable deeds. I have been trying to push for a systemic change. For years. This is nothing new to me. My ancestors have bled on those grounds, their lungs crushed by the stones and the metals.

"But I'm no god. I need you. I need your strength. And although I have received a tremendous amount of support within the past ten years, this ... this is unprecedented. Listen."

The activist was the focal point of all eyes and ears. The faces were suspended in a state of zero gravity.

He resumed, "Today, we begin the *Great Revolution*. Today, ladies and gentlemen, WE ARE RETAKING THIS COUNTRY."

His roaring call sent the crowd into a frenzy. The standing ovation fractured the skies like the condensation trails of planes. The leader's eardrums promised to rupture. But he was willing to embrace his fate, to welcome the disease of the free.

"Thank you. Thank you. Thanks."

The crowd placed its hopes in the man's guidance. The people almost instantly complied. The droning sound reemerged.

"A few items before we start. Enough blood has been spilt on the account of hatred, division, and oppression. For some of those negative factors, we blame the institutions of this very country. The ones designed to crush us with taxes, barriers to entry, legal loopholes, and constant shifts in regulations. But for some of the other issues, *we* are to blame! This is why I urge you not to resort to any form of violence as we navigate through this historical development. The changes we require from others must also happen from *within*. You must renounce to the warped ideas that racism, hatred, or prejudice are exclusive to a specific group. To the idea that those terms aren't interchangeable. You must understand that the betterment of this society can only be achieved if the people of this nation unlearn the toxic generational habits that led us to *this*.

"Second, we have medics with water and dry snacks running a route parallel to ours. Be mindful of one another, be kind, be caring. Let us march."

The televised thunderous applause rocked the country.

The man had chosen his words carefully, concerned with the

tendency of modern movements to quickly become reactionary forces fueled by the very hatred and ignorance they promised to fight; new ideologies that lost sight of their initial mission and added value. Parts of the LGBTQIA+ community, radical feminists, exclusionary think tanks... all drifting away from the core values they originated from: acceptance, tolerance, love, *unity*.

The man with the round-shaped glasses returned to ground level. The mass began moving as one.

From above, it seemed a giant living stream had set its mind on purging D.C. from its filth.

————

WASHINGTON, D.C. - THE PALISADES

The Potomac River's brown waters washed the shiny, glittery soils of the eastern bank. Abeba Solomon and a team of FBI agents were gliding on the artificial waves of the Potomac. Her Zodiac Milpro exercised dominance over the waterway as she lowered her profile to withstand the increasing speeds.

Behind, another inflatable boat followed: three masked individuals with black attires. They were impervious to the shifting dynamics of the watercourse, stoic and solid in their stances.

The group slowed down and approached a waterfront property flanked by a thick web of trees, animals, and landforms. The boats docked at a wooden pier that extended two-hundred feet out in the river. Ahead, a white tower house cast its outline beyond an overgrown garden. Fractured cobblestones led to it, untouched by the wild greens that surrounded the pathway. The perspective was narrow: There was no other opening in the neighboring woods, no secondary structure.

Abeba set foot on the pier. Her eyes fixed on the tower, a structure whose tall windows displayed dark rooms of blurry layouts. She then looked at her team, their FBI athletic shirts flanked by a Glock19M and a black polymer holster.

Her hand raised, and she ordered, "Sweep the perimeter. I want every potential clue within a half-mile radius catalogued. And ... cross contamination protocols."

The agents nodded in approval. One of them carried two forensics kits. She handed Abeba one.

The FBI leader, who was adept at field operations, added, "I have personnel from the DEA here, operating underwater. The property was tied to a big narcotics distributor from the east coast. They'll assist you with forensics. The main investigation takes precedence, but I'd like to help them collect intel before we lock it down."

Abeba walked to the tower house with one of the masked agents. They both drew their weapons out and converged towards a tall metal door, flanking its irregular frame.

The masked man met Abeba's juvenile eyes and nodded. From the left side of the intricate metal carvings found on the metallic surface, she pushed on the pane. Half of the door opened inward. Her quiet partner rushed in, swift and decisive.

She followed suit. Inside, the space was reminiscent of an old lighthouse. The entire layout accommodated the round shape of the stone. Custom black cabinetry and appliances surrounded a central spiral staircase that shot upward through an aperture in the ceiling. There was no apparent movement or recent activity. Rich Persian rugs absorbed the sound of the visitors' steps as they reviewed the room.

Abeba pointed to the upper level. The masked agent gave her a thumbs up.

She engaged the staircase, walking slowly, her low profile like a creeping shadow's.

Upstairs, the room functioned as an art studio. Paintings on the wall were highlighted by picture lights installed at strange angles. Abeba swept the remainder of the space with her provisional partner. She stopped in front of a massive canvas split in ten different portraits of the same subject.

Her, *she.*

Abeba examined the art piece with a trained eye. It was contemporary portraiture. Each of the ten faces featured a different set of eyes. Some were possessed by a black fire, some were upside down, some shattered. The beauty of it distracted from the fear-inducing implications behind the scenes: A domestic terrorist had forged a bond with Abeba Solomon.

She looked at her masked partner and said, "Clear." Then, "Status?" she asked her team through her in-ear communicator.

"Clear. Still sweeping. Nothing of significance yet."

"Understood."

The masked man spoke. His voice was a quiet threat. "DEA. Sound choice for a covert identity. From what I gather, the *Watchmaker* left no other clue through his proxy besides this location?"

Abeba nodded in agreement.

The masked man began walking the place, his uncovered eyes dancing on the paintings.

Abeba's brain was racing. The entire structure revealed its layers to her eyes. The data was overwhelming.

The specifics of the Watchmaker's ideology, his convictions, the transparency in his communication style, the undisputable fact that his motives are neither of economic nor religious nature all point towards a single conclusion: He has no interest in misleading. There must be something here.

Abeba shut the noise out. She focused on the inner workings: the picture lights, the paintings, the colorful stains on the granite floor. The patterns were complex, the tower house's layout vibrant, disorderly, and textured. *It* was telling a story, but the words were drowning in a sea of paper.

This is the work of someone who matches my particular skills, she thought.

The masked man, who had appropriated her forensics kit, returned and stopped right next to her. He said, "Nothing of significance, no code, no braille, no fluids, no body."

Abeba met his eyes and shifted her attention back towards her portraits. The other art pieces shared no common theme, covering various periods, subjects, and movements. The picture lights in their vicinity may have offered a clue, but she could not identify the markers. *Think.*

"I'm aware of your ... capabilities, Miss Solomon. But have you considered that maybe our person of interest is trying to overload you with visual data? The answer may be in a more basic form. An outline, maybe?"

Abeba looked up and mouthed a *possibly.* "There is a legal pad in this first aid kit."

The masked man complied and retrieved a small notebook which he passed to her. She grabbed a pen from her back pocket.

The picture lights, when connected to one another, shaped hundreds of combinations, countless vectors and clusters. It was like receiving God. But the outline of their arrangement, the overall composition, gave birth to a croissant-like figure that looked familiar to her. She drew it on the yellow paper.

Her eyes shifted to the portraits. They were laid out in four columns, with two extra artworks in the first. She drew the outline once more. Both of her shapes were side by side on the legal pad. Her photographic memory felt an interdependence. She connected the columns to the croissant.

Howard. The geometric association resembled a satellite view of the prestigious research university. She was one of its notable alumni.

But the scope was still too broad. She asked the masked man, "Howard is—"

A synthetic voice triggered, somewhere in the high coffered ceiling. The agents' weapons sought the source.

"Howard is a private federally chartered historically Black research university in Washington, D.C. It is classified among 'R2: Doctoral Universities – High research activity' and accredited by the Middle States Commission on Higher Education. Andrew Rankin. Class of 45," the virtual intelligence announced.

Abeba clicked.

Class of 45.

20. THE EXODUS

*Human nature is quite the creature of habit. Certain triggers and
predatory instincts acquired millions of years ago invariably overshadow
ideals of a better... you.*

The thoracic cages behind the membranes of various compositions and thicknesses had a life of their own. They expanded and retracted to the beat of the dead animals and the dead human's foul smell, to the rhythm of the acetous fluids bubbling from the orifices, the melting flesh of the decomposing casualties.

The Lion maintained a safe distance from the filth, but his mind was already contaminated by a crippling anxiety and the sight of a bottomless abyss. Next to him, the Pig leaned on the chamber's main access, shaking. Tears rolled down his porky eyes, magnifying the pink shades of his smooth skin.

The beasts were defeated. They had no leverage, no allies, and the man sitting behind those doors seemed to have suffered another tragic fate, as a victim of the same perpetrators.

The Grasshopper stood on his bulky back legs, next to the Lion, opposite the Pig. He felt the vibrations caused by the President's paws; they were traveling the few remaining blood-stained portions of carpet.

The bug's glassy eyes scouted around for an alternative. He addressed the Lion.

"M. President." The designation made very little sense, but his tiny brain refused to acknowledge the politicians' failure. "There must be an exit. We need to escape."

The others suddenly shifted their strained attention towards the Vice President, the green insect of rapid speech patterns. They all came to the realization that there was no other option but to flee.

Wings flapped, and subvocalizations and strange noises assaulted the space. The chronic craze flared up, worsening from remaining untreated. The Lion roared to assert dominance and avert another deadly outburst. The beasts hung onto the fragile thread of this hierarchical society and complied. The silence that followed became an invisible bonding agent. All creatures tuned in to a shared frequency.

The Lion spoke, pacing back and forth on an elevated platform, looking down on the servile condition of his tribe. "We have the strength of a thousand humans. And a country to run! Where are the profitable voters? We need to save what we have left of this ... poweeeerrrrrr." he thundered, turning internalized fears into an aggressive sound.

"Destroy the flooring. The walls. Crash the ceilings. Open the space!"

The beasts let go of their restraints. The massive hands, paws, and claws targeted the integrity of the surrounding structure.

The marble pilasters and walnut panels flew, shattered. The stone and the fibers of the carpet blended in wild splatters. The noise was sickening, but the beasts of prey had embraced a tunnel vision, seeking their target: an elusive being named *freedom*.

At this very moment, a towering survival instinct trumped all selfish impulses.

Soon, the House of Representatives chamber displayed bare walls and floors.

A dark steel frame surrounded the caged creatures. It absorbed the artificial lights, prompting the animals to quickly find a way out of this claustrophobic darkness. Underneath the podium, a deep hole presented hope. Light beamed from within. It flickered to the frantic blinking of the politicians.

The Bear stood the closest. The aperture was too narrow for his massive stature, but he managed a grip on the nearest metallic panel. It flew open under his applied strength.

The Bear, the disgraced CIA Deputy Director, revealed sharp teeth as he defied others with diseased, black eyes. He turned his back on the tribe and disappeared in the opening.

The Lion's vocalizations boomed through the chamber. He lifted a paw and said, "Go!"

In an unusual display of selfless leadership, the President waited for the crowd to exit.

He looked around, licking his yellow-shaded canines, finding that the chamber was a vision of horrors. Flies and maggots created clusters of moving black matters, some converging towards severed body parts scattered in a sea of stone dust, marble chunks, and wooden panels. The carpet was ripped in giant strips that bore the marks of razor-sharp claws and teeth. Blood was a colorful addition to the blacks, beiges, and greens.

The Lion's nose acclimated to the rancid odors of advanced decomposition, fluids, urine, and fecal matters. *To an outsider, the smell would be deadly*, he thought.

There was no guilt felt in the hearts of the grotesque creatures of a new folklore, however.

The President simply felt like he had lost his edge, like he was caught red-handed because he failed to *conceal* well enough. The stubborn politicians with no good left in them were unaware that an external party had shone a light on their filthiest, darkest secrets.

But throughout the past fifty years in politics, improvement and accountability had become foreign concepts lost somewhere in the process. The animals left the same way they entered: unapologetic, boastful, broken.

The Lion followed suit, swinging his mane as he walked the blue carpet to the final, definitive outcome of his failures.

Thump... thump... thump.

Down below, a maze of tunnels challenged the animals' land navigation skills.

The man-made network of underground pathways angled, sharp-turned, and curved. Some of the beasts were driven by desperation, splitting from the main group and crashing walls in their pursuit of a meaningless freedom.

The Unicorn shone a supernatural light on the tunnels' smooth concrete. He was more measured than the others, less impulsive. His hooves clicked on the inhospitable grounds, echoing through the massive, soulless spaces. The Lion made his way back to the front of the convoy and adjusted to the mythical creature's stride.

He asked, "Where?"

There was a common understanding between the two leading figures. The Unicorn, in his most demonstrative moments, represented a truer, purer form of leadership: one that was implied, not communicated.

The Libyan national answered the President, "The Spirit of Justice Park. The fountain is calling."

In a grounded reality where success translated into numbers and data, their advance was a stark contrast; it was an odd quest to a magical place and a mysterious fate.

Ahead, a metal door with a massive handle muffled the chanting of *many* humans.

WHAT DO WE WANT? CHANGE. WHEN WILL WE STOP? NEVER. WHAT DO WE WANT? JUSTICE. SAID NO SUIT? EVER.

The words were fear-inducing to the cockroaches who, until

recently, fed on the warm droppings of the working class. But the Unicorn continued to the door, and so did the remainder of the core group.

The Panda was in the back of the procession. His calm demeanor cast a benevolent spirit on the band of misfits. The Secretary of State had lost two of his most valuable assets, Andre Seraos and his humanity, but there was still a way to contribute, he thought. He moved through the crowd, slipping through the feathers and furs. His left paw found the handle and applied pressure, pushing it down.

A metallic shriek announced a new world, one full of fears and persecution. At this very instant, *they* became the people they used to exploit, oblivious to the trade.

The door opened. Outside, the blinding lights of the sun triggered a shared panic. Metal birds added to the oppressive feeling, their audio signatures distant yet loud and choppy.

People screamed; the high pitch of their cries sent a chilling warning. They were furies set ablaze by the wrongdoings of the *Hill*'s most recognizable actors.

The picture became sharper and clearer. A fountain of troubled waters provided a soothing score to the chaotic scene. The Pig stepped forward, struggling to find balance on the cobblestones.

Tap.

Tap.

Tap.

He was tensed in fear.

The legal adviser looked at the crowd and stood on his back legs in an unnatural stance.

Ohhhhh.

Next, he spoke. "Do not harm us!" He pointed at the Lion with bloated toes. "This is the President of the United States! We were attacked by …" The Pig's decaying eyes were dancing from body to body. He could not remember the specifics. He then laid eyes on his tribe and found the same realization in their looks.

The protesters were stunned. They had seen the animals online, but nothing could have prepared them for a real-life confrontation. The Gorilla sniffed around and beat on his chest. The mass blenched and gave the creatures more ground.

One man, however, moved forward. He was stumbling, his long, dark, greasy hair swinging left and right. His skin was covered by small black deposits. He reeked of sweat and rubbing alcohol.

Two Chinooks approached the area, their blades growing louder as their outlines began defining their significant size.

The Gorilla ran to the man quickly and stopped a few feet away. The drunk continued his stumble forward, in a careless act of aggression. Others in the crowd urged him to reconsider.

The Lion, the Panda, and the Unicorn were more concerned with the helicopters and the big containers they hauled. But was there any other option?

The homeless man swung at the silverback gorilla. He met the thick membrane of the primate's jawline. The Gorilla grabbed the human's frail body with surprising dexterity and began smashing it against the cobblestones. Blood splatters formed red concentrations on the grey shades. The cracking of the drunk's bones haunted the bystanders, filling a deafening silence with a dreading warning.

The D.C. interns, the flock of migratory songbirds, took off and fled the brewing madness.

Above, rotors produced strong winds washing the paved ground with waves made of leaves and dirt. The protesters who agreed to drive a change from within and from the very institutions leading them had surrendered to panic, self-preservation, and outright cruelty. Their faces told the stories of old lynching mobs propelled by blind hatred and a xenophobia so deeply ingrained in their DNA that no external force could fix.

The animals stood by the maintenance access, stacked in a tight ball. The Gorilla had joined them, leaving the crooked frame of the dead human for display.

Around, eyes of all shapes and sizes swept the changing paved stones and the rippled coats, furs, and feathers. There was a palpable tension, a silence breeding grounds for a seismic event.

In the trees nearby, more birds left their nests. Their wings sang and triggered a response in the Bull: He charged the crowds circling an imaginary perimeter, and the few humans brave enough to reciprocate did so in a mad outburst. They showed less restraint in their attacks, however, instead positioning themselves as apex predators, launching offensive strikes and grazing the bovine's coat with small knives and improvised weapons, unbothered with sustaining a conflict deadly in the flesh.

The activist leading the belligerent crowd was miles away, foreign to the new development. But what was integrity if not exercised when unseen, unrecorded?

Gunshots erupted, echoing in the sunny canopy that made for this ring's edges. Most humans dispersed, some trampled by others who refused to die by the guns they had manufactured and promoted.

A voice showered the mayhem from above. "This is the United States Army. All civilians and non-authorized personnel, please stand clear."

The warning was short and unequivocal. The aircrafts hovered over the transformed beings; the latter had regrouped by the maintenance access, once more, satisfied with the humans' ordered dispersion.

As the crowd cleared the park, another frame painted a red stroke on the cracked cobblestone; it was smaller than the homeless drunk's, the one who willingly plunged into his death.

A child. A young Black child whose angel face was splintered in blunt impacts, bruised and distorted, like a melting wax doll. Blood was pouring from his left eardrum, exposed to the skies. The Pig had spotted the casualty of a brief war. The child was left alone to die.

Where are the offspring's parents? silently questioned the porky advisor, shaking to the rhythm of the loud rotor blades and hurtling waves.

No answer.

In the throes of a nightmarish vision, strings of smoke descended from the metal birds, erecting an immaterial wall around the beasts, like a magical Chinese play.

The dead child disappeared in a dense smoke, adding to the Pig's compounded trauma through a painful confrontation with the dark side of human nature.

Massive metal containers hit the stones after clearing a safe radius for landing, carefully avoiding the corpses, as strange black uniforms rained down on ropes that had established dominance over the fragments of flagstones. These were the last visual memories for the fantastic beasts; they were sedated and evacuated in less than five minutes.

Two soldiers remained on site. They covered the unidentified homeless man's beaten corpse and the child's damaged frame. Soon, DCPD cordoned the area, assisted by FBI forensics.

———

Further east, the Wolf and the Bear wreaked havoc near the GOP-controlled Capitol Hill Club. Protesters were mauled by the claws of the Bear, hitting the nearby white brick building like balled paper.

The Wolf's fur bristled. His lips pulled back, revealing sharp incisors as a group of protesters swung *things* at him. The former National Security Advisor had lost touch with reality. He was a man who genuinely cared about his country, about the well-being of its population and the safety of his constituents. There was no malice in his heart. However, at this very instant, the loss of his *pack* warped his perception.

He had become a frightened wolf released in a hostile city. He jumped at his assailants' throats, rupturing their arteries with expertise. The humans attempted to cover their throat but quickly, they collapsed, blood expanding outward from the points of impact.

Bang.

Suddenly, a hard metal hit the Wolf's cranial structure with force. He collapsed and whimpered, hyperventilating on the hot sidewalk of red herringbone patterns.

Another blow. And another blow. And another.

Blow.

An overwhelmingly persistent fear in the peoples' hearts and minds drove them to abandon their ideals of better... selves.

Stop. It's dead.

The Wolf's fur absorbed the blood dripping from his deep-cut wounds. He was convulsing, fighting the call of death in a state of shock.

Soon, he stopped breathing.

The Bear interrupted the murderers' contemplation with a rushing charge; he was much harder to counter or stop. He rearranged organs and tissue in a brutal fashion, penetrating the flesh of his paralyzed targets.

Tires screeched in an adjacent street.

A DCPD car approached the corner. Three officers stepped out with shotguns, sleek Remington 870s that reflected the bright rays of the burning star above.

"Police! Stop!" one of the officers shouted at the raging bear who was shattering windshields and crushing body masses.

The Bear turned around, teeth out, and growled at his

opponents. He felt a profound hatred for the people he smelled and saw. *They are threatening our strategic interests.*

The officers issued warning shots, booming sounds traveling the brick façades. The Bear disregarded the cautionary note and charged. Shotgun shells fractured the air with ear-splitting echoes and entered the Bear's soft flesh. Inside, organs and arteries imploded, stopping the big body in its tracks.

The CIA Deputy Director fell to new DCPD recruits in a big ball of fur, fat, and muscles. His last thought accompanied hazy memories.

Pathetic.

———

A makeshift bridge was set up to reach the Capitol's main entrance. The visitor center had collapsed in a torrent of dirt after the vacuum bomb decimated the nearby landscapes, effectively compromising water and gas lines. Abeba was on the search for the *Watchmaker*, but most of her tactical teams were dispatched to clear the Capitol of further threats and retrieve sensitive information.

Within the stone walls of America's new relic, a religious silence was observed. The FBI Hostage Rescue Team and Critical Response Group had donned gas masks and tactical gear, moving in with their weapons up. They anticipated booby traps and other theatrics, caught in a struggle they did not fully comprehend.

Tap... tap... tap.

A voice shouted from the House of Representatives chamber. The words were a distorted mumble.

The teams split in half. One detachment veered left to the voice, in a highly coordinated file line. The point man identified a shape past the Statuary Hall.

A man was rushing towards them: the bearer of a suicide vest.

The lead officer issued a warning shot with an assault rifle and ordered, "FBI! Freeze!" The loud shot reverberated in the space and resonated with the hostage. The man stopped, raising shaky hands. His dress shirt was drenched in sweat.

"I—"

The FBI lead interjected, "QUIET! What's your name?"

"Paul. Paul Meinhardt."

"Okay. Pay close attention, Paul. Paul, are there any people left in here?"

"Nnnno. Nnnnottt to ... my knowledge."

"Good, Paul. Stay with me. Is this explosive device armed or active? Keep your hands up, Paul."

"It never. It never. It—" He began bursting in tears. "The countdown never started. I ... dooon'tttt know w ... hy." Paul looked down at a small display unit with four zeroes.

"That's great news, Paul. I have a specialist in explosive ordnances with me here. She's going to look at it. I need you to stay calm and still. Do we have an agreement?"

Paul nodded yes and waited a few seconds. "Yes, sir."

An EOD officer broke the formation in the rear. She wore a bomb suit with an inflated outer layer. Her expert eyes approached the hostage.

She introduced herself. "Paul, my name is Leya. I am an EOD. Are you familiar with the designation?"

"Yes, ma'am." Hope traveled through his bloodshot red eyes.

She resumed, "Great. Thank you for cooperating with us. We'll get you out of here shortly, as long as you follow my instructions. Is that clear?"

"Yes, ma'am."

She motioned a ten with her hands as she ordered the detachment to step back.

"Okay, Paul. It seems the device was not armed. Which is good. You need to remain still, hands up. I will now check for potential countermeasures, alright?"

Paul nodded, in tears. She met his eyes and brought comfort with a benevolent look.

The tan suicide jacket was quite standard in design. Embedded blocks of Semtex, ball bearing sheets, and a basic detonator connected to a timer. It was well-made, however. The EOD swept the stitching and explosive plates, finding that the integration was flawless.

She shone a pen light on the display unit and followed the wires to the blasting cap; the latter was not connected. She sighed and unzipped the jacket.

"Okay, Paul. Lower your hands. Careful."

He obliged. She found anticipation in his beady eyes.

"Good." She carefully removed the suicide vest from his soaked shirt and laid it out on the marble floor. "Paul, I need you to remain still for a few more seconds. A simple precaution."

"Yes, ma'am. Thank you." Tears continued rolling. This time, they were followed by a smile.

The EOD examined the vest and retrieved the blasting cap. She placed a coarse black tarp over the improvised explosive device. Her eyes shifted towards Paul through the polycarbonate lenses of her gas mask.

"You did great, Paul. Thank you. Given the circumstances, and I'm sure you understand, we must take you in. But be assured: If you're not involved in any capacity, you have nothing to fear. Do you have any relatives you need to contact?"

"Understood. Uhh... My wife, Roxanne."

"That's a beautiful name, Paul. We'll make the necessary arrangements."

The EOD gave a thumbs up. The remainder of the tactical unit approached the hostage. Two FBI agents guided Paul back to the exit, to the light at the end of a starless night sky. The others entered the chamber, bracing for a sinister discovery to the hushed beat of ominous drums.

21. PRINTS IN THE BLOOD

WASHINGTON, D.C. - GLOVER PARK

What a wild ride. A Joker-like figure is terrorizing D.C., but a billion-dollar enterprise is on his trail, while the people drown in the chaotic streams of their contradictory behaviors. Sounds familiar? Maybe I should develop new theatrics. Let me try. "I'm Retribution."
Ahahahahah. Ah ah ah. Ha.
Hahahahahaha.

Paul Meinhardt rode on the passenger side of a Subaru Outback, its leather seats creaking under the bodily movements. He wore a blue t-shirt whose chest pocket's white letters read *DCPD*. His face was carved by exhaustion, his flesh pale. His tired eyes sunk in purple bags.

Where were you the morning of the attack, September 6, 2023? Let's start at 6 AM.

How did your kidnappers establish contact?

Did they bear any identifiables? Tattoos, scars, an accent maybe?

Why you, Paul?

Paul reminisced the short but intense debriefing he underwent. On a few occasions, he felt a crippling anxiety take hold of his current situation. The FBI had not found any connection between him and the *Watchmaker*'s mysterious organization; his background check came back indisputably clean, and although there was no video footage retracing his steps prior to the attack, forensics supported the theory that he was abducted.

His wife, Roxanne, was informed. His better half was given the VIP treatment at the FBI's Washington field office, surrounded by armed caregivers who empathized with her state of emotional distress as they wiped her tears and offered a genuine ear. Behind the dripping mascara and the crumbling foundation, Roxanne's heart longed for a single thing: her husband.

Her fingers blanched behind the wheels, pressing tighter and tighter; she was a middle-aged white woman in athleisure wear, a product of an uneventful suburban microcosm. Her tiny frame and short stature accentuated the razor-sharp edges of her bob cut. Black cat-eye frames clashed with her blonde strands.

Although her posture was stiffened and her wheels handling conservative, she projected an opened nature, a welcoming smile that screamed joy behind its imperfections.

Paul interrupted her contemplation as they penetrated a major artery full of glass towers and concrete structures.

"I think we ought to take a trip, my love. If that's something you'd like to do?"

Roxanne nodded with a smile. She was still in shock after reuniting with her husband, who survived very powerful people.

The vehicle stopped under the cover of an oak tree, in a popular neighborhood north of Georgetown. Across the sidewalk, a colorful row house of green and white shades whose front yard featured white picket fences and a massive banana tree offered a heavenly proposition. The couple stepped out of the car and entered through a white round-top door.

Inside, the old-fashioned interior design conveyed a tale of two worlds. Persian rugs and brown leather sofas complemented espresso brown China cabinets and various pictures of faraway places Paul and his wife had explored throughout years of a quiet marriage.

The couple shared deep roots in *Glover Park*, where they were born and raised. Their respective families were prude traditional structures lobbying for Christian groups on the *Hill*; old money from the railroad boom of the 1800s that fueled successful investments and the acquisition of an impressive portfolio of assets. Some of those were passed to Paul and Roxanne, tax-free, courtesy of a broken system in which wealth trumped regulations.

But the two successful CPAs, inspired by the many cultures they had established contact with, were willing to stop over-indulging and promote a more just taxation and redistribution of wealth.

Paul carefully placed his immaculate dad sneakers on a metal shoe rack in the vestibule and, for a brief moment, examined the space. He then asked, "Roxy, sweetheart, is it a bit too early for dinner?"

"Not if you have a sweet tooth, turtle dove."

Paul's tiredness faded to the sharp focus of a conqueror, as he became something *else*.

He walked towards the living room space and moved a small area rug connecting the sofas and love seat. A gentle pressure on one of the wooden planks produced a *click*.

Paul pulled the board; below, a burner phone was sealed in a zip lock bag labeled *AIAZ*. He retrieved the package, removed the bag, and opened the cell.

A bloated finger found the call button.

Ring. Ring. "Operator."

"Hi, PMGP is cleared."

"Understood. Best wishes to you. To a meaningful change."

"To a meaningful change."

Paul hung up.

Roxanne had lost her benevolent smile, joining her husband in the dramatic switch-up. She was now focused, purposeful, deadly;

the suburban innocence vanished, chased by the dark clouds of a secret war. She brought a metallic shredder on wheels, carrying a small aluminum safe underarm.

Roxanne and Paul's eyes met. They nodded to each other.

She turned the battery-powered shredder on; its four shafts began spinning in clockwise and counterclockwise rotations.

Roxanne retrieved the aluminum safe from under her right arm and placed her thumb on the biometric lock. A chime preceded the unlocking. The safe contained a standard Glock19M, a set of golden keys, and two shiny ball bearings. Roxanne poured its content into the shredder. The items cracked and transformed into a fine powder of sparkling accents visible through a gap in the shafts.

Paul threw his burner phone in the feeding pipe. Similar outcome.

Finally, Roxanne moved the shredder back to the kitchen and returned.

She asked, "What now, turtle dove?" Her face was still possessed by a woman of harsher struggles, but the language had remained the same as prior: affectionate and comforting.

Paul smiled at the sound of his *true* love. His hardened face softened into the law-abiding citizen he was known to be.

———

"The hostage was cleared. Nothing conclusive." Abeba's voice echoed through the comms. Below, the streets swarmed with protesters. The masked man sitting across from her in the helicopter's cabin nodded in approval.

She received a text on her encrypted phone.

Still working through that pipeline? Report.

She replied.

Yes, sir. The PAG element proves useful. We are five mikes from Howard U.

A few seconds passed. Abeba received a new text.

Understood. Keep it airtight. Report in two hours.

The helicopter's rotor blades swayed a rich, emergent layer of oak leaves as it approached an improvised landing zone. Abeba and her partner from the CIA touched the ground. They quickly stepped out of the cabin and walked towards a suited-up Black man who did not seem to suffer the scorching heat that plagued the city. He was quiet, composed, and formal in his stance: a scholarly figure.

Abeba extended a hand as they met. "Luther. Thank you for facilitating this search."

His aging beard and lordly demeanor betrayed no reaction. "Don't mention it, Miss Solomon."

He motioned for Abeba and the mysterious asset to follow him. As they walked through a quad of red buildings and a rich history, she reminisced of her days on campus.

Her experience had been positive. Many would argue the thought because she at no time socialized and blended in the crowds of popular Black students, the *Elite*, the bright future of a powerful demographic.

Abeba's autism birthed different desires, divergent paths of discovery. She saw Howard University as a massive pool of knowledge feeding an infinite ocean from upstream. Every day, she would absorb more numbers, more data, more visuals through various mediums. Her brain was insatiable, calling for more and more dopamine rushes from the learning of new processes, the exploration of new subjects, the development of new concepts. She was content, subjected to a peculiar form of addiction.

The Howard alumni fought the rush building *within*. The group reached a small circular plaza whose white stone coat shone on the neatly trimmed evergreen bushes arranged in its perimeter.

At the center, a small obelisk read *Class of 45*. Abeba nodded at the university's president. He reciprocated and left.

The roundness of the structure sent a complex representation of stacked circles and overlapping patterns to Abeba's brain. The *Eye of God* did not notice any specific message at first, any underlying guidance.

The masked man walked around the memorial; there was this... *cleanliness* and an acquired taste for symmetry that brought satisfaction to his demanding OCD.

But there was also a discrepancy, here, laying in a specific spot on the smooth white stone.

The CIA asset crouched and established contact with the ground. It was strangely cold and slightly less rough than the remainder of the area. His spiderlike fingers followed the trail of smoothened granite.

At the edge, by the thick mulch that enriched the soil, another detail struck the operative's analytic eye.

The ground was leveled higher, like it had been covered after a dig.

"Miss Solomon," he called. Abeba joined him and the earth instantly *spoke* to her.

The mulch had been manipulated, changed. She said, "A cache."

"Precisely." The masked man retrieved silicone gloves from his pocket and donned them. He began digging. Quickly, a turquoise enamel stood out in the shaded concentration. It was an egg-shaped object, framed in a constellation of diamond-like stones.

Abeba clicked. "A Fabergé egg."

The object was an exquisite piece of craftmanship. The significant weight and the gray and white sparkle of the stones indicated this could be an authentic creation.

What is the implied message? Its value is irrelevant, Abeba thought.

She knew her colleagues would find this game of cat and mouse counterproductive, but it was the hottest lead to the perpetrator. And her brain enjoyed the stimulation. She refrained a smile.

The masked man asked, "Russian?"

"Yes. 1885-1917. The product of workmasters, if genuine."

Abeba briefly glanced at the blazing sun and its downward course, on the opposite side of the monument.

She *saw an implied direction.* "How did you find it?" she asked.

"Someone used chemicals to clean the stone, leading to the mulch. Some cleaning compounds are heat repellants. The ground was cooler and smoother."

Once more, Abeba separated the layers of this world. The trail led east. *The direction.*

"The Hillwood Estate out east. Former residence of a wealthy heiress. She spent years collecting Imperial-era Russian art. More notably, Fabergé eggs."

The masked man laid glacial eyes on the egg. "Maybe we should bring tactical, Miss Solomon. There is a lot of ground to cover."

She nodded in approval.

Her delicate hand tapped her in-ear receiver. "Control."

"Yes, ma'am."

"Bring the entire team in. I also need five CRGs. I'm going to send you the coordinates. I'll be there in twenty-five."

"Understood, ma'am. The Capitol Eight have been sedated and transported to TF Orange."

"Good. But our priority is still PO1. He went ghost as his main leveraging assets evaded his control. He has two options now. Disappearing for good, or hitting harder in one last stand, in a self-destructive craze. Given the theatrics and the psychological profile, the latter is more probable. Think *Hizbul Mujahideen*. India. May 2018."

———

Virginia - "Task Force Orange" Black Site

Chill-sending screeches. The claws desperately tried to break through the scratchproof coating in the six by eight feet glass box. Eyes extended wide, and pupils dilated. The politicians had lost to the beasts within, now becoming the high functioning drunk clowns of a circus in a state of disrepair.

The animals were deprived of most of their speaking skills as they delved deeper into the pockets of their consciousness, looking for a fix. The robbers, the pedophiles, the con artists, the rats who sniffed the cheese, the rapists... all gone to raging beasts who matched their inner demons.

Researchers from the CDC and personnel from the Department of Defense were commissioned to examine the men and women turned into creatures of odd patterns. In a massive warehouse space that featured gigantic air conduits and high ceilings, sophisticated containment modules kept the monsters at bay; their soundproof glass depicted a visual yet silent struggle.

A tall and slender Caucasian male in his thirties stood at the intersection of the sweat boxes, in the center of the vast space. His aquiline nose, chiseled jaw structure, and bony shoulders were those of a bird of prey, a flying vulture aware of the decaying flesh down below. The man's shadow reached for the edge of one of the cells. He was talking to an even younger Black woman who probed his flesh with piercing hazel eyes. Her white lab coat shone a godly light on his dark suit.

The lady objected, "M. Ruggart, with all due respect, there are human lives at stake. Regardless of the potential applications or their alleged crimes, we have a responsibility. Forgo the game of chess, the politics, the strategic approach. We ought to try."

"Kia, what are the odds of reversing the process? And, more importantly, the timeline?"

She broke eye contact for a second, her eyes scanning the space, evasive.

"It is slim, sir. In the low tens. But we have samples, a controlled environment, dead subjects for autopsies and world-class researchers. It is very unlikely we'd compromise the biological material."

The Vulture stared into the windows of her soul. His shadow was arched, crooked, bent to the will of protruding bones.

"Fine. Let's explore more humane alternatives. We'll circle back in twenty-four hours."

"Thank you, sir."

Across the black site, the transformed struggled vocalizations and single words in a deconstructed speech.

The Gorilla beat his chest, his glassy eyes searching the ceilings. *Evaaaagrineeeee.*

The Lion paced in his cage, analyzing his surroundings. *Orderrrrrrrrrr.*

The Bull laid on the concrete floor, by the drainage. *DC. DC. DC.*

Night-night-night-night-night-mare! the Grasshopper stuttered in a rapid fire.

The soft fur of the Panda sat into the corner of his glass box. *Son.*

Each word and action were recorded, documented, and timestamped. The metamorphosis undergone by the big wigs in D.C. was still an enigma; it was the byproduct of a unique chemical with an otherworldly molecular structure.

At the edge of the *Kingdom*, an autopsy room was concealed by a stainless-steel panel that shot upwards to the artificial skies. Inside, among the dead beasts, a human corpse laid flat on a mortuary table: Andre Seraos.

A forensic pathologist studied the well-preserved body. Scratches on the left cheek bone constituted the only remnants of an unconventional war. The doctor was recording his findings through a lapel microphone mounted on his scrubs. His monotone speech was muffled by a surgical mask and a face shield. As he prepared for an I-shaped incision, he began the review.

"Subject's name is Andre Seraos. Latino male. Forty-one years old. Identification was confirmed through dental records, fingerprints, and vein matching. Subject presents three minor cuts on the left cheek bone, acquired post-mortem. No blunt force trauma. No cardiac arrest. No internal nor external hemorrhaging. Toxicology reports indicate the subject was not under the influence of a controlled substance at the time of death. There is no trace of the chemical compound the other casualties in CH-North had been exposed to. I-shaped incision may provide further details in regard to the subject's cause of death.

"At 02:13 AM, September 12, 2023, the cause of M. Seraos' passing had yet to be determined. Notably, the subject's decomposition is unusually slow. The subject's skin color, softness of the tissue, and the absence of blowflies and flesh flies' activity led to the conclusion that M. Seraos is still in the initial breakdown stage. This is another unusual parameter I will come back to further down the road. Executing the I-shaped incision. Temperature is sixty-eight degrees Fahrenheit. Local time 02:14 AM."

A blade found Seraos' flesh, eager to extract the secrets buried deep within the scientific anomaly.

To hell with the fraudsters and zealous spiritualists! This magic is real!
This change? Meaningful.

The Hillwood Estate Museum flashed its façade behind ramparts drowning in a green opulence. The red brick mansion was eerie in its quietness, a soldier of stone journeying a land of giant greens. Around, footsteps grew closer and closer.

The FBI and three CIA elements operating under DEA cover had swept the outer perimeter in a zigzag pattern. They began converging towards the main building and the greenhouse, a half-glass, half-metal structure full of burgeoning flowers and exotic plants.

Time was of the essence; it was the only variable bringing consistency in the equation, the only one whose outcomes were certain.

Abeba and the three CIA elements approached the mansion from a French Parterre traversed by an elegant fountain with blue water that sparkled under the rising sun. Surveillance on the site had halted the FBI's course; a strong militarized force infiltrated the museum and gardens, unseen, and initiated the transport of art collectibles and essential personnel. Abeba chose to wait for the mercenaries and hostages to vacate the premises before launching a full-scale assault.

The greenhouse and French gardens were cleared by the tactical teams of the Counterterrorism Division. The city's lockdown had facilitated the secret operations on both ends by virtually eliminating any potential traffic in the area, including visitors, dignitaries, and staff.

The masked man who followed Abeba in her pursuit of the *Watchmaker* ran point on the breach, seconded by his two subordinates. The Political Action Group had a more extensive tactical training and was given the greenlight to insert into the world of a criminal mastermind. His cold, icy eyes fixed on Abeba as he posted by a set of French doors and lowered his profile, peeking through the glass.

He motioned a closed fist and a knocking. Abeba nodded in approval.

The door opened, cooperating with the intruders. They entered and split, rushing alongside the walls to the corners. As they cleared the ground level, a strange sight added to the complicated sensory input: The museum was empty. It was expected yet unsettling, odd.

China vases, diamond-studded military presentation cups, intricate rolltop desks carved by the gods, expensive Persian rugs and Renaissance Art; all was gone, leaving the space to winder stairs and herringbone hardwood floor. To Abeba, this world had been robbed of its ability to differentiate; it failed to provide substance in the emptiness of its frame. The reverberating void of an empty shell screamed at her heightened senses.

I was robbed. They took it all. The art. The history I was bound to.

Abeba looked above. Her eyes sharpened, in her own bizarre way of showcasing surprise.

A glass box *levitated* in between floors, at the center of the spiraling stairwell. There was no apparent cable, no net, no connecting pieces. The masked man signaled for the team to move upstairs. In doing so, they gained a better perspective of the magical object.

Abeba saw him first. A white male in his twenties or early thirties. His tortoise frames gave his angelic face a soupcon of sophistication. An elaborated combover shone under the magnifying glass.

The man gave the intruders a warm, welcoming smile. He wore a wetsuit and stood barefoot, leaving no sweat prints in the cooking heat.

A man of another world.

He anticipated any call for reason. "Bring the response groups in, Abeba. They'll be safer with you in here. The glass is bulletproof, and the entire structure is rigged with explosives and water reservoirs. I imagine you can foresee the potential outcomes."

Abeba and the CIA unit remained silent. She tapped her in-ear receiver.

"All response teams, evacuate! Meet at assembly area alpha, with EODs on standby. We found the PO1, but the main residence is booby-trapped."

The man clicked his tongue and shook his head. "Abeba! I'm ... quite disappointed."

She demanded, "Who are you? Do you share any connection with the September 6 attacks on Capitol Hill?" Her innocent eyes were at odds with her sharp tone. She pointed a gun at the transparent container. The rest of the unit obliged.

The mysterious man reciprocated with a wider smile. He clapped, echoing in his glass house.

"A connection? *I am* the connection."

Abeba inquired, "The *Watchmaker*?"

"Precisely."

Field lights triggered from the modified, coffered ceiling. Abeba maintained her aim, but her eyes were called upon by the powerful beams from up above. Heat rained down on the stairwell. *And the glass box*, Abeba assumed. *How can he withstand those conditions without sweating?*

The *Watchmaker* began pacing in his cage, except his feet stomped an imaginary ground a few inches above the bottom surface. He spoke, looking at the masked men and women whose steady silencers were directed at him. "Showtime is near. You're about to witness something that has been in the works for a substantial amount of time. *Quite* substantial."

Abeba sought a logical explanation to the levitating box. It was motionless, godly, *almighty*.

The *Watchmaker* resumed, "Yes, Miss Solomon. But I am no god."

How did he...?

He continued, "I know. I read *things* in people."

Abeba looked around. The world was muted. The patterns and shapes were insignificant, irrelevant, inconclusive. She said, "Spare the theatrics. Lives were lost. Property damage amounts to millions, and an entire city is paralyzed. This has to stop NOW."

The *Watchmaker* stopped pacing. His feet landed back on the bottom of the glass box. He shifted his smart looks and attention towards her.

"Miss Solomon, patience. You see the logistical mishaps. But what about opportunities? The prospect of a better world? For your children, your grandchildren. Generational trauma dead on arrival."

Abeba found the reasoning and prospect seductive. The pigs on the *Hill* were known criminals, scams, but they were necessary to navigate through the system as it was designed. *Unless...*

"Political agendas are not my concern. I am an agent of the law, a neutral party."

The *Watchmaker* tap danced on the hard glass and played the fool, in all its grandeur. He stopped and extended a welcoming invitation with his arms. "Blah blah blah. A brilliant mind like yours and those of our undercover friends here surely understand the importance of what we set to accomplish."

"Who is 'we'?" she asked.

"Irrelevant. Let's talk about what I need from you."

The masked CIA officers climbed the stairs to switch vantage points and examine the box. There was no apparent structural weakness, no breach point.

The *Watchmaker* ignored them and continued, "Actually, let me … let me clarify. I am not leaving this building alive. This is my last stand. I just… I need you to realize the dreams that inhabit your genius soul. You are important, Abeba. You bear the eyes of a goddess."

"I wish no harm upon you. I'm sure we can find alter—"

The *Watchmaker*'s glass box began filling with water. The flow was rapid and the currents conflicting, creating a whirlpool that expanded outward to circle his frame.

"I have very little time left, Miss Solomon. This magic is real. I want you to be a part of the change. Deep down, you know you are destined to greater things than being an executioner for the Devil's clique."

Abeba found a flaw in the demonstration. "This is not about me. You expressed your yearning for a systemic change and launched a terrorist attack on U.S. soil. You are trying to cater to egos."

"Abeba, I knew you and your friend at the CIA were going to find me. But you are correct. This is not about you, or me, or any of us. It's about a sustainable and impactful change. A legacy of some sort. But very few, very few would have found me without lousy clues and a straightforward communication. I had fun. Thank you."

The water was chest high. The *Watchmaker*'s body was still, however: it did not seem to suffer the laws of physics.

Abeba calculated probabilities. Numbers ran along the cube's edges and planes.

The *Watchmaker* smiled. "Abeba, forget about it. This place is going to collapse in exactly three minutes and thirty-one seconds. Look down."

The group looked down the stairwell. The ground level was flooding.

The mastermind behind the Capitol's attack was almost fully submerged.

He spoke his last words.

"I know. You have many questions. But some are better left unanswered. And you may find closure in the future. Focus on the moment, on the *living* things. There is no cure for those diseased politicians. No salvation. Their filth is an entrenched resistance to change. Let their humanity die. Like the millions of working poor who succumbed to exhaustion, mental illness, and crime. Save yourselves. You're still of use in this fight."

His eye frames remained glued to his golden boy face as the water filled the entirety of the glass box. *But magicians never reveal their secrets*, Abeba thought.

Waves began crashing the stairs below, in a roaring surf. Abeba glanced down and saw a current of data emerging from the rising waters. She looked at the CIA officers and urged, "We have to go. *Now*."

They nodded and climbed the stairs, with her running point on the maneuver this time around. The layout guided Abeba in her strides. She opened a door that gave to a narrow hallway.

Behind, she could hear the water waves hum.

The group continued, rushing alongside oak panels and cream beiges. The end of the passageway led to the outside, and a staggered terrace. Their boots and trainers crunched on the gravel as the unit descended.

The explosives, Abeba thought. "Faster!"

A tremor felt underfoot caught the team by surprise. The building behind began collapsing on its own footprint. It was a nightmare, where the bodies of helpless humans suffered the wrath of a giant deity. The rise of a dense smoke brought flying fragments of rocks, concrete, glass shards, and wood splinters. Abeba felt an abrasive assault on her sides, cut by invisible blades as she pursued the CIA elements zooming forward. Smoke caught up in a blast that invaded her lungs.

She pushed through, coughing dark particles on the shifting grounds. The cuts deepened, and the confusion that ensued misled her senses. Was it gravel, or dirt? Where were the CIA elements and their foggy silhouettes?

Abeba ran faster, lowering her profile to dodge flying shards whizzing above head. The ground softened, or so she believed, but the storm still raged. She expelled black bile in a gag, her lungs ignited by a burning drought.

Amidst the chaos and a foreshadowing dry heaving, the backdrop's rumble became louder and louder, sheltering her from the safety of a lost reality. Abeba continued until the fragments no longer launched forward, beating her skin, until she identified the dangers ahead, greater than the ones behind: cliffs, sinkholes, powerlines...

Here's the threshold.

She stopped, curled up into a ball, and disappeared, outpaced and consumed by a giant of smokes and stones.

23. SHATTERED GLASS

WASHINGTON, D.C.

Glass has a particular resonance. A frequency at which it will vibrate easily. If the voices of the people find that frequency, they can shatter the thick layers of a systemic status quo. The vibration issued by the sound waves must be powerful enough, however. And what if... what if the glass is tempered?

Chaos. Burning dust. Mud. The sharp and rough edges of fractured stones. The smell of almonds.

The Hillwood Estate was no longer. The landscape was changed, the gardens burnt to ashes, the skies sunless and troubled. Massive sinkholes left the mark of a cataclysmic intervention.

Abeba jolted awake, coughing dust and fluids. Her mouth was dry, her ears ringing. An acute pain hammered her skull.

Helicopters' rotor blades shouted her name beyond the veil of smokes and fine particles. She remembered: The others had reached the edges of this forsaken world.

Tap... tap... tap.

A hand appeared in her peripheral vision. She extended her own, eager to stand and assess the damages.

It was the masked man, covered in a thin layer of a white powder. Abeba stood and surrendered to his guidance. He walked with intent, his frame holding her own with remarkable ease. Above, flying metal birds' shadows glided on the impenetrable clouds, like demons in a hellish sky.

The almonds smell was soon replaced by Iron Ochre, a foul scent of rotten eggs and sulfur. *Different types of explosives.* They both trod a chaotic pathway to the light, to a small aperture beaming its hopeful message through the darkness of these desolated lands. They crossed the threshold to a cleaner air, and a downward slope leading to a river stream.

"Miss Solomon, a few more steps. This stream is pure. You can clean up before the rescue teams hit the ground. Are you injured?"

Abeba felt nauseous. She fought a gag. "No. I thought I … could … reach saf … ety faster."

"It's okay, Miss Solomon. We still succeeded." Their eyes met and they nodded.

The stream was cold to the touch and crystal-clear, with a strong current. Abeba crouched and let the water pass through her delicate fingers. The place was peaceful, ages from the weathered landscape up the slope. She poured some water into her mouth and swished for thirty seconds. She then spat the liquid out on the wet soils of the bank. Her mouth regained some semblance of integrity.

The masked man was alone. She asked, "Where are the others?"

"Safe. They already left the perimeter. I stayed back."

"Thank you."

"Don't mention it. But I must leave now, Miss Solomon. I'm sure our paths will cross again."

She nodded in approval and continued washing the ashes and cuts that made for the outer layers of her beaten body.

The CIA element disappeared in the woods, his slender silhouette absorbed by a nearby tree line.

———

Bodies occupied the streets of D.C. They were moving around like the shifty patterns of the rising tides.

Behind bars, an old man watched the waves stretch on a small TV screen. Beads of sweat passed through his gray beard as he reached for the only window in the forty-eight-square-foot jail cell.

Cling. Cling. Cling. Anticipation built up outside the tank as other inmates on death row had closely followed the most recent developments.

The leaks originating from the *Watchmaker* included a report on the U.S. correctional system and its profitable model. It relied on the incarceration of Black Americans at five times the rate of other demographics and the absence of sensible, effective rehabilitation measures. Some transcripts in the leaks contained audio logs and calls between lawmakers and executives in the private prison sector.

We need them right back in. It's a numbers game.

John, an 82% recidivism rate. It's good. We're not trying to work ourselves out of business.

As long as these Black folks keep killing each other, we'll stay in the green.

The documents provided by the *Watchmaker* were unequivocal: Prisoners were profitable, while education and rehabilitation were not. And in this country, profit ruled over the betterment of social standings.

A fire was set ablaze in the prisons, the county jails, the glass houses and super-maximum-security units. Although the general population was distracted by what they considered more pressing subject matters, inmates demanded answers as the information made it to them through accomplices and connections.

The old man in the sweat box was Jesse Jones, a sixty-eight-year-old Virginia native who had spent forty-three years on death row.

He took his red top off and blacked out the small vertical window hanging above his bed.

Mike won't tell; he owes me a hundred favors.

There was no climate control system in the overcrowded prison that reeked of piss and burnt ashes. Jesse had grown accustomed to the inhumane treatment he received. For the past seven months, he had even begun doubting his innocence after being caught into the lies of murderous Klan members who raped and murdered the victim he was associated with.

"Hey, Mike! Boss man, it's *hot*," Jesse shouted at the hallway across from him.

Steps grew louder, rapping on the cold concrete floor.

A slender correctional officer with a buzz cut appeared in the frame of his cell. He noticed the blacked-out window first, then switched his attention towards the inmate.

He frowned and answered, "We know, Big J. We have maintenance folks on standby."

The steps grew feebler as his handler continued his rounds.

Jesse Jones, a poster child for prison reform, spotted strange inflexions in his correctional officer's voice. Cracks.

They're trying to kill me before the revolution begins. Or reaches us.

M. Jones stripped to his underwear, agile despite his age, and hopped off his bed. He threw water from the stainless-steel toilet onto the cement floor of his cell, careful not to flood the space. Jesse then grabbed a towel and wet it with more toilet water.

He laid on the cement and covered himself with the towel, praying. The antique TV monitor still sang praises and celebratory shouts in the background, but the fight was here, in this bullpen, on the smoking floor of a scaled-up broiler.

Father, give us courage to change what must be altered, serenity to accept what cannot be helped, and the insight to know the one from the other.

———

Miles away from the dying man, the Capitol was a ghost of the past, its shattered windows giving views to a hollow core, to darkness and nothingness. Around, the lawns told the story of a cursed land: Underground tunnels laid bare their secrets, the smooth steep sides of a massive sink hole began cracking under the heat, and a deafening silence supported the absence of life.

Further out, on 1st St NE, a man spoke to an edgeless crowd, in front of a divisive symbol, the warped vision of a broken justice: the Supreme Court.

The activist guided his people through the axial route of a defining battleground. He met his partner at the rendezvous point; she was a brilliant Black woman whose actionable insights built a social justice empire.

They were a far cry from the corrupted race hustlers who monetized *#BlackLivesMatter* and profited off of the anger and oppression endured by the battered minorities of a profoundly racist country. These two represented a better way forward, individuals who had healed and gained a broader perspective on various matters through higher education, travels, and a healthy dialogue with outsiders.

They both led very diverse people to this pivotal moment. The mass soon shouted, *WHAT DO WE WANT? CHANGE. WHEN WILL WE STOP? NEVER. WHAT DO WE WANT? JUSTICE. SAID NO SUIT? EVER.*

On a wooden platform, the man, Charles, extended his arms to the West, where the sun began setting. The loud chants and side conversations stopped. His partner walked forward.

She raised a megaphone to the masses and spoke.

"Today is the beginning of a new era. The shakedown of the biggest criminal enterprise in the world: the old America."

Shouts of support and praise thundered in the late afternoon.

She resumed, "I would like to ... thank you for lending us your voice, your resources, your convictions. We are grateful. But the battle onward isn't about us. It is about this country, about a better future where decisive actions will shape better opportunities. The military took the perpetrators turned victims away as they escaped the Capitol to spill in these streets, but our resolve has not faded. However, I ask that you please remain safe as we navigate through the *Agenda*. So ... what's next?"

She stepped back and let her ally speak. He readjusted his frames and accepted the megaphone from her.

"Thank you, Kenya. We all want the same thing. A comprehensive reform of the U.S. political, social, judicial, and economic systems. But how do we achieve that herculean task? Nine steps."

He paused to let his tribe absorb the information.

"Step one. A response from the interim government addressing the recent developments and leaks of incriminating documents suggesting many members of the government were involved in illegal schemes and criminal behaviors. Step two. A promise on delivering a thorough review of the current shortcomings of our outdated Constitution and the members who swore to protect it. Three. The dismantling of all political parties in favor of individual candidates with no affiliation to nefarious lobbying forces like the NRA, Goldman Sachs, and Monsanto. The list is not exhaustive.

"Four. The streamlining of the regulatory system. Federal enforcement of all laws and the dissolution of state agencies, regulations, and governing bodies. Five. An audit of our annual budget and the reallocation of funds towards infrastructures, healthcare, and education. Six. The televised prosecution of all parties mentioned in the *Watchmaker leaks*. Step seven. A complete makeover of our law enforcement agencies, with better hiring practices, a higher education requirement, and better tactical training. Better oversight in the intelligence community, as well, and the trimming of its tentacular structure. That includes the CIA, NSA, parts of the FBI, JSOC and the NGA. A modernization of our armed forces to maintain superior capabilities without having to feed the ever-famished monster of an ever-growing expansionism.

"Eight. The promise of a well-funded environmental policy including recycling, sanitation, zoning, and anti-littering measures. Finally, step nine. A precise timeline for all of the above."

The crowd erupted in a passionate pledge to the activists' vision. The man took a deep breath, looking up to the skies. The press was covering both air and ground. He hoped he had been heard.

"We will remain here for as long as needed. Our financial partners poured millions into this operation to ensure your safety and well-being during this phase. As mentioned prior, we provide food, water, medical assistance, and security." He paused. "Before we conclude this announcement, I'd like to clarify one thing: We do not exist within the restrictions of partisanship. Our ideas and vision for a better America are not motivated by democrat or republican, liberal, communist, or socialist ideals. They are parts of a thought process supported by logical reasoning and the pursuit of a better quality of life. Let go of the counterproductive comparisons and arguments, and let's move this country forward, together."

The words were like glue; the two activists were the binding adhesive holding the fractured porcelain together.

The hearts and souls of those standing before them roared in content, grateful to have been purged of the toxic beliefs and nonsensical lines of inquiry that favored storms over clear skies.

24. THE FOOLS

VIRGINIA - "TASK FORCE ORANGE"
BLACK SITE

First, there were two sets of footprints in the sand. Then there was one set of footprints in the sand.

oom. Pounding on the tempered glass.

Click! Upper mandibles seesawed.

Bang. The beatings of the chest to ward off rivals.

Bleat! The federative vocalizations of the Panda.

The detention site became a loud, chaotic jumble. The cacophony of wild animals gnawing their own flesh, frantically itching and targeting the boundaries of their captive state painted a more familiar picture: the humans who were once within lost to creatures of more primitive aspirations.

The Vulture had returned to the makeshift zoological garden. There were no more spoken words from the beasts, no observable signs of self-awareness.

At this very stage of the metamorphosis, they simply yearned for freedom, food, mating opportunities, and a more favorable climate.

Kia, the lead researcher on site, contemplated the extent of her failures.

She and Ruggart, the Vulture, approached a glass box: the Lion's den.

She pressed her fingers against the coated surface.

Rrrrrrrrr.

It was a threat formulated by an apex predator who was not conditioned for captivity. She remained there, pensive, numb to the demonstration of force.

"Kia?" the Vulture asked.

She turned around. Her eyes found him. "Yes, sir."

"Report."

"Yes, sir. We have a general idea of the science behind the transformations. Unfortunately, we are lacking environmental data and source samples from the gas compound used in the attack. I won't have all the answers, sir."

"Fine. Break it down for me." He was perched on his two stick-like legs, still as the night.

"What is happening is ... is unfortunate, but the technology that was employed is ... path-breaking. Initially, we thought the changes they underwent only occurred at genome level. The manipulation of their DNA. We were wrong. Some of our autopsies revealed that the Capitol attendees first reacted to the aerosol like it was an environmental modifier. Think mutations endured in Chernobyl, for instance. But their proteome was altered first, which is strange given that DNA usually drives changes in the proteome, or proteins. Basically, those are what provides a structural and functional framework for all cellular life.

"Energy production. Movement. Reproduction. Then, gradually, changes applied to their genome, their DNA. And that explains their shifting behavioral patterns, the regression of their cognitive functions. However, there are still many unanswered questions. The main one is ... how did they receive different attributes and characteristics? There was no clue in their genetic markers."

Magic, she thought.

The Vulture laid spiky eyes on her. He inquired, "So, if I understand correctly, there is no clue as to why they transformed into various animals as opposed to a single, common species? It is one of our main interests. I'm sure you can foresee the possibilities, the implications. Or applications."

"Indeed, sir."

He was of cold stone and glass. "We'll extend the research. Any progress on an antidote?"

"Well, technically, antidotes are for poisons. It would be more of a genic manipulation. But I'm afraid the process is irreversible. The mutations have deeply altered their genetic framework. There are no more 'human' markers left in their shells. Did you receive my recommendations?"

She defied his threatening shadow. He answered, "Yes, Kia. I have. You mentioned a possible alternative. Care to expand?"

They began walking among the raging beasts, now accustomed to the aggression and desperation coexisting in this fragile ecosystem. A fine mist flooded the glass cages, hissing like the paralyzing warning of a King Cobra; the creatures laid down and answered the call of the *Sandman*.

Kia resumed, "Yes, sir. We would either need a sample of the gas to break down its composition and effects. Or take the genic modification's route, but it could take years as we do not possess sufficient knowledge on the matter. There are theories but nothing actionable. At this point, I'm more concerned with their living conditions. They weren't acclimated to or raised in captivity, and it shows. Some are pulling their fur out, digging through their flesh; we witnessed repetitive motor behaviors. Our lead zoologist issued recommendations for the next steps."

"I'm aware. Look, Kia. I'm willing to work with you on this, but I need insurance. Guarantees. Do you have enough samples to pursue your studies? Before we ship them out."

The word choice struck Kia as insensitive.

"Yes, sir. And since they would be *taken* to a reserve, a controlled environment, we have room to maneuver. We can still monitor behaviors and collect more samples should the need arise."

"Fine. Let's move forward and find them a home. Last question."

The move confused Kia. What was the Vulture? Good, evil, or neutral? The latter seemed more plausible. "Sir?"

"What about our humanoid subject, M. Seraos?"

"It is a strange case. No reaction to the gas, despite confirmed exposure. No deadly injuries, no cancer, no immunoexpressed condition. But we are working hard at it. I expect another update from our forensic pathologist in twenty-four hours."

The man probed her flesh, searching for a hidden breakthrough in her body language, unsuccessful, and nodded in approval. He turned around and left the warehouse space, his heels clicking like the unavoidable beat of life itself.

———

Washington, D.C. - FBI Washington Field Office

Her hands attempted to match the rate at which the data flowed through her brain. Abeba's marker painted broad strokes on the think board.

WATCHMAKER. DECEASED. NO ID MATCH.
RASHID. TRANSACTIONAL IMMUNITY. NO FURTHER
INTEL.
?? PAUL MEINHARDT. CLEARED.
GAS CANISTERS. ETHIOPIAN MANUFACTURER.
FORENSICS??? NO RESIDUES. NO EVIDENCE OF FORCIBLE
ENTRY.
WHO COORDINATED INSIDE? DCPD AND USCP
COMPROMISED.

BOMB THREATS? DISTRACTION. CALLER UNKNOWN.
WHAT DO WE KNOW? AMERICAISAZOO.COM. RETRACED
IP TO TURKMENISTAN. INVESTIGATION IS IN PROGRESS.
CLASSIFIED.

The FBI had reached a dead end. Miss Solomon, one of the brightest investigators the Bureau had ever employed, could not connect the dots. The bridges between causes and effects collapsed from crumbling foundations.

Someone had outsmarted her. She felt like she was chasing her own figure, an alter ego driven by a commendable motive yet potentially dangerous quest.

Abeba left her corner office and clapped. On the floor, the hive quit buzzing.

"I need more forensics. Coordinate with DARPA to find anything of relevance with the Capitol survivors and the ones KIA."

"Ma'am?"

Abeba acknowledged. "Yes, Jones?"

"Preliminary field tests on Hillwood were completed. Post-explosion residues indicate RDX and nitroglycerin were used in conjunction."

Abeba interjected, "RDX is known to be used for steel and denser materials. Nitroglycerin is used for concrete, mostly. Controlled demolition 101. It was the work of a professional. Did you locate the provenance?"

Jones jotted notes on his legal pad and answered, "No match with any local stockpile. Chromatographic analyses are inconclusive."

She sighed. "Okay. Keep digging everybody. There must be a clue, somewhere."

The zombified gazes nodded in agreement.

————

Washington, D.C. - Eisenhower Executive Office Building

New money stormed the old executive office. The checkered floors, spiral staircases, stained glass ceilings, and other French-inspired additions screamed architectural grandeur and historical significance. But a young woman walking a marble hallway to the former VP's office chose efficiency over opulence and representation.

A grasshopper. Her brown skin elegantly complimented a conservative black pantsuit and cream silk shirt. She turned left to a massive conference room packed with austere men and women. They raised at the sight of her.

She addressed the panel. "Please sit."

The woman's tone conveyed authority and confidence. It was sharp and swift.

Some voices erupted as the committee members sat down.

"Madam President."

The acting president of the United States remained standing. She was reviewing a report, flipping the pages as her heels enjoyed a quiet embrace with the carpet underneath.

"Good evening. Order of the day, ladies and gentlemen. Reinstating a strong, functional government following the attacks on the *Hill*."

She continued walking around, gathering thoughts as she reached the opposite edge of the conference table. Her evergreen eyes found the audience.

Madam President resumed, "I have laid out a plan. My office drafted a proposition."

The new cabinet members reached for the manila folders placed in front of them.

She continued, "As you review the specifics, take three factors in consideration. One. I do not care about optics, nor do I care about public opinion. Often, effective and necessary measures meet resistance from individuals who are not qualified or equipped to understand why those measures need implementation. Two. We are going back to assuming our true role. One of being public servants. Emphasis on *public*. You were all picked because you have the qualifications and skillsets I need. And the insight to drive meaningful change, the visibility on what's actually going on out there, in the society we should be protecting and nurturing. I do not care about your looks, your connections, your level of wealth, your skin color, your speech patterns, your fashion statements or personal brand. I want actions. Actions that will benefit the people.

"Three. We are going to start running this country as a sustainable business model. And yes, I said business, but let me clarify. This is not a pledge to ultra-capitalism, which has already destroyed the lives of millions and compromised many social and environmental initiatives. Think more … *business* operations. I want this country to run smoother, to adopt certain procedures and models that make sense. I want the dysfunctional and overcomplicated administrative machine to be replaced by a centralized platform that will lead to cost-cutting without compromising on the delivery. This country was built off of slavery and industrial expansionism, no matter the costs. It is time we shift the narrative and employ our ingenuity and resourcefulness to birth a new nation. A nation where the well-being of its general population constitutes the top priority matter for its high-ranking officials.

"If any of you lacks the commitment to carry this mission, or have some sort of … ideological reserves, please see yourself out."

The speech left the cabinet in awe. There was no fear, no resentment, no discomfort felt. Madam President simply radiated a new type of leadership in D.C.: one beyond appearances and angles.

One of tangible output.

25. OPTICS
WASHINGTON, D.C. - THE WHITE HOUSE

"This is a new dawn. A new era. Consign most of what you've learned to oblivion. Every preconceived notion stemming from the violent culture we fostered. And this is not about me being the first Black woman in this unique position. I do not plan on running a circus, assuming the title of the greatest showman on Earth to satisfy your craving for virtue signaling. This is about unity, a healthy progress, and love. We the People of the United States will cross a new defining threshold. Together."
- Madam President.

C amera flashes sieged the brilliant mind of the new leader of the free world. She was waiting the storm out, ready to sail forward past the massive wave.

The James S. Brady Press Briefing Room was boiling, numb to the romantic gestures planned by the state-of-the-art climate control system. The temperature was set at a cool seventy-one degrees Fahrenheit, but the hearts and minds occupying the space were blistering, set ablaze by the magnitude of this extraordinary turn of events and the countless questions that haunted them.

Madam President chose a neutral approach. She bore no smile, no frown on her delicate facial structure. Her security detail was in the background, looking for primers to a potentially explosive reaction.

As a former U.S. diplomat and political science buff, POTUS had reached the position following a unanimous vote of confidence from the survivors of the crusade led by the *Watchmaker* and his collective.

Born in Miami in the crack era, Madam President used to lay on a soiled mattress stuffed with syringes and needles, dreaming of a better life as she met the eyes of her mother, a drug addict whose mouth was foaming white and eyes had rolled back in a destructive climax.

Raised by the streets, she learned to adapt and protect her neck, yet steered clear of drugs, scams, and violent crimes, unwilling to become the monster who had brought her into this world.

As she defied all odds, graduating from Stanford Cum Laude and climbing the ladder of U.S. diplomacy, the Dade County native began considering a transition to politics, where she believed she could carry a broader influence. But the barriers of entry were many for a young Black woman with a logical approach.

Until recently, when someone, or something, opened the pearly gates.

———

It was now public knowledge that Abeba Solomon had survived the Hillwood Estate collapse and shut down *americaisazoo.com*.

She knew the leaked documents published on the portal would resurface and agreed, deep within, that the *Watchmaker* had won the public relations fight with what most called a *selfless sacrifice*.

However, she still felt compelled to tie the loose ends and lay the groundwork for the reinstating of a critically essential order: *the removal of distractions*, as she expressed it.

A few miles away, at the White House, Madam President intended to capitalize on that newly freed space in the mass media. The exercise was not planned for her own benefit, nor to gain political capital, but to instead achieve the results that were required, to oversee the realignment of crooked teeth: those of a thin, sickly nation.

She raised a hand, and the camera flashes stopped.

"Good morning."

All across the globe, billions of viewers shared a blood-rushing anticipation.

Numerous cultures, sensibilities, beliefs systems, and social classes gathered, hopeful for a nation foreigners often perceived as unilateral, imperialist, expansionist, and obtuse.

"There are One hundred thirty-two rooms, thirty-five bathrooms, and six levels in the Residence. There are also four hundred twelve doors, one hundred forty-seven windows, twenty-eight fireplaces, eight staircases, and three elevators. At various times in history, the White House has been known as the 'President's Palace', the 'President's House', and the 'Executive Mansion'. For those of you who can read between the lines, those facts lead to one conclusion: Parts of our history and some of our past decisions reeked of an egocentric culture that stemmed from the reactionary nature we adopted during our fight for independence.

"I am here not only to drive change in processes and lead this country with integrity and consistency, but also to educate and promote healing. Often, we were told our failures resulted from a lack of raw output, from being disobedient to an almighty Constitution, from the colors and shades of our skins, from a lack of patriotism. This country is full of misguided spirits stuck in between planes, between a legacy of blood and a better state of affairs. I am taking us back to the basics. To a better education. To a broader perspective, to the cultivation of critical thinking skills. It is time you leave the warped realities of your destructive upbringing and seek true unity.

"As I stand in front of you today, I can confidently say that I am a true patriot. A servant who has her country's best interests in mind. Anyone who stands in the way of the prospect of a healthier society, one built on verifiable knowledge, love, compassion, and logical reasoning, will be treated as an enemy of the nation. Make no mistake: I'm an independent. I have no political affiliations. This warning is not aimed at any particular group of individuals but at *all* enemies of the United States of America. I'd also like to clarify that I was chosen because I was qualified to execute the mission. Being a woman of color, I want to make sure that message is clear. I am no token. No placeholder. No consolation prize. Questions?"

The press corps unleashed the *Kraken*. Questions hammered Madam President with a frequency of sounds that did not quite match her resonance factor yet.

All over the world, the audience was stunned: the aggressive lingo, the neutrality, the bluntness and the uncompromising nature of this new leader who emerged from the ashes of an archaic political machine impressed.

Madam President pointed at a young red-headed reporter.

"Madam President. Emily Forthwith, *The Washington Post*. I understand the situation is unique as far as the state of the Executive Branch goes, but what are your plans for a future presidential election? We have democratic measures in place designed to avert abuses. The people must be given the ability to choose their next leader."

Madam President remained stoic. "Thank you, Miss Forthwith. Currently, constitutional requirements prevent the postponing of a presidential election. Certain loopholes and legal specifics between the Congress and the states could be used to delay it, but ultimately, an election would happen. This is going to change. I will define narrower specifics in a future address, but at this very moment, my cabinet and I have initiated a complete overhaul of the judicial, legislative, and executive branches. We are also going to revise the articles of the Constitution to serve our people better and support a more just society. Which leads to your question. To answer clearly and concisely, there will be no presidential election until further notice. Right now, our top priority is to rebuild the foundations with more sustainable and durable materials."

The world shook. Foreign leaders struggled to comprehend the implications and how she was able to create those parameters.

Madam President remained inflexible, unbothered by the frozen faces and bodies rooted in their places. She met the gaze of a tall Black woman in a pencil skirt. Her evergreen eyes spoke of a sophisticated beauty and a deep intensity. Madam President pointed at her.

"Madam President, Jhene Oliwe, *The Guardian*." Her British accent sang to the ears. "Some components of your speech bear striking similarities with the *Watchmaker*'s, a terrorist who claimed responsibility for the deaths of at least twenty-five U.S. nationals. Are you in any way, shape, or form associated with him or his organization?"

The question was bold. Madam President appreciated the effort. She smiled inside.

"Thank you, Miss Oliwe. I am not affiliated with the *Watchmaker* or his associates in any way, shape, or form. Although some of the beliefs we both expressed may be similar, mine are rooted in a logical reasoning, not an ideological preference. I condemn the *Watchmaker*'s actions, and our counterterrorism services successfully neutralized the threat, despite a dramatic conclusion. Yes?" She pointed at an older white man with an elaborate blow-dry.

"Madam President. Gary Tdranhniem, *Le Monde*. Will there be any consequences, any charges brought against the U.S. officials mentioned in the *Watchmaker leaks*? And where have you taken the Capitol Eight?"

The last question triggered side conversations. Madam President raised a hand. The noise shut, obedient.

"Thank you, Gary. *Gourmand*." He smirked at the French term. "We will seek prosecution for any citizen involved in criminal activities, regardless of their position, status, or connections. We also made the decision to revise our enforcement of diplomatic immunity and reduce its scope of support to promote accountability. I invite other nations to consider a similar approach. As far as your last inquiry, it is still classified."

Madam President. Madam President. Madam President.

The immaterial assault on her position held no weight, much less frightening and unpredictable than the childhood she was given. Inside the fortress of her mind, the outside commotion was deflected by the reinforced layers of her past trials.

She raised a hand and pointed in the direction of a young white female with boyish features. Her piercing eyes defied the quiet authority of the President.

"Madam President. Fran Carter, *Outside the Wire*. You laid out quite a few drastic measures, and I understand that the process is complex, and you may not have all the variables yet, but do you have an outline of your first one-hundred-day plan?"

"Thank you, Miss Carter. First, I would like to elaborate on my decision to postpone presidential elections. My cabinet is composed of individuals who are highly qualified and share my vision of a more consistent governance. They have been handpicked and display the highest integrity in the exercise of their function. More information on their backgrounds and track records is available on the White House website. I do *not* wish to establish a dictatorship. But sometimes, reality calls for difficult decisions. I am the one willing to assume responsibility for those decisions. Ultimately, it is in this nation's best interest.

"Once the modernization and transformation of the political machine, system, is completed and the plan executed to the highest standards conceivable, I will organize elections. As far as an outline goes, I want to have all the data in hand before formulating a definitive version. We are working with community leaders, economists, foreign liaisons, and other highly qualified professionals to ensure the best outcome. Thank you all."

Tap... tap... tap.

As she turned around and disappeared behind the White House signage, the shutter sounds of expensive cameras and the delirium of rapid-firing speech patterns washed ashore.

She had returned to the mainland. It was time. Something had to shake.

26. SEQUENTIAL PATTERNS
WASHINGTON, D.C.

The cards are falling in a precise pattern, birthing ripples rocking the flimsy, collapsing house. Strangely, they do not sway out of bounds in their fall; their print is heavy, like the bones, pieces, men, stones of a domino effect.

hump! In his hideout made of giant screens and minimalist furnishing, Mark Wagner threw a bouncing ball at the ceiling, exercising dominance on the immutable concept that was gravity.

The Egyptian cotton of his white t-shirt was soft and threaded in a premium fashion; its satin finish glowed under the dimmed lighting. The comfortable attire allowed a broad range of motion as he laid on an off-white linen couch.

Thump! The German was exercising his brain, patiently waiting for the final act to open to a new, grandiose decor. *Fischers Fritze fischt frische Fische; Frische Fische fischt Fischers Fritze.*

Thump! He ran the probabilities in his head, the shortcomings, the unpredictable developments, environmental contributors. The plan was masterful, he thought. *Brautkleid bleibt Brautkleid und Blaukraut bleibt Blaukraut.*

Thump! The ball found his palm once more.

A ring followed. Wagner sat up straight and pulled a burner phone out of his pocket. He flipped it open and answered, "Sugary cravings?"

"Maybe after an early dinner."

Wagner smirked, cool and composed. He asked, "Are we ready to close on the deals?"

"Yes. The properties have been surveyed."

"*Danke.*" Wagner hung up and headed to his small Swedish desk, reaching for a pen and paper as he sat on an ergonomic chair. *The Americans must be precise.*

He retrieved his phone and dialed #347. He began writing on the yellow paper, effortlessly gliding with a scholarly dexterity. *T1. RS.*

A voice answered the call, "The swimmer?"

Wagner replied, "In his natural element." The call disconnected.

On the other side of the line, a masked man of tall stature was fixing a silencer onto the threaded barrel of a handgun. The elevator he stood in was shaky and loud, but there was no one else here.

The man soon reached the fourth floor. The cheap vinyl underfoot squeaked as he advanced towards the target, at the peak of a steamy night.

424. The hitman retrieved a lockpicking set. He began applying a slight torque on the mechanism from two angles.

Click.

The door unlocked. He infiltrated the space, shutting the entryway behind him.

A few steps through the unpretentious setting bridged the gap between him and the target. Rashid Saeati was sleeping, still and peaceful. Outside the bay windows to his left, a pitch-dark night provided concealment for the man in black.

He fired a quiet headshot. Rashid briefly twitched and began his journey to the afterlife, his face frozen in discomfort. The hitman picked up his shell and retrieved a small cylindric container from his cargo pocket. He poured its content on Rashid, the clear liquid soaking the victim's white undershirt. The killer flicked his lighter and set the body ablaze. Flames began consuming the flesh, fabrics, and woods, their sharp edges scraping the ceiling.

Out west, Wagner received a text from *#347*.

The water is warm.

Wagner struck the small keys of his burner and replied.

Good.

He found his notes. *T1. RS.* He added, *Check.* Line break. The German's pen continued gliding in an elegant exercise.

T2. PM. Mark Wagner once more pressed the keys of his burner phone. *#602.* He pushed the call button. The phone rang. A delicate voice answered, "Quiet souls."

Wagner replied, "Uneventful." The call disconnected.

On the other end of the short exchange, a curly-haired woman of afro features waited in a SUV whose tinted windows concealed her presence. She was parked a few properties down from the colorful row house of the Meinhardts. Inside, Paul and Roxanne slept peacefully, comforted by the reassuring prospect of a reemerging daily routine.

The young woman across the street had entered their home earlier, from the foundations, unseen. The building received an unwarranted upgrade.

The contracted killer pressed the call button on another burner. A Glock19 laid on the passenger seat as a contingency.

Carbon Monoxide began diffusing in the Meinhardts' bedroom at a furious rate. The odorless gas left the couple no chances. They surrendered to the *limbo*.

Thump! The ball hit a wall opposite of the giant displays and returned. Mark Wagner received another text from *#602*.

Uncle had some footage of the cookout. It was fun.

Wagner replied. *Good.* He jotted down another *Check* next to his most recent words on the yellow legal pad.

#404. The call button was pressed down by Wagner's manicured thumb.

"Nana's home."

The German nodded in approval and said, "Thank you for escorting her, Lily."

The call ended. In this *Deutsche*'s brain, the pieces of a giant chessboard moved to reach the impenetrable defenses of the *Queen*, his final target. The lives of those who partnered with the cause were of no significance to him, a result-driven machine that only spared the final product.

Near the Capitol, masses of brave revolutionaries camped on the grounds of a historical protest. *Mama Joy*, a staple of her local community, was looking at the crowds from inside her bucolic setting. The pharmacy was closed, the inventory updated and the shelves restocked.

Her assistant had left after sanitizing the store. She turned around and walked to the stairwell access in the back. Her smile radiated the dimly lit place.

As she engaged the staircase to her private quarters, a shadow found her. A needle penetrated the thin layers of skin covering her neck. She collapsed under the numbing effect of the powerful anesthetic.

Thump.

The shadow snatched her and took her to her grave.

Thump! Wagner's analog watch indicated it was time. He received a text from *#404.*

Remember her master recipe?

Yes.

The German produced another addition to his notes. *Thump!* The bouncing ball hit the wall again.

———

President Hall's address has shattered media ratings as the country is undergoing what experts refer to as a transfiguration. The President's call for the rebirth of a new nation took the world by storm as she presented strong arguments for massive reforms in the judicial, executive, and legislative branches.

Michael, what are your thoughts on the address?

Jenna, there are so many talking points. First, the angle. The White House seems to seek a new ... business model. It's bold, strangely apolitical and practic—

Abeba drank in the words as she ran on an incline. Her treadmill program challenged her lung's capabilities in a grueling pulmonary test. Her face mask accentuated the hardness in her eyes. Abeba's juvenile gaze had been replaced by the inevitability of a deadlier character. She continued running, a smoldering fire reaching for the steep sides of her airways.

A voice interrupted the news broadcast that boomed through the workout room. "Administrator. Security breach in E7. Back access, ground level. Tango is on an interception route. Forty-five seconds."

Abeba pulled the emergency stop cord on her treadmill and rushed to a floating storage behind her, stumbling and heavily breathing. "Zoya. Con ... tact emergen ... cy center and ... request EMS."

"Noted."

The head of the FBI Counterterrorism Division pressed on a wooden panel that opened upon contact and retrieved a Glock19M and a loaded magazine. She slammed the mag in her pistol and loaded a round in the chamber. *Thirty-two seconds.* Abeba found a corner and leaned back, looking to regain her bearings. She inhaled, paused, and exhaled. *Seventeen.* The lights shut. She heard footsteps nearby.

I'm cornered.

The sliding panel of her workout space opened wide.

But no one entered.

She braced for contact on the far end of the panel. A light beamed through the dark, sweeping the walls and floors.

Still, no one entered.

Abeba felt vibrations. Her world projected the data of sounds, movements, and sequential patterns. For a fleeting moment, time and space froze. *Throu—*

Two shots hit her lower legs through the separation, sending hot blades to her delicate tissue, and a pulse acting as a reminder in her damaged flesh. She collapsed and blindly fired back. The subsequent stomping of feet grew feebler as the assailant vacated the premises.

Outside, the red and blue lights of the DCPD shone on the brick buildings of adjacent houses. However, the colorless outline of the aggressor had already fled Abeba's property, regaining anonymity in the city's night.

Further east, Mark Wagner, the German fixer, received another text from an ID numbered 312.

Hey Martin, have you checked the news?

Wagner replied. No, why?

A mining incident in the DRC. Tragic.

How many casualties? The German typed.

One confirmed.

Let us pray.

Thump! Wagner's ball hit the bare wall in one last dance. He grinned, in a sophisticated spin on the *Big Bad Wolf*.

27. THE CHEMIST

ATLANTA - HARTSFIELD JACKSON AIRPORT - JUNE 2010

"It was Allah's doing. Like your burning bush on Mount Horeb. Or the Jews' Witch of Endor."

Atlanta. *The New York of the South.*

Andre Seraos reminisced of his first time in the city. It was a leisure stay. The vibrant crowds of an artsy downtown, the block parties in Old Fourth Ward, and the flavorful soul food on the southside had demanded his unconditional love on a yearly basis. This time around, however, he would not leave the black sprinter van he rented.

The men sitting by his sides were quiet and devoid of emotional cues; one of them drove the big body from their duty station in North Carolina to Hartsfield Jackson Airport, seeking to blend in with the masses in transit. The drive was relatively short, but the upcoming mission could bear repercussions spanning over decades.

A needle in a haystack. Andre Seraos reviewed the travel arrangements in his head, emboldening the lines, textual content, and shapes of a mental blueprint.

Hartsfield. Heathrow. Tripoli International. Al Jawf. Harat. Service members blowing up steam on the Sicilian coast.

The plan was simple in structure, but Andre relied on shadowy human assets. His men followed him to the edge of *this* world, but he made sure they understood: The line between exposing the U.S. destructive foreign policies and high treason was a fine one of blurry contours.

"Rental center. We're here, ladies."

The sprinter passed a checkpoint, and the tires bounced on traffic spikes. The big black Mercedes van found its return spot in the rental center.

Inside the garage, the men shifted facial expressions; their neutral looks became the faces of a genuine excitement. Smiles opened wide, shoulders relaxed, and eyes turned dreamy. They were now playing a new role, that of unsuspected vacationers.

They stepped out of the vehicle into the hot, muggy afternoon. The driver left the keys on his seat and closed the door. The group retrieved their luggage in the back and closed the ramp. They were dressed casually, with a soupcon of sunny accents. Andre elevated his narrow-cut pleated shorts with a beige waffle-knit polo and rectangular shades. He looked both ways before leading the group to an elevator access across the road.

The men chatted about family, overseas attractions, and foods as they entered the domestic terminal. Their purposeful steps led them to the SkyTrain.

Seraos did not participate in the side conversations; the implications of recent discoveries had challenged his views of the armed forces even further and occupied his sharp mind rent-free.

He still believed in his men, in the skillsets they acquired, in the outcomes they shaped, but what if... what if the latter were tarnished by human rights abuses, covert programs whose lackluster oversight led to fatal transgressions, political agendas of expansionist nature? A stranger from the Libyan countryside had planted the seed in his brain, but he did not feel swayed, manipulated.

He felt... *significant.*

Concourse E was a buzzing hive, a swarm of travelers: the wealthy and their yearly trip, the working poor who, for years, saved in order to escape the hellish routine of their perceived-to-be-meaningless lives, the childless couples backpacking in the wild, the social media influencers running on private donations and credit lines.

Tap... tap... tap.

A thought occurred to Andre Seraos as he appreciated the deconstructed patchwork; he realized the issue he was called upon was bigger in scope than the wrongdoings of an intelligence agency.

The men checked their luggage at the airline's counter and soon boarded. The economy plus class they were provided by Bin Allah's discreet proxies was intended to match their income levels and avoid raising suspicions within their command.

Ladies and gentlemen, welcome aboard Flight 1EVG7 with service from Atlanta to London. We are currently fourth in line for take-off and are expected to be in the air in approximately thirteen minutes' time. We ask that you please fasten your seatbelts and secure all baggage underneath your seat or in the overhead compartments. We also ask that your seats and table trays are in the upright position for take-off. Please turn off all personal electronic devices, including laptops and cell phones. Smoking is prohibited for the duration of the flight. Thank you for choosing Delta Airlines, a SkyTeam partner. Enjoy your flight.

Seraos checked on his men once more. They seemed joyful and full of life.

They may never come back, he thought. Seraos was still appalled by the sacrifice his soldiers were willing to commit to, leaving relatives and supportive spouses to pursue an elusive dream. It was something he could not quite explain.

He finally closed his eyes and surrendered to a deep sleep, hushing the thoughts of his racing brain.

London - Heathrow Airport - June 2010 - 8 ½ Hours Later

Seraos woke up from an eight-and-a-half-hour drowse. There was no dreamworld he entered, no pitch-black plane. He was walking onto a fine thread between the lively grounds and the dozing skies.

For a second, time was a foreign concept. He regained his bearings and checked on his men. They were patiently waiting for landing, consuming in-flight entertainment.

The seats' screens faded to black. A delicate voice sang to the cabin.

Flight attendants, prepare for landing please.

Cabin crew, please take your seats for landing.

Another soothing delivery took over.

Ladies and gentlemen, we have just been cleared to land at the London Heathrow airport. Please make sure one last time that your seat belt is securely fastened. Flight attendants are currently passing around the cabin to make a final compliance check and pick up any remaining cups and glasses. Local time is 4:55 AM, and the temperature is twenty degrees Celsius. Thank you.

Gravity shifted as the plane began its descent. Some concerned looks from beginner travelers met Seraos' benevolent gaze and eased up; he felt compelled to help those who'd never had the opportunity to travel outside their local boundaries, outside the walls that housed ignorance, biases, and prejudice. He prayed for a brighter future, so that the victims of a debilitating way of life could heal and thrive.

The plane bounced on the well-lit runway. The sun was still shy, hidden behind the dark purple shades of a persistent night.

Seraos' men left the plane at various intervals. Under the glass dome of their terminal, they spread and reached their assigned locations. The group's newly donned dad hats compromised any potential facial recognition.

Seraos sat on a cushioned bench and waited. He kept a low profile, observing the flow of footsteps clicking on the immaculate marble.

Beep, beep. An electric cart approached from the left. Andre rose and jumped on. The driver betrayed no apparent reaction and continued forward. The point man could see his soldiers stationed in various spots, waiting for their transport.

The ride was long, but it allowed Seraos to map exit routes and study airport security, as a contingency.

Terminal 4, he read internally.

Further out, the front desk of *Dnata Private Aviation Services* constituted the main objective. The leading man sought active cameras in his peripheral vision, finding there was no surveillance operated in this part of the terminal.

Check. Seraos relaxed and left the cart. A tall and radiant attendant whose beautiful sepia complexion inspired excellence greeted him.

"Please, this way." He gave her a nod of acknowledgement and a polite smile. They both engaged a small boarding bridge and walked the downward incline to the runway.

"Any particular accommodation, sir?" the attendant asked with a flawless smile.

"No, thank you."

She nodded as they reached the runway. The temperature was cooler here, yet still pleasant.

It was the peak of an English summer.

Ahead, a Gulfstream G800 shone its curves. A well-dressed man waited before the private jet. His double-breasted Prince-de-Galles jacket projected an elegant gray that matched the silky dark blue of his Seven-Fold tie and the off-white tone of his premium shirt. The liaison's grooming and posture suggested a quiet yet tangible wealth.

The attendant turned around and returned to the terminal. The man met Seraos' neutral stare and extended a hand. "Andre, Ali. It's an honor."

"Thank you for accommodating us."

The mysterious liaison waved the display of courtesy away with a smile. They both entered the private jet. The inside displayed a refined comfort. It featured rift-sawn European white oak, hand-tufted wool, cashmere bouclé, and Belgian linen.

This is not a standard configuration. It's custom, Seraos thought. He attempted to maintain his composure in the grandiose décor of an experience far beyond his tax bracket.

Seraos found a seat facing the cockpit and entryway. His liaison sat in front of him.

The latter asked, "Care to begin? We have a few options for breakfast, all detailed in this menu."

He pointed at a brochure laid straight on the solid wood table mounted between the two men.

"I would like to wait for my men."

"Naturally. Refreshments?"

"Yes, please. Sparkling water, Perrier maybe?"

The attractive Middle Eastern man of a chiseled jaw line and a refined nose bridge raised a hand. Another flight attendant came to serve them.

"Two Perriers please."

"Yes, sir."

A few seconds later, the attendant returned, flashed a smile at Seraos, and poured the beverages into crystal glasses with grace. She left the green Perrier bottles on the table.

Andre inspected the glass and took a sip; the flavor and taste transported him back to childhood, where sparkling water was a commodity, even for slums' roaches like him. The refined taste and citrus accents were dopamine-inducing rewards, as poverty infiltrated his life like a cancer. Bin Allah's partners did not seem to share the same past.

The liaison remained quiet as the other special forces service members arrived and discovered the opulence of a world-class jet. Their eyes expanded wide as they found seats next to Ali and Seraos. Some fingers discreetly ran through the premium textiles and woods.

Andre spoke. "We are ready. I'm going to opt for the Moroccan baked eggs. Thank you."

Ali once more raised a hand. The flight attendant produced another flawlessly engineered smile and took notes. The others ordered.

"Thank you for putting your trust in the *King of Kufra*. He sends his regards and is looking forward to working with you."

Andre answered, "The trust is not yet earned, and this partnership is conditional. But I will say one thing: We are men of values and principles. If I notice one instance of deviation from the original plan, I will lead the hunt for Bin Allah myself."

Ali politely smiled. "Naturally. Breakfast will be cooked fresh to order, after takeoff."

The plane began maneuvering on the runway. Ali raised both hands. "The takeoff is much smoother than the commercial airliners', by the way."

Ten minutes later, the G800 was reaching for the clouds. The men barely felt the upward shot.

Andre inquired, "I saw a G800 painted on the frame. I must have been mistaken since they're not available to the public yet."

Ali smiled a bit wider. "A connoisseur. You're traveling in the first unit ever cleared to fly. I can't say much more."

Seraos nodded in agreement. The smell of a flavorful cuisine soon enhanced the cabin's sensory input. Ali began a review as the guests appreciated the freshness of their lavish breakfast meals.

"[...]Every box was checked. Your flight plan will show you boarded Delta 2ST3 to *Leonardo Da Vinci Airport, Rome*. The feeds have been altered, and you did a remarkable job concealing your print. This aircraft is unregistered, and all the personnel involved were handpicked. Your final destination is *Tripoli*, where you will drive to *Al Jawf Kufra* and reach *Harat Zuwayyah* via a secondary transport. Your tactical equipment awaits in the back of this jet. I figured you'd feel more comfortable acquiring your gear early."

"Understood. What about the package?"

"I know Bin Allah mentioned a delivery, but I am not aware of its contents. You will be given more details on the ground."

"Fine. Flight time?"

"This is a remarkably fast aircraft. Seven hours."

Andre Seraos finished his breakfast and thanked the attendant, complimenting her on the service and quality of the products. Fine cuisine was one of his guilty pleasures.

He waited for his men and began walking to the back storage compartment. Behind a sliding door, a small armory was set up with mounted racks and hooks. Tactical vests, backpacks, camelbacks, combat shirts, pants, boots, first aid kits, and state-of-the-art assault rifles with cylindric threaded barrels awaited procurement. The special forces team began gearing up for a silent war. A clearing barrel was set up in the back room.

"Ali, are we cleared for test shots?"

The Middle Eastern facilitator nodded and raised an index finger.

"In a pressurized cabin, at high altitude?"

Ali nodded and spoke one word: "Trust."

He pressed a button above him. The cabin dimmed its lighting, and a red glow invaded the space.

Andre Seraos shouted, "Test shot!"

His men repeated the order. He shot a round in the barrel's ballistic gelatin block.

Bang! The weapon behaved to expectations, generating very little recoil.

Seraos' men followed suit. Soon, the red glow vanished to warm ambient lights. The men found their way back to their seats.

Ali added, "Any adjustment?"

Andre answered, "No, thank you, Ali. It's quality gear. Up to mission specs."

The men tilted their heads in agreement, and quietness settled in the cabin.

An hour before landing, the team performed another gear check and cleaned up.

The next twenty-four hours promised to be unforgiving.

Ali was composed and contained. He was absorbed in a novel whose crimson-red front cover depicted suited up animals in a business setting, strangely human in behaviors and gestures.

Soon, he laid the book down and addressed Seraos. "My partners own the private aerodrome in Tripoli. We set up sunshades with thermoregulating layers. Your friends from the NGA and NSA won't spot much through their satellites. You'll be transferred to an armored car, which you'll then drive to Al Jawf Kufra, as per your request. Any questions?"

"No."

Andre began calculating opportunities and potential risks. His team had designed contingency plans funded out of pocket. But how far-reaching was Bin Allah's network? Would they ever feel safe again if they decided to withdraw? Or to follow through?

The private jet operated a surprisingly smooth landing. The wonder of engineering transitioned from an open runway to a covered path and maneuvered on the tarmac to park next to a G-Class Mercedes Benz, all blacked out. Ali remained put as Seraos' men began disembarking the plane with their gear.

Andre nodded to Ali. The liaison replied, "*Al-Baraqa*. Best of luck, American."

The searing heat produced rising waves outside the sunshades' perimeter. The shadow of a big-bodied truck hid in the shaded mass. There was no human activity within a mile radius. His potential partner had been careful.

The Five entered the G-Class SUV. One of Seraos' soldiers pressed the start button and initiated the onboard navigation. An address was pre-recorded, and the route mapped out; it ran south.

Andre spoke from the passenger seat.

"Before we leave, I need to make sure. You understand that we do not walk in with the flag on our shoulders. There is no going back from whatever we may set in motion. This is covert ops territory. No protection. No backup. No contact with relatives until we are cleared. Any injuries we sustain, we're walking out with."

The men sought their leader's commanding eyes and nodded in approval. The mission was supposedly low-risk. A meeting, a proposition, and a delivery. But the men knew that good occasionally shapeshifted into evil, and vice versa. The SUV drove off to a nearby interstate access and blended in with the congested traffic.

Libya - Al Jawf Kufra - June 14, 2010 - 20 Hours Later

The G-Wagon stood out in the narrow streets of Al Jawf. The luxurious SUV's sleek contours towered over the beaten frames of Toyotas and Nissans. The twenty-hour drive was challenging, but airspace was compromised after the U.S. military incursion a few days earlier.

Seraos surveyed the compressed earth buildings whose light shades of a clayish color scheme partly reflected a blazing sun. Behind the tinted ballistic glass, he felt confident about the outcome.

The black SUV steered right to an even narrower alley. Ahead, two armed men stood under arched openings on opposite sides of the street. They nodded at the invisible ones inside the vehicle. A massive gate opened inward to an equally massive property. The off-duty military men parked in a covered courtyard and dismounted.

A young woman waited a few steps ahead. The door behind them closed. Revealed string lights gave the space a magical feel; the location was a safeguarded heaven preserved from the heat of the nearby desert.

Lush trees and magnificent marble fountains created an ecosystem of colorful shades and flowery scents. The greeter was young, maybe in her last teen years. A deep tissue scar ran from her left eye to her upper lip. She had a dominant stance to her and a hardness that could have only been acquired through painful trials.

"Gentlemen, Bin Allah is waiting for you." She pointed at a cylindric machine set up on a monorail structure in an aperture leading to unknown territories.

Seraos tilted his head forward. "Thank you."

The men advanced and entered the spacious cabin. The glass frame offered a breathtaking view of the high ceilings, elaborate light fixtures, and creative carvings in the concrete surfaces the train was surrounded with. The backdoor of the strange transport closed, and the hands of the soldiers found hanging straps attached to metal bars above head. The train's departure was swift yet soundless, and no swaying was felt underfoot.

The technology is unique. Their pool of assets and resources. Unparalleled.

All around, streams of grays and browns mixed with specks of yellows, lights stretched by the perspective of a fast-moving object. The commute was inexplicably short. Eighty-three miles covered in less than twenty-two minutes. Andre Seraos quickly exited the glass module upon arrival.

A spectacle of grandeur made for a vision of a thousand

wonders. The underground cave ahead was a natural structure with a water stream at its center. The black bedrock chiseled by a timeless monster bled colorful murals depicting epic scenes of three-headed monsters spitting fire, Merlin-like wizards flying skies of oversized stars, outlined shapes of humans walking wavy dunes, the birth of a child whose halo radiated over his genitors, a maze, strange eyes peeking through a plush jungle...

The amount of visual data was overwhelming, stretching even further out, beyond Seraos' visual field.

Ahead, a man in a white satin robe stood by the stream, contemplating the artwork of a god.

Seraos led his men without a command, pointing his barrel at an individual he could not identify yet in this feebly lit passageway.

A few steps bridged the gap. The height, the slender frame, the noble wisdom exuded by neutral eyes and a beard shaped by the ages.

Bin Allah.

"I pose no threat, Mr. Seraos. I would have never supplied you with those ... purveyors of death, otherwise."

Andre lowered his assault rifle. The others followed suit. The leader sought Bin Allah's focal point; the *King of Kufra*'s eyes were dancing on the silhouette of a faceless monster painted on the bedrock with humanoid features. Various drawn animals were attempting to evade his grasp, frozen in their pursuit of freedom.

Andre asked, "What is this place?"

"Sacred grounds. Those weapons should only be used in a life-or-death predicament."

"Care to elaborate?" Seraos pressed, his eyes surveying the endless waves of shapes and perspectives surrounding them.

"*Muhammad* the prophet discovered those caves. They are a gift from Allah. A place where His flawless hands engineer the materials for a world of stronger foundations. Allah entrusted my ancestors, my clan, with the responsibility and duty of employing ... *deploying* them."

Andre Seraos remained skeptical but connected the dots. *A gift. Engineers materials.*

"The delivery."

Bin Allah nodded in approval. "Precisely. But I want to make sure your intentions are pure, American. Allah spoke to me, and as he cleansed my soul of selfish, earthly considerations and feelings like fear, hatred, resentment, lust, greed ... he assigned me to a mission. But being the vessel of His work is no easy path. You'll have to challenge the culture you were brought up in, the very people who raised you, the preconceived notions and falsely godly beliefs you acquired in a society so often beaten by the sharp claws of the *Shaytan* it now continuously bleeds. There will be sacrifices to make, casualties. But make no mistake, I am no terrorist. I believe my people need as much healing as yours. I share no anti-American sentiment. My purpose is simply to shape a better world for our future generations and for Allah to return."

Andre and his men processed the implications and message.

"What do you propose?"

Bin Allah replied, "Come with me."

The group journeyed through the caves, their steps leaving volatile prints on the fine sand. Bin Allah guided the others in a purposeful fashion, his stride increasing in length with every step.

They soon reached an auxiliary chamber that featured a bottomless pit at its center. Lab equipment was set up on marble platforms running alongside the walls. A man in a white lab coat jotted notes on a small white pad.

He muttered to himself, "So that no useful compound is inaccessible to practical synthesis. Geometric factors are more important than the intrinsic reactivity of a molecule. Exploit combinatorial methods. Synthesize new substances that can spontaneously self-assemble into complex organized systems with important properties. A symbiotic relationship." The lab rat peeked over his shoulder and returned to his notes. His abnormally fast speech patterns matched the craze of his pen.

Bin Allah expanded. "This is the Chemist. Another vector for Allah's greatness, and a Kufran brother." The Chemist raised a hand, distracted. Bin Allah pointed at the pit and resumed, "You are the first outsiders to witness one of Allah's greatest gifts. The moon of a thousand suns. The peace at war. The sweetness others call bitter. I discovered it during my surveys of the caves a few years back. It gifted me an amber gemstone of flawless honey shades, among other things. Inside was trapped a compound. One that will frame a new world."

Bin Allah directed the men's attention towards canisters stored opposite of the lab instruments, across the pit.

He resumed, "I offer you my resources, protection, and support. Before I expand, I want to clarify, American. I am not a delusional old man with a history of violent transgressions in the name of a warped version of the *Jihad*. I only wish to improve this world, and, as stated by Allah, for people of all faiths and classes."

Andre Seraos attempted to connect the dots, but the mission remained unclear. Some data clusters lacked connectivity. He asked, "What is this compound? And why us?"

"I studied your records, your interventions. You and your men are brave soldiers, highly adaptable, strong yet cultured and intelligent in the broad sense of the term. You also have a particular background that fosters a broader insight many Americans and even locals here do not share. The compound." Bin Allah snapped at the Chemist and shouted, "*Yallah!*"

The scientist turned around. His face was partly covered by a N95 mask and antique goggles. His voice was muffled.

"Yes. The compound. In layman terms, it alters the proteome and genome of your very molecular structure to drive physical and cognitive changes. *Afwan*, not really layman. Imagine a human transformed into another species. Which one, specifically? It would depend not only on the physical and physiological blueprint but also the moral orientation and subconscious motives of the subject, as Allah wished."

Andre's comprehension skills fed a fragmentation process.

Transformation. Men to animals. Biochemical weapon. How?

Questions cascaded into the staggered waterfalls of his intellect.

Clinical trials? Reversible or permanent? To what application? How?

A humming sound called from the pit. It was a patchwork of competing pitches, the trance-inducing notes of foreign sirens, but they formed a cohesive voice altogether. *Magical. Godly.*

The Chemist's fast speech regained dominance in Seraos' space.

"Quite literally, the men become the beasts they cage within."

28. THEY WATCHED US

The Boogeyman is the very embodiment of fear. He is inevitable,
preying on those who sunk in the muddy grounds of their inner
struggles. Or those who have precious valuables.

adiqat Maydan Alshuhada'. The Garden of Eden. Seraos
was Christian by faith, yet he knew Allah had spoken to
him. There was no logical ground to Bin Allah's hidden
treasures.

The most funded research teams in the world had barely begun
scraping the surface of DNA and proteins manipulation. The
Chemist, however, had reshaped a God-given gift. And his Kufran
brother, the *son of Allah*, had entrusted Seraos with it.

The *King of Kufra* gave few details on how he planned to employ
the aerosol agent. He told Seraos, *Allah requires a patient hand and
a flawless execution.* The operation would target the highest
echelons of the U.S. political system to then trickle down onto
smaller governments and sovereign states.

Bin Allah mentioned a shadow network years in the making,
loyal soldiers bound by a central ideology, the codified tribal culture,
unlimited resources, and unique technological assets.

Seraos' men had trusted his judgment call, stunned by their life-altering discovery. Andre felt a crippling dizziness flood his sight as he walked alone alongside colorful fruit stands embedded into a nexus of utile trees.

He inhaled. *An opportunity.* Exhaled. *Treason.* The service to his country still held weight in his heart but he thought, *What if actual patriotism, a truer love for our nation, resided in the fight against status quo?*

Time and again, Bin Allah had assured him that he was in no shape or form anti-American. He provided verifiable intelligence and public records that all pointed towards a man who rather wished to educate the world on the message of unity embedded in the *true* Islam. The *King of Kufra* also openly condemned the actions of known terror movements some of his files proved to have been funded or trained by the U.S. in some capacity.

Wool yarn ran on a pin board, and the web grew more and more complex. But Bin Allah's solution appeared to be the most transformative, the least compromising.

To the right, further down the wet red stone, an arched opening led to a glorious lobby whose white marble floors skillfully complemented the red tapestry and mahogany woods. Accents of gold and indoor plants conveyed the stories of the majestic, mystical Arab world.

Andre Seraos veered left past the fabricated smiles of the hotel staff. He continued down a courtyard split in two by a running stream, one cycling through an underground circuit. *The caves.*

At the opposite end, a door stood in all its highness. The gold geometric patterns reminded him of Bin Allah's compound, the starting point to his new quest.

This time around, however, Andre was no longer an executioner. He was a decisionmaker, the architect of a *new* America.

His golden key found the lock mechanism, and the door opened to a clean-looking unit. The Islamic architecture gave the small space a cozy feeling, a warm ambience.

A burner phone vibrated in Seraos' pocket. He retrieved it and locked the door behind him.

"It's a bit early for dinner."

A voice answered through the phone. "Sweet tooth."

The call disconnected. Seraos headed to the shower and undressed, anxious to wash the offshoots of his initial thoughts away. He stood in the hot, steaming water, seeking balance against the tiled walls.

Foreign born.

I can't drive a change of this magnitude the conventional way.

No one can.

He shut the water, dried off, and found a white undershirt and cotton pants neatly folded on the double sink.

Through the bedroom's bay windows, rain drops synced to the swaying of giant banana shrubs. A private garden offered serenity: The thick foliage filled the space, its leaves crawling on the outer walls.

Tears welled up in Seraos' intense eyes as he engaged his rest space. His thoughts were clouded by conflicting agendas, by a fear that was then foreign to him.

Tap... tap... tap.

A silencer found his right temple around an edged corner, pressing on his flesh. The steady balance suggested the intruder was a seasoned shooter. Seraos took no risk and stilled.

But inside, deep within, he anticipated a potential struggle. Triggers from combat theaters demanded he be ready to force the gun's slide back and hit the attacker's carotid with the knife edge of his hand.

The man's voice was cold, shutting down the slightest possibility of a response from Seraos. The speech pattern was methodical and the tone quietly threatening.

"Face me."

Seraos obliged and faced the man. He wore round-shaped eye frames and a black and white striped shirt. His melanated skin highlighted the glacial hazel of his eyes. He was a killer, Seraos thought.

"Now, take this seat." The mysterious aggressor pointed at a love seat in the opposite corner. Andre complied and sat down, silent. He had already mapped an exit route, but the towering shadow of this tall beast obstructed the pathway to safety.

The intruder stood still, reviewing the space.

He tossed the pistol at Seraos. The latter fought to betray surprise, tensed in his facial movements, and grabbed the gun. *Heckler and Koch.*

The visitor resumed, "Michael Hoover. We'll spare the theatrics of blackmailing and leveraging. This is not a negotiation. More like … an offer."

Andre refrained from pointing the barrel at Hoover. He asked, "Who do you work with?"

"I'm a JSOC contractor. I supplied ground intel for your direct action on Bin Allah's compound."

"CIA?" Seraos asked.

"PAG." The three letters rang like the raspy call of the *Boogeyman.*

"I'm on vacation. Took a detour."

Michael Hoover smiled. He said, "You and your men have been particularly careful with your trip's itineraries. Remarkable display of spycraft. The agency is unaware. I found you on my own. I'm off-duty. Now, hear me out."

The character was strange. He was almost… *synthetic* in motion.

Hoover resumed, "I was at the forefront of a training program in 2006. A classified operation in the basin of Kufra. The operation you led a few days ago was a masquerade, a false show to justify the capture or killing of one of our ex-associates. Bin Allah."

Andre found comfort in the confession. Hoover added credibility and weight to the Kufrans' claims.

The CIA officer pursued, "During operation *Green Spear*, Control lost communication with you for seven minutes and forty-seven seconds. You then left the compound with the HVT. Your reports mentioned equipment failure. Plausible. But Bin Allah failed to realize how deeply ingrained I was in the DNA of this beautiful nation. I dance in the shadows of these streets, looking for my next partner and the right beat." He paused. The rain intensified. "I know he's alive. And you came back, with your men."

Seraos contemplated killing the spymaster. But Bin Allah had exhorted him to choose peace in adversity. His own beliefs tended to align with this approach, outside of his military service.

Hoover continued, unbothered. "I want in. Whatever the *King of Kufra* is set to accomplish, it is going to be significant. He has the resources. And more importantly, he was able to provide you with a body that matched his biometrics. This is beyond our current knowledge. I'd also like to cite ... irreconcilable differences with my employer, mostly of ideological nature. Think *righting the wrongs*."

Andre Seraos was given precise instructions on talent acquisition. Bin Allah needed to vet Hoover personally. A network of shell properties and underground tunnels would be used to smuggle the candidate.

Andre asked, "This is an interesting theory. Do you speak Arabic?"

Hoover nodded in approval. "Yes."

"Great. Ask the front desk for a coffee. Coarse grounds. Black. It may help you with your delusions." Andre stood and gave the pistol back. "I don't carry weapons on vacation."

The two reached a mutual understanding. Hoover left the room of warm accents.

Washington, D.C. - September 6, 2023 - 13 Years Later

Andre Seraos counted the seconds leading to the incursion. He readjusted his microphone, appreciating the froggy figure of the Chairman.

Fifteen. Bin Allah had shared a universal truth. The oversight hearing committee featured attendees whose shadowy characters would soon shape into the beasts they, sometimes, "caged within".

Five. A gas mask was taped underneath his seat. He confirmed by readjusting his chair and running his fingers on the polycarbonate lenses.

Now. The doors behind him opened and two light thumps broke through the crowd's astonishment. The Chairman drew a long face whose double chin formed melting smiles.

To Andre's left, the Secret Service had donned their masks. Behind, a green smoke was filling the space as the politicians, officials, and sly lobbyists ran to the exits.

Seraos grabbed his mask from underneath the chair's frame and adjusted it on his head. The fog almost instantly cleared from his coated lenses as he navigated through the panicked crowd to join the ranks of his allies. No one noticed his maneuver in the mayhem.

The main access and two other side entryways were locked by the infiltration team. The only remaining egress was guarded by heavily armed soldiers who held key positions in the President and Vice President's protection detail. The gas reached the distressed mass of cowardly beings and weak frames.

They froze.

The Secret Service left through the unlocked access they had blocked. Seraos followed suit and disappeared in the inception of a painful metamorphosis.

His cloned shell, a product of Bin Allah's mysterious technology, was brought inside the chamber by one of the bodyguards. It bore the same hairstyle and an identical outfit, down to the black stripes of his cotton socks and the silky touch of his tie. The reinforced entrance was locked behind the last man, closing the chapter of a wild development.

Tap... tap... tap, tap, tap.

Outside the House of Representatives chamber, one of the Secret Service men lent Seraos an in-ear receiver as they all progressed through a maze of intersecting hallways. A voice came through the miniature device. "All secured. PM is waiting with the EO."

Seraos answered, "Copy that. Moving to first speech. Deploy the asset and standby. The CTD is taking over."

Andre's escort veered left to a high-ceiling hall while he continued forward to an antique elevator a few feet ahead. He opened the yellow gold doors and entered. His fingers found the lowest button, *-4B.*

The ancient lift descended into the abyss of a lesser-known Capitol. A few seconds passed. Andre checked his analog watch. *T minus thirteen.* The cage screeched to a halt. He opened the barred door and engaged a poorly lit tunnel. Bags of concrete mix were staggered along his route. A heavy steel door unlocked to his left and slammed back shut after he entered what appeared to be a radio and broadcast studio.

Andre was formally trained to handle the setup of his equipment, now familiar with the many knobs and switches that greeted him. Lights blinked in the darkness of the soundproofed room.

He began a mental checklist. *Output channel and network connectivity. Voice modifier. Equalizers. Speech.*

His fingers danced on a printed paper. A silent power generator sat in a corner, shining a soft blue light.

A few minutes passed before Seraos gave one final look around and sat down.

He took a deep breath and remembered Wagner's words.

Your delivery is beats and steps.

Andre pushed a red button on a console nearby and approached a suspended microphone hanging at mouth level.

"This is the Watchmaker. Today, at 01:45 PM Eastern, D.C. Police Department received an anonymous call reporting that two bombs were planted east and southeast of Capitol Hill. The Capitol Police, which has jurisdiction over a 200-block area expanding outward from the pits of snakes that are the House of Representatives and the Senate, has proved surprisingly effective in cordoning the sector and taking appropriate measures towards a potential evacuation. It's almost like … January 6 was never a thing.

"But like everything in this city, the truth is always concealed, or at best, underlying. The suits and decisionmakers shaping your lives exercise a narrow vision, preoccupied by the preservation of their benefits and a position of power that allows them to build generational wealth through questionable practices. Politicians lost their humanity a while ago, when the system became a rat race where the fat worms now justify status quo under the pretense of a new form of 'body positivity'. I'm aware this message outlasted your average seven-second attention span, but it is necessary. You have been fed content from ill-advised medias controlled by a handful of wealthy partisans who fight one another to drive favorable optics for reelection.

"When's the last time you questioned the system? The last time you took action, tangibly and purposefully? This country is broken, shattered by a tale of two worlds on the opposite extremes of capitalism's spectrum. The men and women ruling this nation feast over your decaying flesh. You are served at their table, medium-rare, by systemic design. Drink those words, reread my transcripts if necessary; we will make them available online at americaisazoo.com."

A pause provided a dramatic effect.

"A prime example of this State being a house of lies: The incidents reported earlier this afternoon are nothing but smoke screens. The real fight broke out inside the walls of your Capitol, once more. This time, however, it was executed with consideration and professionalism, with pure motives lightyears away from the nonsensical actions of uneducated demographics born into generational racism. Further details are coming. Note to law enforcement agencies: Do not breach the U.S. Capitol or interfere with our process. M. President and his VP, trapped inside, would face grave consequences."

29. THE SPECTER OF A SHIFT
VANUATU

This was his final curtain call.

he pale cream sand slipped through his arachnidian fingers, raining down on Vanuatu's immaculate beach. The *Watchmaker*'s public face, Seraos' elaborate decoy, looked nothing like the man who floated in a glass cage stormed by supernatural waters, embracing the rising tide as the FBI and CIA evaded his planned demolition of an American symbol.

The Hillwood Estate.

The man smiled. His new jaw structure, cheekbones, and nose line felt foreign to him, however. Small waves crashed his bare feet, bringing a rejuvenating ocean breeze.

Vanuatu was a safe haven for warlords and international criminals. The national government had taken a few steps to align with global criminal laws and statutes, but it was still behind, dragging its feet, held back by a partly justified resentment for the international community.

The *second Watchmaker* spread his fingers apart, palms facing up. His fingerprints had been altered, and so was the remainder of his unique identifiers. He was changed by Bin Allah's technology, like the Capitol animals caged in their own nightmares.

The smile expanded. The *other Watchmaker* chose the right side of history, unlike them, and gave a stunning performance to an audience that would have waved him away under different circumstances.

They can't comprehend how vital art forms are.

He also helped with constructing the blueprint of a better society and was rewarded with millions in the process. Soon, when his recovery was total, he would return to the States and witness the birth of more favorable parameters for people like him, neglected artists, strong and resilient minds all relied upon, ostracized men who gave but never received. Misunderstood creative geniuses. Visionaries facing the high walls of the narrow-minded.

The beat of the waves became a pattern of standing ovations.

The imposter syndrome is dead. Long live the art!

Before the decoy's eyes, the beaches turned into a grimy New York City. His memories led a recollection.

Tap, tap... tap, tap.

"And this, ladies and gentlemen, is a new spin on gravity. Pun intended."

A few patrons laughed and echoed in the small cabaret. A supportive woman shouted, "Yes, Ehrich!"

The percentage he negotiated on ticket sales would allow him to cover a few meals until his next appearance. At this very moment, however, he felt whole through his passion. His powdered face and slicked-back hair were an homage to his role model, the great Harry Houdini.

Although he shared the same work ethic and creative talent, Ehrich never gained the traction of a *Blaine* or a *Copperfield*. He was too invested in his magic, his illusionism, rejecting soul-crushing branding efforts. He carried the belief that art should connect with audiences if it was well-thought and executed, innovative and bold, with or *without* publicity. Show after show, the world had proven him wrong.

He faked a wide smile and began pacing around the frail frame of a small stage in South Manhattan.

Suddenly, he was aboveground, walking an invisible stairwell. The crowd was awed with the physics-defying performance. Ehrich reached a high point and called out his audience.

"Join me!"

They first hesitated, gauging each other's commitment.

"Don't be afraid. It's magic. You can trust it, right?" Ehrich added.

The people approached the stage and awkwardly stepped on it. They tried to retrace the performer's steps but found nothing. There was no cable, no subterfuge.

In their minds, one question subsisted. *How?*

Ehrich was satisfied, looking at the astonished faces of his twelve spectators down below. He addressed them. "Forgive my manners. Why not bridge the gap?"

Gravity no longer applied to him as he returned to a lower section of the stage, *upside down.* His eyes were now leveled with those of his crowd. Some timid claps filled the shoddy space.

Ehrich smiled and rotated back to touch down on the squeaky boards. He shook hands and ended the show without a final curtain call. Management had deemed it "too old-fashioned".

A few minutes later, the closet space that served as backstage saw the illusionist clean up. He was wiping down the foundations of a heavy makeup, trying to make sense of his progress through a scratched mirror. As the layers peeled off, Ehrich's dopamine levels dropped. Hunger creeped in on him, as well as a self-perceived failure. Tears were wiped with the remainder of the cracked greasepaint.

Years later, on Vanuatu's heavenly beaches, those tears welled up in Ehrich's eyes again.

This time, they conveyed joy, pride, and self-significance.

30. CAGED IN THE WILD
BRAZIL - SERRA DOS ÓRGÃOS NATIONAL PARK

In the jungles made of concrete, subspecies rose from the underworld. Thieves, liars, murderers, rapists, sociopaths. They are now literal animals, endemic to a new ecosystem.

The drier season of the southern hemisphere's winter brought mild temperatures and moderate precipitations. From the gorgeous valley of white orchids, red tulips, and pink ballerina flowers, *God's finger* pointed towards the Creator: the world-famous geological formation shot through foggy layers of a fine mist. In a clearing down a colorful path, black containers of various sizes laid on the hard soil.

They were marked *AIAZ* in yellow lettering.

Local Park Rangers with long guns and U.S. intelligence officers gravitated around the boxes. Eyes were shifting between the beasts' cages, the surrounding rainforest, and the mountain range peaking in the backdrop. It was heaven on earth, chosen to become the sinners' last sighting before Hell.

A few U.S. and Brazilian scientists coordinated the effort, as a link between their respective security forces.

A local zoologist addressed his American counterpart. "Here, in this valley, we have this ... patchwork of microclimates. The higher the altitude, the drier the soil. They'll look for more favorable conditions and take separate routes, naturally."

The American answered, "Which makes sense since we've noticed more individualism. Behavioral patterns expected from their classification. They lost this 'esprit de corps' as their humanity and associated cognitive functions crumbled. Fascinating. We may have a couple of competing apex predators, but that's also part of their judgment."

The Brazilian smirked and combed the valley with his eyes. "What did the U.S. Department of Justice decide? We only received a brief report with transportation guidelines."

"It's classified, I'm afraid."

The Brazilian frowned. "The reason why I'm asking is because my government needs to be made aware of the parameters of this semi-captivity. Are we authorized to introduce other females and males for mating? Any other restrictions?"

The American lifted a finger and scrolled through a tablet she held with a firm grip. Around, all eyes were on the two decisionmakers.

The U.S. zoologist finally answered, "No mating authorized. I understand the prospect could lead to breakthroughs through breeding, but *this* is also their sentence for the crimes they committed before transforming. There was quite a debate on whether or not they were legally responsible entities. Our decision was to lay the groundwork for a new judicial model and proceed forward with the judgment. Otherwise, no other restrictions beside the ones in the brief you received. The unmarked box is classified content. We'll deal with it ourselves, but no residuals will be left on your site."

The Brazilian, a local native, or *Carioca*, nodded in approval and consulted with his team, including the Park Rangers.

Birds of a million colors flew over the emergent layers of the tropical paradise, casting shadows on the humans. Stingless bees sought the juicy nectar of surviving flowers. The sky was gray, but the temperatures were still relatively high for the Americans and their preconceived idea of a winter.

The Brazilian camp gave a thumbs up, and the U.S. intelligence officers approached to provide support and monitor the releases.

The first container opened. In the darkness of its confines laid the Pig. He retreated to a back corner, possessed by a tremor as the sun penetrated the thick polymer.

A Ranger entered the container and approached. He grabbed the Pig from underneath his twitching belly and took him out of his cage, with control and firmness. A new world appeared in front of the animal's beady eyes, wider, panoramic yet lacking depth and details. There were flowers, strange species, mountain ranges breaching the mystical skies and... mud.

An area to his right had preserved the last precipitations in a small depression. The soil was softer and spongy. The Park Ranger let go of the Pig, who bolted to the intriguing scent of wet dirt.

"Weird demise," one of the Rangers said with a strong *Carioca* accent. Laughs erupted as they all maneuvered to the next sweat box.

Another container further right began swaying under the thumping of an angry beast, but *this* one was quiet, despite its massive size.

A Park Ranger returned from a nearby vehicle with a bag of bamboo stems. An automated system opened the windowless cage. The giant Panda, a former figure of integrity who fell to the dark side, was laying on the back panel heavily breathing. The Park Ranger knocked on the side walls until he woke up. His sad eyes looked at his handler and spotted the canopy behind. The fresh air and sweet scents triggered a self-realization. *Food.*

On all fours, the Panda left the cage, moving surprisingly fast. The Ranger swung a bamboo stick in the air and followed a path to a nearby downward slope. The black and white mammal followed as they both disappeared in the jungle, in a bizarre game of cat and mouse.

The scientists examined their watches and directed everyone to the next cage. The lead Brazilian zoologist said, "The conditions may not be optimal for this one. But he'll find food in this ecosystem and since breeding is not a concern, the ecological balance is not threatened."

His American counterpart now understood why he needed further details on the release conditions. They all nodded in approval. The cage's door slid open as four Park Rangers stood to its sides. The remainder of the personnel stepped back behind the container. The Lion was trying to scrape the walls of his prison with sharp, stained claws. The polymer was scratch-resistant, but he had continued in an inexplicable craze.

The sudden light triggered his predatory instincts. He began pacing in his box, evaluating the outside world. Sensory markings like urine, feces, and pheromones formed a blueprint for the apex predator. He walked out and saw the strange beasts on two legs in his peripheral vision. A loud noise thundered through the objects they held. *Bang.*

Predators. The Lion ran and followed the scent of smaller preys, escaping to survive while hunting to thrive.

The scientific personnel demanded a precise timing; they needed to orchestrate a sequential release based on species-wide behaviors. The four Park Rangers who issued warning shots remained where they stood, monitoring the Lion's progression with binoculars.

The rest moved to the next cage. Inside, something was stomping with a clicking noise. The door opened.

The Bull charged forward, blinded by the sunlight. He ran into a downslope and was taken by a small mudslide. Vocalizations indicated he was still alive, a few feet down, stuck in a massive depression.

The Rangers looked down. One of them confirmed, "He can't go back up."

The personnel, anxious to finalize the release, continued to the next cage, silent. The procedural process was a monotone beat, a tensed thread, a fragile equilibrium.

The small box was opened without hesitation or preparation. Inside, the Grasshopper stood still on his back legs. He jumped at the sight of light and quickly disappeared in a patch of tall grass hugging the steep side of a mountaintop.

Earlier on, the Brazilian camp inquired about the missing Falcon, who was part of the surviving Capitol Eight in the initial reports. The U.S. government communique stated that he died from sustained injuries during transport but there was no factual evidence to support the claim. The mystery remained as the men and women who were parts of this historical development moved to the last marked cage. The pounding inside the container was heavy and continuous.

Thump! Thump! Thump! Thump! Thump!

"*Porra*," shouted a Ranger. His colleagues surrounded the cage's access while the others positioned behind, once more. The door opened and the pounding ceased. Above, rotor blades grew louder and louder, from a distant rumble to a sharp cry.

The Gorilla stood in the darkness, assessing the threats outside. Captivity bred anger. He advanced and beat his chest, his black coat and silver back shining under the beaming lights of his new home.

Suddenly, he attempted to rush one of the Park Rangers, the ground shaking under his course. But warning shots drove him to run the other direction. There was no fear in his adversaries; they had earned the right to be left unharmed. The massive black frame vanished in the wild, his stomping of the soil lost in the loud rotor wash straight above.

U.S. intelligence agents rushed to climb all marked containers. Seven helicopters hovered over in a file formation. The CIA paramilitary officers began sling loads hookups. They quickly jumped out and motioned for the pilots to fly off with their cargo. The site was mostly cleared; the mysterious unmarked box was left untouched.

The lead U.S. zoologist addressed her Brazilian counterparts, "*Obrigado*. We'll take it from here and let you know when the site is cleared. Thank you for your help and hospitality."

The local Rangers and scientists, brave men and women of few fears, nodded in approval and soon drove off on a dirt path.

———

A few hours passed and the darkness rose on the diverse Brazilian ecosystem, forming one with the all-black mystery box.

The lead U.S. zoologist projected a different persona at nightfall. Her friendly demeanor had left place to a cold determination. Her smile faded, and her eyes sharpened. She looked at her satellite phone and read a text. Her attention shifted towards the CIA paramilitary officers on standby in their trucks.

She said, "Hoover gave the green light."

The men, quiet professionals, unloaded their trunks with rolls of a black material and metal poles. In less than ten minutes, the unmarked cage was concealed from satellite views and from its surroundings. A CIA agent manually opened the cage.

Inside, a magical beast shone his light in the dark. A myth turned reality.

The Unicorn, Abdul Baaqi, slowly stepped out. He stopped in front of the officer, docile and still.

The CIA element raised his left hand and drew circles in the air. The Unicorn nodded.

A needle found the mythical creature's thick membrane, right below the neck. The paramilitary officer gave the Unicorn some space and ordered others to comply.

The creature laid down on the dry soil and began panting. His white coat blistered. Bones shifted under the tissue as a shriek of pain pierced through the moonless night. The muzzle retracted. The eyes shifted colors, going through a broad spectrum of reds, blues, grays and greens. The sounds of fractured cartilage and osseous matter made for the beat of a foreshadowing clock.

For a few, the transformation triggered painful changes. Final adjustments occurred as the white hair follicles shrunk to reveal a tan skin.

In a fetal position, the Libyan national, an attendee at the Kufrans' oversight hearing and a distant relative of the tribe itself, came back to life. His breathing was chaotic and his gaze lifeless. The CIA officer approached again and injected him with an adrenaline shot.

The pupils retracted; the flesh pulsed as blood coursed through veins faster. He twitched uncontrollably and eventually stabilized. Another member of the scientific team approached with a medical penlight.

She addressed the Libyan national, "Good evening. My name is Kia. Can you state your name?"

His brain was rewired, building new psychological constructs, bringing new realizations forth.

Through his eyes, the quasi-360-degree vision was no longer. He saw further but in a narrower fashion. *My skin, it burns.* The tremors resumed.

Kia was stoic, indifferent to the compulsive shaking of her patient. She repeated, "My name is Kia. Can you state your name?"

Inside the Libyan's conscience, memories flooded a dark, rugged plane. Allah had chosen him to cross the *Barzakh*, a veil between the living and *others*, and come back to this world, as one of the architects of His will. He remembered his name, a variant of the Arabic term for everlasting, permanent, eternal.

He answered, "Ab ... d ... ul Baaqi."

"Good, M. Baaqi. Can you please sit and look straight ahead?" He nodded and obliged. Kia shone her penlight onto his pupils, finding that they had regained their normal sizes. "Thank you, M. Baaqi. We have clean clothes and hot foods at your disposal, but it will be provided while on the road. For safety reasons, you cannot stay here any longer. Do you understand?"

"Yes, Kia. One thing?"

"Yes, M. Baaqi."

"Did we succeed? Did we fulfill Allah's wishes?"

She looked at his dreamy eyes, the tears flowing on his pale gold complexion, and answered, "Yes, we have managed so far. You were instrumental in creating a false investigative lead to follow while we campaigned for a new administration."

Abdul was a resilient individual born and raised in a war zone. He had dealt with harsh conditions before and reemerged from the dark body of muddy waters, richer in possessions and spirit. Like the many soldiers of this holy army, his identity would be altered, and he would exist as a new man living within a new order: a byproduct of his contribution.

He rose, covered by a black thermal blanket, and followed a concealed path to his transport. The paramilitary officers were already working on dismantling the screens as he stepped in the armored truck. They loaded the metal poles and shades into the massive container where Abdul was held captive.

One of the agents shouted, "Vacuum. Clear?"

All personnel on site answered in unison, "Clear!"

The agent twisted and pulled the pin of an unmarked white grenade. He threw the ordnance in the container and ran back to the truck to find cover.

A warp-sound preceded the wavy motion of a vacuum bomb's

blast, the same mechanics observed around the Capitol, on a smaller scale this time around.

In less than thirty seconds, the container had vanished, leaving a print on the soil. The scene was rid of compromising forensics, left in a virgin state.

The armored trucks drove off in the night, leaving a trail of dust in their wake.

EPILOGUE: GOD IS A BLACK WOMAN

The ploy was elaborate, sophisticated. It matched the visionary perspective of those who were quietly shaping a new world. As she stood at the edge of an alternative reality, one she could almost touch, Abeba thought, I am no longer accepting the things I cannot change. I am changing the things I cannot accept.

Two miles off Ivory Coast's shore, a sailing boat of rich glossy woods was anchored into the crystal-clear waters of Monogaga Beach. The blue skies competed for brightness with the white sands drawn afar.

Abeba, Hoover, and another unidentified individual enjoyed light breakfast options and freshly pressed juices. They raised their glass to a toast.

"To a brighter future and a better process. To Bin Allah," Abeba managed to articulate slower.

Clinking glasses celebrated the architects of a new world. The three were masterminds who drove a nationwide systemic change in the upmost secrecy, while being celebrated in their prior careers. Abeba and Hoover had retired. The third individual, whose facial features were altered in a beautiful reconstruction, was officially declared dead.

Andre Seraos smiled, looking at his partners. He had joined Abeba's new non-profit organization, *Zoya*.

The trio charted a new course through the stars of a fractured sky. Healing was a lifetime pursuit that expanded beyond the U.S. borders. Africa was the next breeding ground for a better model, a more humane society in which love, active listening, and a sustainable progress reigned over the hearts and minds.

This time, however, there were no subterfuges, no forced entries, no meticulously planned assassinations. Bin Allah's mentorship and a successful shakedown of a then-diseased America had convinced other nations to follow. Simply put, Abeba was the forerunner of a foreseeable development.

A few minutes later, she stood by the bow of her sailing lady. Her tropical print cutout dress shone in the sun, the *soie sauvage* texture aligning with her petite frame and complimenting her dark skin.

Andre sat beside Hoover, contemplating her beauty. He was the only one capable of love on this ship, partnering with individuals whose brilliance and efficiency concealed, offset their inability to *feel*. Abeba's Kanner's syndrome made her a goddess on Earth, with its intrinsic lack of emotional accessibility and availability to mortals; to Seraos, the realization was saddening.

From the first encounter with the former FBI Counterterrorism Division's director, he knew. She was an elegant display of brain and raw beauty; the dream girl for men who valued genuineness and substance. His heart was racing and his mind fantasizing, considering an alternate future where they shared a love-filled home.

Andre failed to repress a tear. Hoover laid a comforting hand on his shoulder.

At this very moment, both men were convinced: God was a Black woman.

Abeba paid them no mind. Before her eyes, the world spoke to her. The waves' velocity, the currents' directions, the wind speeds, the refractive index... it was melody to her ears.

Then, she found *you*.

"Africa. The motherland. A heaven on Earth fractured by the fallen angels of colonialism. One last war will be fought here, against the remnants of ethnical cleansings, greed, corruption, the appropriation of natural resources by foreign states and political instability.

"In these jungles, the demons lurk in the shadows, monsters of a different breed than those who ran America and other westernized nations. But there is a high level of adaptability to *Zoya*, my non-profit organization and paramilitary force. While I purposely misled my former team during the Capitol's investigation, I'm no longer tied to feigning incompetence. I am me again. *Alkebulan*, Africa, the mother of mankind, the Garden of Eden, will rise to prominence, freed from the shackles of evil spirits."

Waves crashed the hull, relentless, inflexible.

"We used proxies to drive changes out west. U.S. President Hall, high-profile activists, a German fixer, special forces, local assets, foreign nationals, you name it. While they served their purpose, the methods we'll employ here widely differ.

"Seraos, Hoover, and I no longer hide in the dark, moving pawns attached to our strings and threads. We're doing this with the *People*, in broad daylight, marching in the wake of a loud revolution. Amid these shifting dynamics, one main conclusion transpired from the exercise. Whether covert or public, day or night, the *push* of a collective body can move mountain ranges, revealing new landscapes of lush greens beyond.

"Be the change. Find the strongest bonding adhesive for your collage of hopes, energies, cultural backgrounds, and ideas and demand it be displayed in the offices of those who run your country."

AFTERWORD

America is a Zoo. Beyond the shock value and aggressive angle of this title lays a bleak reality. This country has gone mad, embattled in a struggle between walking contradictions, a class divide, corruption, ultra-capitalism and systemic oppression.

There is hope, however. But it is conditional to us, the general population, changing the way we approach and view this world.

Within this (hopefully) thrilling story dramatized to allow me to take certain creative liberties (it was incredibly fun, by the way), there is a central thread: Polarization has become a cancer that prevents the healthy cells of innovation and progress from growing and developing in the sickly body of this nation.

Yes, polarization. Initially designed to identify various schools of thoughts and ideological, political movements, terms like "liberal", "conservative", "LGBTQIA+", "POC", "left", "right" and many others are now used in a battle of bruised egos and shouting contests. It is no longer about the cause itself or the country's best interests, but about dominance in the landscape, about the emergence of ONE, SINGLE survivor. Before I expand on that, please understand that I speak from the point of view of a foreign-born with an interest in American politics, yet still apolitical by conviction.

Liberals have become social justice warriors competing for cancel culture's throne and instrumentalizing economic and social hardships. Most conservatives are associated with generational racism, gun lobbying, a growing rejection of science, and the targeting of federal institutions and regulations. The LGBTQIA+ is radicalizing, slowly but surely becoming a reactionary force that no longer promotes the tolerance and love they initially formed to fight for. People of color are used as tokens, or leveraged, by "allies" who never considered educating themselves on the needs and cultural specifics of the communities they never grew up in or shared challenges with.

The list goes on. Everyone has gone mad. Racism is still institutional, but it is also now carried and promoted by a vocal *minority within the minorities*. Even more importantly, this confusion is preyed upon by our incompetent leaders so they can apply cheap countermeasures to problems that need actual solving without facing any resistance or constructive criticism; they themselves are drowning in the tumultuous waters of partisanship and destructive power dynamics, the deadliest enemies of good policymaking.

I am a neutral party. This story was not intended to support any of the actors in this theater.

I believe in logical reasoning, in semantics, in my faith, in true unity, in science, in verifiable information from cross-referenced sources. I do not believe in virtue signaling, in reverse racism, in attempting to extinguish a ravaging fire with lighter fluid.

But this is what America has come down to: a divided body of lost souls ordered to disperse by a subpar educational system and toxic patterns ingrained in the very DNA of this State.

It is time we shift dynamics in our interactions, in the shaping of our perspectives. There is data to correlate the aforementioned elements and the state of disrepair in which this country finds itself.

As of September 3, 2022:

1. Gun violence deaths (suicide, homicide, accidental discharges) amount to 30,001 this year alone, the highest ever in our history. Mass shootings and mass murders respectively peak at 453 and 19. (**Gun Violence Archive**. https://www.gunviolencearchive.org/)

2. Half of people 12 and older have used illicit drugs at least once. 700,000 drug overdose deaths since 2000. (**National Center for Drug Abuse Statistics**. https://drugabusesta tistics.org/)

3. 1 in 5 U.S. adults experience mental illness each year. Suicide is the second leading cause of death among people aged 10-34. (**National Alliance on Mental Illness**. https:// www.nami.org/mhstats)

4. The U.S. has the world's largest economy. Apple is the world's first corporation to reach a market capitalization of over $1 trillion. On Jan 6, 2020, Apple reached the $1.3 trillion market cap. Yet inflation averages 8.6% while wage growth averages 5.2%. (**Facts.net**. https://facts.net/us-economy-facts/ and **Statista** https://www.statista.com/chart/27610/inflation-and-wage-growth-in-the-united-states/)

This speaks volumes. But beyond the numbers and charts, I mainly wanted to speak to you as a writer, as a father, as a Latino who grew up in an Afrocentric culture, as a U.S. Army veteran, as a human being with flaws and inner demons. I wanted to touch your souls and (maybe) make a small difference in this world, *your* world.

And this is what drove me to work, tirelessly, on this piece of storytelling; to find a way to convey my thoughts on the current state of politics and economics in this country while educating and (maybe, again) sparking new conversations.

A significant amount of research was involved in the making of *America is a Zoo*. It was critical for me to stay true to the cultural parameters of the groups depicted in my story. Growing up in a house of Jamaicans, Europeans, West Africans, and Brazilians, I wanted to portray Black people as drivers to innovation and excellence with complex souls, to explore the complicated history of Islam, a religion of peace and brotherhood too often instrumentalized and used as the catalyst for xenophobia and ignorance.

I wanted to show you the world as it is, lightyears away from trauma porn, the criminalization of minorities, and this (mostly observed in the US) tendency of mistaking ethnicity for color, as well as associating certain groups with harmful stereotypes.

Now, yes, I made a passionate pledge to you, but who or what is causing this polarization? These warped views of a reality that is being changed by equally misled individuals? How do we prevent the ship from sinking?

The root cause of this growing cancer and the path to entering remission both lay in the lines of this novel. It is an increasingly intricate patchwork of variables. But if we decide to isolate the primaries and auxiliaries, two things transpire from studying American society and its shortcomings: Our education is lackluster, and the administrative machine running this country needs modernization and streamlining. Attacking those two issues could produce many positive results such as a more just judicial system, better infrastructures, cost savings, a more responsible financial strategy, a more cultured population, the eradication of generational racism at the source, and, of course, a deadly blow dealt to polarization.

How do we achieve that? That is the difficult part. Unlike France's revolutionary spirit or the Scandinavians' innovative social policies, for instance, America does not YET possess a common trait or weapon that could drive systemic changes of this magnitude. It is a reality: Division, a performance-driven culture that subjected to unregulated capitalism and consumerism, a lack of knowledge on foreign affairs, and many other variables prevent us from marching the streets together and demanding MORE from our leaders. We witness more and more protests organized and a generational voice begins taking shape, but it is still mostly temporary and reactionary.

However, it is not a permanent disability.

By finding the courage to let go of our fears, our insecurities, our prejudice and preconceived notions, we can move forward together and "cross a new, defining threshold."

Wake up, America.

PS: Chapter 23, "Shattered Glass". How do you envision Jesse Jones' fate? A sixty-eight-year-old Virginia native who spent forty-three years on death row. Tag me on social media and share your input with the hashtag #americaisazoo. I have a few surprises for those who join me on this journey of discoveries.

Oh and, don't forget to leave a review! E-commerce retailers, independent and chain bookstores, libraries, The StoryGraph (a better, Black-owned alternative to Goodreads), social media... Yes, indeed. I cannot, in good conscience, remain active on Goodreads (they support review-bombing and the blatant extortion of indie authors, the very same ones who provide value and content to their platform).

WHERE TO FIND ME?

Website: *https://www.thesoaresprotocol.com/*

 facebook.com/thesoaresprotocol

instagram.com/thesoaresprotocol

BY THE SAME AUTHOR

The Forerunner: A Vice Versa Series

C1: A Vice Versa Series

Alidala: A Vice Versa Series

CPSIA information can be obtained
at www.ICGtesting.com
Printed in the USA
BVHW051942210223
658948BV00012B/189

9 798987 615300